Orchid Blue

Eoin McNamee was born in Kilkeel, County Down, in 1961. He was educated in various schools in the North of Ireland and at Trinity College, Dublin. His first book, the novella *The Last of Deeds*, was shortlisted for the *Irish Times* Literature Prize and his novels include *Resurrection Man*, which was later made into a film, and *The Blue Tango* which was longlisted for the Booker Prize. He lives in Sligo.

Orchid Blue

EOIN McNAMEE

~

ff
faber and faber

First published in 2010
by Faber and Faber Limited
Bloomsbury House, 74–77 Great Russell Street,
London WC1B 3DA

Typeset by Faber and Faber Ltd
Printed in England by CPI Mackays, Chatham

A CIP record for this book
is available from the British Library

ISBN 978-0-571-23754-8

2 4 6 8 10 9 7 5 3 1

To Marie

PART ONE

Mr Justice Curran had just finished his summing-up and the court precincts had barely cleared when the tipstaff told Curran that the jury had reached a verdict. Some of the reporters had stayed in the vicinity of the courthouse. Others had gone into the town to file copy from public phones. There was no expectation of an early verdict in a capital murder case.

Twenty-six-year-old Robert McGladdery of Damolly in Newry was on trial for the murder of nineteen-year-old Pearl Gamble, also of Damolly. The case had been heard in Downpatrick Courthouse because of defence fears that an unbiased jury could not be empanelled in Newry.

The prosecution alleged that McGladdery had lain in wait for the girl on her way home from a dance at the Henry Thompson Memorial Orange Hall in Newry. It was maintained that McGladdery had beaten Pearl, stabbed her seven times and then strangled her. Her naked body had been dragged over half a mile, through a stubble field, and partly hidden at a place known locally as Weir's Rock. The Crown was represented by the Attorney General, Brian McGuinness, QC. James Brown, QC represented the defence. Mr Justice Lance Curran presided.

The trial had lasted for seven days. Brown said afterwards he thought that the longer the jury spent on their deliberations, the better it would be for his client. The evidence against McGladdery was entirely circumstantial. The prosecution had no direct witness or forensic evidence to connect him to the crime. McGladdery had been in the witness box for six hours and, in Brown's opinion, had done himself no favours, although he had been adamant that he had nothing to do with the girl's murder. Brown hoped that the jury would take time to consider the fact that there was no direct evidence. He hoped that they would address themselves to the absence of motive. Pearl had been stripped naked but in the words of the lead detective, John Speers, 'it was a mercy she was not outraged'.

In any event Brown had already started to consider grounds for appeal. Any appeal would be difficult. Lord Justice Curran had conducted the case with icy impartiality. It seemed that he had thought of every eventuality. Brown sought to open legal issues hanging in the air, to leave certain avenues unexplored in order to provide grounds of appeal. But Curran had anticipated each move, restricting Brown's room to manoeuvre in the future. The judge was soft-spoken and implacable, and the final portion of his charge to the jury had been, in the words of Eddie McCrink, Chief Inspector of Her Majesty's Constabulary, 'sabotage'.

Curran's presence in the courtroom would not have been tolerated in any other jurisdiction. In 1952, the judge's nineteen-year-old daughter Patricia had been murdered in a case which attracted massive publicity. In 1953 a young airman, Iain Hay Gordon, had been found not guilty by reason of insanity, and incarcerated for the killing of Patricia Curran. It is unlikely that any of the jury members would have been unaware of the murder of Lance Curran's only daughter. In any other jurisdiction Curran would have been disbarred, or would have disbarred himself, from presiding over a capital case involving the murder of another nineteen-year-old girl.

In the first few days Brown could see the jury members glancing towards the bench. They knew the judge's history. As the trial progressed Brown thought that they had become attuned to the judge and to the subtle shifts in his demeanour. At the beginning he appeared abstracted, lost in grief, having to drag himself back to the moment, to the business in hand. As the days passed, unlooked-for sternness crept into his attitude. When Speers said that Pearl had not been outraged the jurors looked at the judge. Although his daughter had also been stabbed she had not been sexually assaulted either. Witnesses at the trial of the man charged with the murder of Patricia had reported Judge Curran's remark at the time that 'thank goodness there was no interference'.

When he was arrested there were fresh cuts on McGladdery's hands. Curran questioned him closely from the bench as to the origin of the cuts, which McGladdery explained as being from the tools he had used in his apprenticeship as a shoe-maker with a local cobbler, Mervyn Graham. The questioning served to draw attention to a vital part of the prosecution case – the contention that Pearl had been stabbed with a shoemaker's file.

The crime scene now adjoins a traffic interchange with a retail park to one side. There is a grimy, out-of-town feel about it. Foster Newell's department store where Pearl worked was destroyed by firebomb in 1974. The brasswork and ornate plaster is gone, the garment racks and lingerie displays consumed in the flames. Vortices of flame carried upwards into the incendiary night. A large gospel hall has been built on the northern side of the railway embankment. The house of the godly. Bible texts are displayed on the gable of the building. The Wages of Sin is Death. Trains pass nearby on the viaduct. Diesel fumes hang in the air.

Pearl Gamble is buried in the Friends' Meeting House grave-yard. The cemetery is on the hillside looking down on North Street and the head of the lough. Old North Street was demol-ished in 1963. A dual carriageway and blocks of flats were built on the site. Their gone-to-seed modernist facades with washing on the balconies hide the cemetery. Traffic dirt hangs in the air. One row of original buildings remains as though to illustrate archetypes of business in decline. On the second storey of a barber's shop you can see the faded lettering indicating that the building was once a temperance hotel. A ghostly proscription against appetite and excess. The traffic streams past.

A formal photograph of Curran had been published in local newspapers on the opening day of the trial. Curran was review-ing a guard of honour of the First Battalion of the Royal Sussex Regiment at the opening of the Downpatrick Assize. Curran is wearing the garb of a High Court judge. A horsehair demi-wig. A starched white collar reaching down over the breastbone. A dark red cloak or surplice with ermine collar draped over the shoulders and a red gown underneath reaching to the ankles. A tipstaff comes behind him holding an umbrella over his head. The pleated folds of the soutane fall precisely. You can see the downturned mouth, a characteristic which he shared with his murdered daughter. His features are set. An eminence. A sou-taned cardinal set at the head of some baleful congregation.

The usher ordered the court to rise and Judge Curran entered.

One

Monday 30th January 1961

Eddie McCrink's Heathrow flight landed at 8.15. When he was in the air he liked to close his eyes and picture the air traffic control radar screen. All this speed and velocity monitored in dim-lit rooms by people in headphones, the terse clipped phrases of passage being exchanged between the tower and aircrew. Bearing headings. Westbound. Northbound. McCrink wondered if the travel itself was the point. Being airborne. Ranging between the aviation hubs, tracked across the vectors. There was a mystic element to aircraft crossing the radar screen, the ghost traces they left.

McCrink had worked in London for fifteen years, rising to the Murder Squad before being appointed to fill the vacant post of inspector of constabulary in Belfast. When he had applied for the job he had expected a formal interview process but instead had been called to the Cavendish Club by Harry West, a prominent member of the Stormont government. The talk about West was of buying up land ahead of zoning change for new motorway development. Re-drawing council boundaries. McCrink met him in the foyer. West had the look of a countryman about him, bluff and shrewd, the skin wind-reddened. He was wearing a tweed suit. He shook McCrink's hand. He showed him that evening's Belfast Telegraph. There was a photograph of Pearl Gamble on the front page.

'Dreadful event,' he said, 'the poor girl.' McCrink could read the look that West gave him, the steady corruptible stare. 'Was she of the minority faith?' McCrink knew what he was getting at. Lynch-mob politics. Hoping the killer was a Catholic. The miscreant underclass sunk in the perversion of their faith.

'The dance was in an Orange hall,' McCrink said, 'so it's not likely.'

'Someone laid in wait for her on the way home?'

'That'd be the way of it all right.'

'You think the man will be caught.'

'It's up to the local police. Under the supervision of the Inspector of Constabulary.'

'You'd better get supervising then. The job's yours. Make this a priority. And bear in mind we don't want another Curran case.'

'It won't take that long.'

'That wasn't what I meant, Mr McCrink. I want Allen to have him. Send out a signal.'

'Allen?'

'Harry Allen. The hangman. What goes on the mainland goes in the province. Shows we're upholding the rule of law without fear or favour.'

The terminal was empty except for passengers waiting for a Palma-bound charter delayed in Spain, grounded on some far-off sultry apron. Outside McCrink could see the lights of Belfast reflecting off low cloud to the east. The land fell away towards the conurbations to the west. Aldergrove had been a wartime aerodrome and it retained some of the improvised feel of those times, a windswept plateau and a feeling that, if you listened for them, lost callsigns could be heard in the radio buzz and clutter, whispery ghost wordings in the radar operators' headsets. Oscar, Whiskey, Zulu.

He took a taxi from the rank at the front of the airport, crossing the drizzly flatlands of Nutts Corner and Dromara, parts of the old aerodrome being used as a motorcycle race-track, blue lines of two-stroke exhaust hanging in the evening air. Wistful post-war landscapes, driving through the slobs and flax dams, dropping down towards sea level and into the late-evening traffic heading into the city. He had been booked into the International Hotel in the University area. The taxi driver left him there at ten o'clock, the thoroughfare empty at that hour except for couples walking home. There was a television lounge in the hotel. A boxed set that stood in the middle of the floor. The picture was poor, but McCrink sat up when he heard the newsreader menton Pearl Gamble. The screen showed the murder scene at Weir's Rock. The flickering rudiments of television. There was a different texture to the crime-scene photographs he was used to. The utilitarian six-by-tens, the darkly functional allure they brought to their subject matter. The hunched dead. The lingered-over poses. They were sombre and darkly themed.

McCrink left the hotel and walked down past the Botanic Gardens. He passed the end of a small cross street. A woman beckoned to him from the darkness. She was in her forties and there was a smell of gin on her breath, but in the late evening's balm she could be recast as a melancholic altruist, an archivist of arousal and desire, the city's carnal memory embodied.

9

He went into the York Hotel. He ordered a pint of ale and sat in an alcove to the side of the bar. The clientele was middle-aged. Men in blazers with the names of rugby and tennis clubs on the breast. There were club ties and crests. McCrink was familiar with this society, the emblems and allegiances, the coded and shifting structures. There was hearty laughter from the group at the bar. It depended on types. There would be hearty types, aloof men who defined themselves through sporting feats. There would be seducers of other men's wives, sly flatterers of pale dissatisfied women.

In the morning he drove down through the woebegone roundabouts and artificial lakes of Craigavon, its stained concrete overpasses and shuttered estates, its hinterland of failed civics.

John Speers was waiting for him outside Corry Square Station. He hadn't seen Speers since he had left Belfast for London twenty years before. Speers's skin had a grey hue. He looked ashen, exhausted, an apostle of bad faith. He shook McCrink's hand.

'Good to see they're keeping an eye on us, sending the big city boys down,' Speers said. Letting McCrink know there was no way round the resentment, that there would be a subtle and lasting rancour.

'It's your case, John,' McCrink said.

'You must have put the crusader's sword away then,' Speers said.

'A long time ago. Maybe we should proceed.'

~

Pearl's body had been concealed at Weir's Rock. Her clothing had been discarded between Damolly Cross and the murder scene. Speers had made inventory of the clothing. McCrink noted the labels. The word Ladybird on her slip. Playtex on her brassiere. The nubbed fabric. Lejaby. There were things he didn't understand about women. How they measured themselves and what rule they used. McCrink wondered if that was why her clothing had been removed. If the man who had killed her had found himself in study of these garments. If he had strained for understanding of them like a medieval theologian, head bent over an unfolded codex.

'This is Sergeant Johnston,' Speers said. Johnston was a stocky man in his fifties. The kind of provincial policeman that McCrink had expected. Jowly, resentful, shrewd. 'Where was she that night?'

'At a class of a hop in a hall. We have the boy. We have him nailed for you. Just haven't took him in yet.'

'Who are you looking at?'

'Local hood by the name of McGladdery. He's got some form. Convictions for breach of the peace and the like.'

'Any sexual previous?' McCrink asked.

'Not recorded anyhow. I'd say he was just working his way up to it.'

'Any witnesses place him there?'

'The whole town knows McGladdery was at the dance. Him and Will Copeland. The two of them full of drink. He got up to dance with the victim. Pawing her by all accounts. Hands all over her.'

'Common enough at a dance, I would've thought,' McCrink said.

'There's common and there's common. McGladdery takes off after the dance and nobody sees him till the next day.

There's a bicycle missing from outside the hall. We reckon he took it,' Johnston said.

'He spent time in London. He's into bodybuilding and the like,' Speers said.

'We should pick him up,' Johnston said.

'No,' McCrink said, 'leave him out there. Give him the chance to slip up. But we need to start interviewing the witnesses. Bring them up here.'

'We can do it in Corry Square.'

'I'd suggest doing it in Queen Street. Off the home patch. Who found her?'

'Some boy out walking greyhounds. He seen clothing by the side of the road. There's bloodstains between the field and the road. By the look of the face he bust her nose and she took to the fields.'

'I got out of London to get away from this,' McCrink said.

'There's no getting away from any of it any more,' Johnston said. 'As thou sowest, so shall thee reap.'

'Spare us the tent mission, Sergeant,' Speers said.

'I seen it written on a gable on the way up to Weir's Rock.'

'Don't tell us we're in that territory,' said McCrink.

'Clean-living to a man. You worked this kind of case before?' Speer said.

'I did.' McCrink thought about the girl sprawled in the reeking grass. 'In London. Toms killed and dumped.'

'Toms?'

'Prostitutes.'

In 1959 McCrink had worked on the first cases in what became known as the Nude Murders, the killing of eight prostitutes in London. The body of twenty-one-year-old

Elizabeth Figg, also known as Ann Phillips, was found in Dukes Meadows in Chiswick. McCrink had accompanied her to the morgue. A lab technician had propped her eyes open with matchsticks so that she could be photographed for the late-edition Star. She was identified from the photograph.

The photograph was published in the morning editions the following day, given prominence in the Daily Mail, the Mirror and the Express. Elizabeth Figg doesn't look dead in the photograph. Her look is thoughtful. She seems to have spotted something just out of frame that has given her pause. She looks wryly amused.

The Krays and the Nude Murders. Gangland killings and backstreet procuresses. A Reggie or a Ronnie in a lounge suit. The societal weather for the next decade seemed set at steady rain.

Pearl's nude, butchered remains on a fell hillside seemed to funnel these dire times into people's lives, reaching out from the distant metropolitan sprawl and clutter. Weir's Rock and the stubble field taking its place in the dead landscapes of the corpse dumping grounds, the dingy parklands and ashpits and canal banks.

'Same kind of thing then,' Speers said.

'Yes and no.' The Nude Murderer had used only the required amount of force, just squeezing the girls' windpipes, drawing them gently downward, removing them from the squalor of their lives, the thievery and poncing and edgy living. McCrink looking for connections. Pearl's body partly concealed behind bushes on the stony uplands above the town at the head of the lough. The distant scene hidden by coal smoke as if by a miasma of ill-intent.

'Who was the band?'

'A crew by the name of the RayTones. From the city.'

The RayTones. McCrink wondered what they had been doing in an Orange hall more used to stark upcountry gospellers, men with a wintry eye fixed on eternity. He had seen a picture of the RayTones in the Reporter. The band wore winklepickers and narrow trousers. He pictured them standing in the doorway of the Orange hall, peering out warily as though the night was full of hayseed murderers, populated by the interbred and the homicidal.

'There'll be reporters from the city down for this one,' Johnston said.

'There'll be reporters from all over the shop getting a look in,' Speers said, 'they'll go capital. It'll be the rope for whoever done this.'

'There was very little blood where she was found,' McCrink said.

'None here,' Johnston said, 'but I've got blood in plenty for you if you want it.'

'What do we know about her?'

'Girl by the name of Pearl Gamble. Works in Foster Newell's department store in the town. Never come home last night.'

The two men knew what was required of them now. That they be hard-eyed, open to revelation. There were new sciences of detection. There were laboratories where microscopic traces of flesh and matter were examined.

The body had been found in the morning but it had been evening before it was taken away, drawn into the night by motor hearse as the carted bodies from the close-by Workhouse had been drawn. She was driven through Newry

14

and the people of the town came out in the dark to view the hearse, and record to themselves the macabre night scenes as the black car with the dented steel coffin made its way through the rainy streets.

A single constable was left to guard the murder scene. The shadows of cloud moving across the moorlands. A place for the nocturnal transport of the forsaken. For their abandonment, left naked unto the night.

'We'll go to the morgue and give you a look at her,' Speers said.

The nose appeared to be broken and the tongue lolled from her mouth as though the manner of her death had forced her to some final abandon. There was blood and matter around the septum. The neck was marked and bruised. There were seven stab wounds on the torso and neck. McCrink noted that the punctures were small and of a regular shape.

'Made good and sure of her anyhow,' Speers said. Beaten, strangled, stabbed. The girl's eyes were open. She lay on her side with her hands cupped between her knees, a nude and butchered pieta.

The police photographer was Mervyn Graham, a local shoemaker. Graham was the kind of man who could turn his hand to anything. He wore a brown knee-length coat. He had the look of a bystander caught up in insurrection, a crumpled figure on the ground in the aftermath of street fighting. He did wedding photography for the Newry Reporter as well. Formal interior shots that made the bride and groom look like members of some lost peasant class, sombre with the burdens of forgotten worlds.

Graham looked down at the body and lit a No. 6. He knelt down, opened the back of a black Hasselblad and began to spool film in.

Graham started to shoot. McCrink could hear the sound of the shutter, the hair's-breadth clearances. He started to see the photographs as they would appear. Stark compositions lined up in the viewfinder. The nude unadorned body transfixed in the developing fluid, silvered and flickering. The shutter blades like something shuffled, as if a game of chance took place off-camera. A glamour brought to the scene as though staged for some deathly burlesque.

As they left the morgue an attendant approached them.

'Minister West on the line for Inspector Speers,' he said, 'wants an update on the investigation.'

'Fear and favour's what them lot is all about,' Johnston said. 'Rule by fear, reward by favour, isn't that it, sir?'

'You may keep that socialist stuff to yourself, Johnston. They'll have you for a commie. If there's anything they hate more than a taig, it's a commie,' Speers said.

Two

In the twenty-four hours following the murder known sex offenders in the area were brought in for questioning. The flashers, the stealers of underwear from washing lines. Hollow-cheeked, solitary men. Johnston interviewed them.

'Fucking saddle-sniffers is all. I can't see none of them doing the youngster. They wouldn't have it in them.'

McCrink parked at the courthouse and walked down past the Stonebridge and onto Hill Street. He walked past the mercantile buildings on Corry Square. Sugar Island. Buttercrane Quay. Places named for forgotten trades, the canal silted up, the railheads deserted. Sheets of sleet blowing up over the Marshes from the lough, McCrink trailing the dead through the January streets. Finding himself in the back lanes and shambles. Tuberculosis still rampant in the town, disease of the poor. He walked in alleyways lined with one-room cottages where the women were shawled. It was what he always did. He walked the streets, went to the victim's workplace, trying to find a way into the story of their lives, the gritty small-town textures of the story.

At the canal basin two cranes were unloading coal from a Polish coaster into hoppers. A black dust cloud rolled across the water. The cranes bent to their task each in turn like some articulate beast from the dawn of time, as though something it craved was abroad in the dark and filthy hull of the freighter.

There was coal spilled on the dock. Tinker children gathered the spilled fuel into sacks. McCrink put his foot on a piece of the brownish coal. It crumbled under his foot.

'Pure shit, that is.' McCrink looked up. One of the dock workers was standing over him with a spade. The man's face was black with dust, seamed with the worked-in grains. The whites of his eyes stood out against the black.

'You're the boy that's here to hang someone for Pearl Gamble,' the man said.

'I'm not here to hang anybody.'

'Somebody'll be hung though.'

'That's up to the courts.'

'Courts are made up of men. There's a mood in this town for somebody to pay with their neck.'

Across the basin McCrink could see the town gasometers. These were the textures of the town. Coal-dust. Rain-soaked meal spilled on the quayside train tracks. The dark forsworn canal waters.

McCrink walked up the town at closing time. He had left the girl's place of work to the end. He passed the old market. Stallholders were packing their vans. There was a smell of meat from a butcher's skip and gone-off vegetables lay in the gutter. The market gave way to stone buildings. The Northern Bank, the General Post Office. There were brass plaques for solicitors and dentists. People relied upon to be stalwart, to espouse well-worn value systems. There were small groups of workers at bus stops.

He stopped in Margaret Square and looked up at the lit frontage of Foster Newell's. The late-evening customers just leaving. Women in hats with small veils attached, a sombre, monied gait as they walked to their cars. He could see the staff locking up inside. Through the rain-smeared windows the uniformed girls looked elegant and yielding, their movements ritualised, their eyes downcast. They moved easily in the formal interior of the shop, the gilt mirrors and empty counters, and McCrink imagined a sorrow in the air, the knowledge that one of their own had fallen, a caste awareness.

There was a phone box across the street. McCrink phoned Speers. Holding the whorled mouthpiece and waiting for the connection.

'McCrink. Anything new?'

'Preliminary autopsy. Seven stab wounds. None of them fatal. Death caused by crush wounds to the trachea. Bruising.'

McCrink found himself staring at the facade of Foster Newell's. Listening to the line clutter. The information routed through the far-off exchanges, the copper and bakelite contacts, the deep subterranean connections. The death-nodes.

'Any prints lifted from the body?'

'None so far. She was lying out all night in the rain. Wouldn't be many traces left.'

'You finished at the barracks?'

'Nothing I can do for now.'

'Meet me in Nummy's. The Crown Bar. '

On his way up Hill Street McCrink saw the municipal library. He pushed through the mahogany and brass doors. The lights had been turned off in the main part of the library apart from the librarian's desk. It was what he had expected, a shabby and bedimmed provincial interior. He could see a figure behind the desk. He thought he knew what to expect from a librarian in a place like this. A woman with mousy hair, flat-shoed, spinsterish.

'I'm sorry, we're closed.' He moved closer to the desk. The woman was in her late thirties, McCrink thought. Her hair hung to her shoulders and she was wearing gold hoop earrings and a blouse with a gypsy look to it. She had a long nose and a way of tilting her head to one side when she talked to you. There was disillusion in her face, a look that had traded off wry self-forgiveness for too long and was ready to settle into resentment. The kind of woman he was drawn to.

'Police,' he said.

'O God,' she said, 'the murder. I bought some make-up from her last weekend. She was in the chorus in the opera. You never think . . . I'm sorry. I'm making a story of it. You must have listened to a hundred of them.'

'That's what people do. Tell stories when something like this happens.' Their stories all they had to set against the dark.

'Is there something I can do?' She had a way of tucking her head into her shoulder as if to suppress a smile, turning her hands palm-up in surrender, lifting an eyebrow in sardonic bemusement. Murder was abroad in the town.

'Have you got maps of the area?'

'You'd need more than a map to find your way around this place.'

'Why do you say that?'

'You know what people in this town are called?'

'No.'

'Nyuks.'

'What does that mean? The accent?' He'd noticed it in her speech. The mudflat drawl with a kind of disdain in it.

'No. Most people think that, but it's a gypsy word. Cant. It means thief.'

'The town of thieves.'

'It had a history as a trading town. Markets. Goods imported and exported. And it's close to the border. Maybe that's where it comes from.'

'It's not doing much trade now.'

'Place has been starved of investment for decades. The government would rather see it fall into the canal.'

'Why's that?'

'Maybe they think we're all thieves.'

She brought him into a small room at the back of the library. The maps were in drawers against the wall. He wanted to see the distance and terrain between the Orange hall, McGladdery's house and the murder scene, but found himself staring at the lough, the shoals and high-tide lines, the charted murks. He traced the inked-in depths. The town clustered at the head of the lough, the buildings and enclosures hand-drawn. *Nyuk.* The spat-out word, drawing the psychic undertow of the town with it. The secret languages. Tinker's cants. The town rising away from the centre. North Street, Abbey Yard. The gaunt precincts of the town. This was the oldest part of the municipality, the narrow streets and lanes turning into each other. Margaret put her finger on the map.

'Gallows Hill. It always sends a shiver through me.' The place of execution. Gibbeted footpads hanging in rows, birds pulling at their flesh.

'Is it true that whoever did this will be executed?' she said.

'Capital punishment is still on the statute book.'

'I debated repeal in school. Capital punishment has no place in a civilised society. Discuss.' There was an earnestness in her voice which reminded him of his wife.

'The Gamble family would probably love to discuss it with you.'

'Sorry, I didn't mean anything. I'll get my coat.'

He watched her move away into the unlit library. When she had gone into the shadows his eye fell on the Abbey Yard on the map. The mendicant orders. Hooded monks walking in procession chanting.

He found his finger tracing the line of the coal quay where he had seen the tinkers earlier. Bivouacked in the shadows. The Orange hall. The stubble field. Weir's Rock.

'Did you find anything?' The librarian had put on her coat.

'Not much.'

'People forget that they're close to the border. There are unapproved roads. Smugglers pads over the mountain.'

'Maybe that's where the thief name came from. The smuggling.'

'Maybe.'

'Smugglers and excise men. Coming in over the mountain and the lough. Contraband borne by night.'

'You aren't local.'

'I'm from Belfast. I was in London. I came home to be Inspector of Constabulary.'

'So what are you doing here?'

'I wanted a job at home and I got it. They sent me down from the city to supervise the investigation.'

'We have to be supervised, do we?'

He waited while she locked and barred the library doors.

The clank and ring of bolts and bar as though some dire mechanics were at work in the empty square. He watched as she walked to her car, a left-hand drive Renault. She looked at it and looked at him with a half-grin. If he questioned her about it there would be stories about holidays in France, bringing the car back to show herself as unconventional, her life become a thing of self-mocking gestures. If she was afraid of a murderer she didn't mention it. She got into the car and pulled off without looking back, driving alone out into the maverick night.

There was a stillness to the town. McCrink noticed it every time he stepped off the main streets. Haunted spaces. Spaces waiting to be filled.

He walked back up to Trevor Hill and went into the bar. There was a smell of damp coats in the air, a bar-room atmosphere of low-key duplicity. McCrink recognised Nummy's for what it was. A place where people drank to keep at bay the damage they had caused through drinking. Everything else was left outside the door. The bartop was chipped Formica. The stools were shabby. But you could stay there as long as you liked, and the small doorway seemed to be sealed against judgement.

He sat at the bar and ordered a vodka and tonic. Speers and Johnston came in and sat beside him.

'Johnston is still keen on the local for it. Boy by the name of McGladdery we talked about,' Speers said.

'What do you think?'

'There's something about it doesn't add up.'

'He doesn't act much like your regular villain. Mad into

bodybuilding and the like.'

'Doesn't act much like anything I ever seen.'

'The bodybuilding fits,' McCrink said, thinking how a murderous self-regard could develop from it.

'There's a lot that fits. The petty crime. The difficult childhood. The man's a danger to the world by all accounts. It's the criminal arc.'

'The criminal arc?'

Johnston said, 'Inspector Speers's got these theories about the architecture of the criminal mind, sir.'

'What's your theory about the criminal mind?' McCrink said.

'A bad bastard is a bad bastard is my theory, sir.'

'Johnston can be crude but it works sometimes,' Speers said. 'I'm suggesting that he takes the lead in interviewing witnesses.'

'What's your qualification for the job, Johnston?' McCrink said.

'I learned at the feet of a master,' Johnston said, 'I worked the Curran case. I seen Chief Inspector Capstick interviewing Gordon for the murder. Got a confession out of him in a day.'

'Gordon?'

'For the murder of Patricia Curran, the judge's daughter.'

Johnston told them how Capstick had gone about it. Capstick had told Hay Gordon that he was aware of his homosexuality. He referred to undercurrents of deviance in Gordon's person, the weakness of the jawline, the limpness of the handshake. Capstick had referred to his own experience in dealing with the pallid deviants of the London underworld, the queers and poofters, scions of arse banditry. He had filled

Gordon's head with dark visions of night streets peopled with the children of vice.

'At the heel of the hunt, Capstick told him his loving mother would find out he was a pervert. Scared the little bugger half to death to make him confess. The gents of the bar library had to bend over backwards to stop him getting his rightful deserts which was a rope around his neck. Cried like a baby when the ma's name come up. Couldn't wait to write out a statement.'

'It's a distasteful way to get a confession,' McCrink said.

'He got a conviction,' Speers said.

'He got a conviction but he left a fishy smell in the air.'

'Never mind a fishy smell, sir,' Johnston said; 'around this town we do what works.'

'You want to see McGladdery?' Speers said. 'Johnston's men's got him under surveillance at Hollywood's bar.'

They drove down Merchants Quay. They parked the Humber along the canal.

'There he is,' Speers said.

Robert McGladdery was standing outside the bar. He was wearing a Crombie and a porkpie hat pushed back on his head. He was smoking, holding the cigarette cupped in his hand, an untipped Black Cat or No. 6. In the glow of the cigarette McCrink could see a pale face, half-smiling. There was a long scratch on one side of his face.

'A dissolute,' Johnston said. 'Stood there same time every day. Sits at the bar until he hears the mill hooter then out he comes. Watches the night shift coming off the tram. Making lewd and filthy remarks in their hearing.'

'Where'd he get the scratches on his face?'

'That's the question.'

'He never got the glad rags here.'

'Spent a year in England.'

'That would be right.' The clothes garish for this town. Made him look like a fairground barker. As if some lewd carnival attraction was concealed within the pub confines. A grotesque. A caged imbecile whimpering in the dark.

'Do we lift him?'

'Let him lie. He'll come to us in his own good time.'

'Likes of him wouldn't turn himself in.'

'That's not what I meant.'

Three

An incident room had been set up at Corry Square barracks. There were Ordnance Survey maps on a pinboard in the middle of the room. Space had been cleared for Mervyn Graham's crime-scene and autopsy photographs. A bank of telephones linked to the exchange had been laid on by the Post Office. There were photographs of the dead girl cut from that evening's Belfast Telegraph. They were waiting for the full set of crime-scene photographs to be developed, and for the results of the autopsy. Johnston's men had started to bring in witnesses for questioning.

The locals wouldn't look at the girl's photograph. They kept their heads bent over their desks as though they were reciting some personal office of the dead. McCrink examined the photograph. The gap between her teeth. Her mouth turned down at the corners in a way which suggested a mean-spirited sensuality.

'Faulkner's been on again. He wants to see whoever done this hanged.'

'I thought they done away with the rope.'

'Only across the water. Not here. Capital punishment is still on the books. Hangman's not signing on yet.'

'Faulkner's a modern man. He'll throw whoever did it a pardon,' Speers said.

'He'll throw no pardon,' Johnston said, 'Faulker would no more pardon a man who left a girl in that state than he would pardon a weasel in a snare.'

'There's a lot of argument across the water about abolition of the rope,' McCrink said.

'Place is still on a war footing, Inspector. Bear it in mind.' Speers said.

McCrink looked at him. They knew what was going on. Execution still on the cards for those attempting overthrow of the state. McCrink could see the witnesses through the meshed firedoor glass. They sat in benches along the distempered corridor. There was a small-town look to them. Jug-eared youths. Big-boned girls holding patent handbags on their knees. The mill girls with needle marks on their hands from the looms. He could imagine them at a Saturday-night dance. Dressed to the nines, sinking into the myth of it, the band playing Presley and Bill Haley, the Americana seeping in, Pearl in the middle of them catching McGladdery's eye across the hall, down-home lonesomeness dragging danger into the room. Finding a home in the plank-built hall, the dust-seamed walls. The dancers hadn't come far from the tent gospel missions and itinerant preachers, the god-struck hinterlands.

'We should start,' McCrink said.

'Leave them be for a bit,' Johnston said. Let the feel of the station seep in. Let the weight of the town bear down on them, the mass and substance of the teeming municipality. Outside it was growing dark. Rain was falling. The station doors opening and closing, the evening traffic growing until the noise of its passing was felt in the fabric of the building, the witnesses glancing at each other nervously now, feeling the town bestirring itself, the darksome thrumming.

It was eight o'clock before Speers indicated the interviews were about to start. He used a basement interview room, the table notched and scarred. He knew that they would expect this. He was hard-faced, abrupt. He gave the impression that events beyond the station walls were hastening to an inevitable conclusion.

McCrink walked past the interviewees in the corridor. The process would have to be gruelling. They would have to move through the stages. Acceptance and repentance. They would be turned out into the darkness, shriven. He opened the door of the interview room then turned in the doorway and beckoned. A young man got uncertainly to his feet. Come in, McCrink thought. Lay bare your pilgrim soul.

The interview rooms were in the basement of Corry Square. The witness was meant to feel the weight of the building pressing down on him. The rooms were bare, the pipework exposed. There was a table in the middle of the floor with a chair to each side. McCrink thought that the purpose was to intimidate the witness. To draw wrong to themselves, repent of sins they had not yet committed.

'We'll bring the backwoods Prod out in them,' Johnston said. 'We'll rattle on the roofs of their fucking tin gospel huts. There's nothing to distract them. The only thing they can do is talk. They start to tell you stuff they didn't even know they knew.'

Hesitant at first. Then a story starts to take shape in their heads. They start to see the possibilities of narrative, the interwoven stuff of their lives. How things have shaped themselves around the defining moment. How they found themselves in an Orange hall, the dramatic building, in the dark and thrilling proximity of a sex crime. They try to piece the night together, how seemingly meaningless events become part of the weft. They start to ponder the interrelatedness of things. They are grateful to the interviewer for helping to find the patterns.

The telling of it alters what happened. They start to see everything as laden down with consequence. Searching their memory for detail. The dream-sequences. There are digressions. The narrative falters.

'They start making it up,' Speers said. 'If they can't remember they make it up. You got to keep a handle on them.'

They begin to see the victim's passage through their lives, the unearthly progress. Every action fated.

'You wait till you see the whites of their eyes,' Johnston said.

'They're thinking it could have been me,' Speers said, 'the killer could have picked any one of them.' He laughed and lit a Gold Bond. 'They're thinking what's so special about her?'

'That's not it,' McCrink said. The witnesses became panicky, words spilling out of them. They had felt the presence of death or some attendant to death in the hall, a louche cold figure who gave the impression that he had been there for some time.

'They have to tell the whole thing because they're terrified,' McCrink said. Searching for the formula of words that would protect them. The telling. The incantation of story.

'I'd hang them all,' Johnston said, 'hang them all and let God sort them out.'

Johnston put a telegram on the desk in front of McCrink.

The lettering dark and inky, the characters unevenly spaced. Kennedy. Tonight. 8.00. HQ.

'Looks like the Chief Constable wants you,' Speers said.

'We'll be busy here, sir, don't worry,' Johnston said, 'I'm always busy anyhow, isn't that right, sir?'

Busy at what? McCrink thought.

~

McCrink drove to RUC Headquarters at Castlereagh on the outskirts of Belfast feeling he was leaving mischief behind him. The headquarters were low grey buildings, flat-roofed with a Soviet-era look to them. McCrink was led through distempered corridors, feeling he was out in some far-flung spy post. He imagined operatives crouched over radar screens, looking for incoming missiles, parabolic flights coming in over Siberia.

Kennedy's office was leather and wood. The Chief Constable was wearing full dress uniform. A career policeman, McCrink thought. He shook hands with McCrink.

'Congratulations on your appointment.'

'I'm sorry I didn't come straight away.'

'Of course, of course. It was an emergency. You'll find your duties here are light. There is little inspecting to be done. However Minister Faulkner has expressed a wish that you keep a close eye on this Pearl Gamble business.'

Brian Faulkner. Minister for Home Affairs. Faulkner's picture in the Telegraph. Pitching himself at the urbane but you looked at the mouth, the downturned corners, the big-house dissatisfactions written all over him, the epic disdain. Faulkner rode to hounds. Faulkner knew the structures of rotten boroughs, redrawn ward boundaries, electoral carve-ups, zoning scandals going unaddressed. Faulkner was a big-house Unionist. He had estates in the east and on the border. An air of feudal rancours about him. Disdain in the gene code.

'What is the state of play?' Kennedy said. 'A sex crime?'

'Looks like it.'

'What's the story with the girl?'

'She left the dance on her own about 1.30. We're inter-viewing witnesses.'

'Witnesses?'

'The man who found her. The crowd who were at the dance. No eye-witness to the crime.'

'What sort of crowd?'

'Local girls. Mill girls. Crew of wide boys from the town.'

'Murder weapon?'

'None so far.'

'Was she interfered with?'

McCrink had worked in London, Denmark Street. Soho and the theatre district. Areas that were described as vice-ridden. He had seen women dead in alleys, beaten by lovers in shabby flats. He had seen a Maltese tom with her nos-trils slit. Sex crimes with an Edwardian slant to them, gaslit, looming out of the fog, Whitechapel lurkers at work in the night.

'She was stripped. Bare to the world.'

'Anything else?'

'She was stabbed and strangled. He wasn't taking any chances.'

'I'll say again. Any sexual interference?'

32

'He never laid a hand on her person. Bar the beating and the stabbing and the strangling. That's the preliminary finding anyhow.'

'I hope the locals are giving you a steer.'

'They say they've got a likely candidate.'

'The gathering of evidence is the responsibility of the investigating officer,' Kennedy said. 'They have failed to find the murder weapon or any eye-witnesses to the crime.'

'Either he has them well concealed or we're barking up the wrong tree, sir. Might not have been him after all.'

'You do not seem to have considered the possibility that the suspect might be cleverer than you give him credit for. Perverts often are, you know.'

You wouldn't know a pervert from a hole in the ground, McCrink thought.

'I find that an appeal to the public is often effective in these cases,' Kennedy said. 'Encourages good citizenry.'

'Yes sir.'

'We have to apprehend the beast,' Kennedy said. 'An example will have to be made.'

You're an example of something yourself, McCrink thought.

'You'll have full access to Special Branch files in order to familiarise yourself with the province and its people,' Kennedy said.

McCrink stayed in the city that night. He slept badly, the names of the Nude Murder victims going through his head. Elizabeth Figg. Gwynneth Rees. The unmarked corpses, nude and profane. The killer easing them into death and dumping their bodies. Drawing them into his narrative, their stories retold. Their old lives were discarded. All the cheap flats and

33

sex acts in the backs of parked cars. You could see it in the arrest files. Their pale demeaned faces. The autopsy reports pointed to venereal disease, evidence of alcohol abuse and malnutrition. The killer seeing the possibility in them that they could redeem themselves in death.

The body of Pearl Gamble was transferred to the Royal Victoria in Belfast for full autopsy. Photographs in the Newry Reporter and the Belfast Telegraph show the hearse leaving the hospital grounds. There are knots of people at the hospital gates. They have the look of a defeated populace. Sullen, huddled. There are photographers from the city papers, PA reporters in Aquascutum coats. There are no photographs of the hearse arriving at the Royal. The car directed to a rear entrance. A concrete ramp down to the mortuary. The body removed from the coffin and placed on a wheeled gurney by aproned attendants. They wheeled Pearl through the waiting area to the pathology room, the men talking quietly among themselves. The instruments of dissection are waiting for her. The scales to weigh the organs. Pearl's substance and matter accounted for, weighed and assayed. The place tiled and sluiced. Cabinets of stainless steel and high-wattage strip lighting to keep the dark away, the cadaver shadows.

~

McCrink drove back to the coast that evening. He had been booked into a hotel in Rostrevor. He went as far as the Great Northern Hotel opposite the coal pier. Along the coastline there were many hotels named for train companies. The Great Northern. The Great Western. They were built in the style

34

of grand European hotels. There were high-ceilinged foyers, uniformed porterage. The mouldering ballrooms and damp shrubberies seemed to have decays catered for, lingered over. There were still framed posters on the walls of the hotels, the mass-tourism reveries of the mid-fifties. Outings and excursions, charabancs and trains carrying families from dreamed-of industrial belts. The lines shut down. The railway companies went into receivership. The vast hotels could be seen for miles around, gaunt and ill-lit termini on the lough's wintry shore.

McCrink checked in and telephoned Corry Square. Johnston answered the phone. McCrink asked for Speers.

'Inspector Speers has gone home, sir,' Johnston said.

'How is the investigation proceeding?'

'I'm not inclined to judgement.'

'For Christ's sake, Johnston, I'm not asking you to send somebody to eternal flame. I'm asking you how the day went.'

'Since you ask, sir, the finger is pointing in the direction of McGladdery. Since you speak of eternal flame.'

'Go on.'

'We have witnesses saying he danced with Miss Gamble. We have witnesses to vulgar acts on his part. He disappears after the dance. It turns out that a bicycle was stole from outside the hall and the bicycle turns up at Damolly Cross.'

'What does McGladdery say?'

'Denies it. Laughs in the face of jeopardy and right thinking.'

'Laughs?'

'Thinks it a joke a woman laid out indecent and dead in a field like a beast.'

Four

Judge Lance Curran was at the table in the billiard room of the Reform Club on Royal Avenue. Judge Curran played with his election agent, Harry Ferguson. They played French billiards at one guinea a ball. Theirs was the only occupied table in the room. Ferguson racked the balls and broke. The billiard room was in the turreted peaks of the building. A fire burned at either end of the room and there were coats of arms and portraits on the walls. Each time he was invited to the room to play, Ferguson felt as if he had wandered into a storybook castle, a place of shifting perception and nursery cruelties. The windows were white with fog. The city was fog-bound, muffled, inward-looking. He felt as if he had come upon some abstraction of weather.

Curran studied the arrangement of balls on the table, the random disposition from the break. He ran his hand along the chalk-scored nap of the baize. They played as night fell and there were only the lights above the tables. The judge in his pinstripe trousers and white shirt and tie like some master of ceremonies set to fashion and prepare the onset of night. The Belfast Telegraph with the story of Pearl Gamble's murder lay on the table below the cue rack and score board. Curran kept score. Every time he went over to the board he had to see the photograph of Pearl Gamble but he made no mention of it. Curran had a way of letting things hang in the air.

Halfway through the evening Curran excused himself. Ferguson went out onto the landing and saw Curran enter the phone kiosk in the entrance hall. He thought he knew what the phone call would be. He envisaged Curran standing in the kiosk, the heavy bakelite receiver in his hand. An instrument to give weight to your words, a moral heft.

When Curran returned he removed his cue from the rack. He sighted along the ash shaft and brass ferrule.

'I am going to try this case,' he said.

'Do you think that is wise?'

'Wise, Ferguson?'

'A nineteen-year-old girl has been murdered. Your own nineteen-year-old daughter was also murdered nine years ago.'

'Are you suggesting prejudice?'

'The appearance of prejudice.'

'I will try the case even-handedly.'

'I've no fear of that.'

'Then what do you fear?'

Curran leaned over the table. He made a bridge of the fingers of his left hand and laid the cue across the raised knuckles. He studied the balls then put side on the cue ball to kiss the yellow ball into the middle, the cue ball coming to rest against the cushion beside the top-right pocket. Over the years Ferguson had come to understand that the judge believed in pattern. That things were mapped out, that matters were underlain with strange cartographies. Things were not random. Ferguson had gone with Curran to the planetarium. He had sat with him while the alignments of the planets were represented to him. The announcer described the movements of the planets as a dance and Curran turned to look at him as if to say is this in fact a dance, this cold gavotte, the streaming nebulae, the stars of ash?

~

Lance Curran's daughter Patricia had been murdered in November 1952. She had been stabbed thirty-seven times and her body left under trees on the driveway of their house, the Glen, in Whiteabbey. The body had been found by her brother and her father. There were reports of tension between Patricia and her mother, Doris. Patricia was independent and during the summer holidays before her death she had taken a summer job driving a lorry for a builders' supplier.

In November 1953 Iain Hay Gordon was found not guilty of her murder by reason of insanity. Gordon had known the family. Interviewed by Inspector John Capstick of Scotland Yard, he had confessed to killing Patricia with his service knife.

Gordon had been incarcerated in Holywell Mental Hospital. The superintendent of the hospital had said that he could find no reason to detain him. In 1958 Gordon was quietly released. He returned to Glasgow and changed his name. In 2000, forty-eight years after the conviction, Gordon had his conviction overturned. One key strand of his appeal was his oppressive interrogation by Inspector Capstick.

The other strand of the case which resulted in the conviction being overturned concerned the phone call which was made by Judge Curran to the family of John Steel, the young man who had accompanied Patricia to the bus which had carried her home from college that night. Steel's father was adamant that he had answered the phone at 2.15 a.m. and had been asked by Judge Curran if 'he had seen Patricia'. It was

38

conclusively proven that Patricia's body had been discovered shortly before 2 a.m., fifteen minutes before the judge called the Steel household to ask if they had seen her. The discrepancy has never been explained.

The murder of Patricia Curran and the murder of Pearl Gamble were separated by nine years. Patricia was the daughter of a judge. Her family were prominent in political and legal circles. Pearl was a shop assistant. Mystery accrues equally to them. Their tenure in the darkness is assured.

Five

Interrogations resumed at Corry Square the following morning. McCrink stood at the back of the interrogation room.

Mervyn Graham was the first to be brought into the interview room. He rolled a Golden Virginia from a tin using a rolling machine. He confirmed that he had offered Robert an apprenticeship as a shoemaker. That he was due to start soon.

'McGladdery never done it.'

'Why do you say that?'

'He doesn't have it in him.'

'Everybody has it in them.'

'Not this buck.'

'The whole town seen him acting the hard man.'

'Acting isn't being.'

'What makes you such a judge of character?'

'I was in the war. I seen enough men die. Talking about judges, I hear tell Curran's going to try the case.'

'That's up to the DPP.'

'DPP my eye. If Curran wants to try it, he'll try it. And I do believe he wants to.'

'He might disqualify himself.'

'He should have disqualified himself many a long year ago. He's hunger's mother, that boy.'

'The case will be tried according to its merits.'

'If Judge Curran takes the bench, it'll be the rope for McGladdery.'

'What was McGladdery wearing that night?' Johnston said.

'I don't know. I wasn't there.'

'You've got eyes in your head. Did McGladdery own a light-blue suit?'

'I don't know.'

The next witness was a small man called Donaldson who wore a white shirt buttoned to the collar, the sleeves rolled down to the wrists. One side of his face was covered by a port-wine scar.

'That McGladdery was a bad lot.'

'Why do you say that?' Speers said.

'Conceived out of wedlock.'

'Did you know the girl?'

'I never knew her nor any of her kin. She reaped what she sowed.'

'What about the boy that killed her?' Johnston said.

'An instrument of the Lord.'

'Do you do the bit of pulpit bashing yourself?'

'I am a lay preacher at the Church of the Risen Christ, if that is what you mean by your reference to the pulpit,' Donaldson said.

'What he means,' Johnston said, 'is would you ever consider yourself an instrument of the Lord? I mean would you harvest what was sown in the way of nineteen-year-old girls on their way home after a dance? Are you a deviant, Mr Donaldson?'

'You do not number yourself among the godly, Sergeant,' Donaldson said.

'I leave it up to God to do the numbering. That way there's no mistakes made,' Johnston said.

'What do you do for a living, Mr Donaldson?' Speers said.

'I fix cars, lorries, anything with an engine.'

'You like to get in among the innards, is that it?' Johnston said.

'It's honest toil. You do work that you have a gift for. Mine is engines.'

'Mine is thieves and murderers,' Johnston said. 'I labour among the vineyards of the depraved. Did you see McGladdery at the dance?'

'I seen him dancing with the dead girl and others.'

'What was he wearing?'

'I don't remember.'

'A light-coloured suit maybe?'

'Could have been.'

'Jesus, we landed ourselves in Bible country here,' Johnston said afterwards. 'The kingdom of heaven.'

'What was he doing at a dance if he's so God-fearing?' Speers said.

'They like to keep an eye on proceedings. Tongue hanging out for it if you ask me,' Johnston said, 'the forbidden fruit. Who's next?'

The girl had a fringe of greasy blonde hair which almost covered her eyes. She kept her head down as she talked. There was dermatitis on her hands. Her name was Susan Hanna.

'What is it with this town and skin?' Speers said. McCrink thought it was something to do with the damp earth under their feet. There were wreathing vapours on the Marshes at night. You saw people with psoriasis and eczema, all kinds of skin flare-ups.

'Looks like a medieval town,' Speers said, 'you think you're going to see weeping sores and cankers.'

'What do you do, Miss Hanna?' Speers asked.

'I work in the valley dyeworks. In the soakpits.' McCrink looked at the girl's hands again. You could see where red dye had seeped into the skin.

'You were present in the Robert Thompson Memorial Orange Hall on the night of 28th January.'

'I was there. I seen Robert McGladdery and Pearl Gamble. I seen them dancing together. She did have him tormented.'

'What do you mean?'

'Teasing him. Leading him on.'

'Teasing?'

'Beguilement.' McCrink tried to see the girl's eyes but she kept her head down, talking in a monotone.

'She slowdanced him dead close till she had him brave and roused and then she rose up and laughed in his face. She pushed him away. She scorned him. It was like death laughed at you the way she done it.'

'What did he do?'

'He walked after her as she went back to her friend. He had a black look on him. He was like a tale of vengeance from the testament.'

'You're making this up,' Johnston said, 'you've some detestation against the victim. Maybe you set your hat at McGladdery and you saw her dancing with him. Maybe you're glad she's dead.'

'By the risen Christ I had no ill will towards her. I brung the plain news to you as we are bid. You bear witness. What else would you do? The day passes as it must. All that remains is for to tell it.'

'What else did you see?'

'Nothing. I heard about her dying. There was a narration of slaughter in the night. I got up the next morning. I went to work in the dyeworks. I went on my knees in the soakpits.'

'What was he wearing?'

'What?'

'McGladdery. What was he wearing?'

'I don't recall.'

'If you had to take a guess.'

'Guesswork isn't called for.'

The girl lifted her head for the first time. The dermatitis had affected the skin around her eyes, the eye itself reddened and sore and the skin broken so that she looked at them through a mask of affliction. The wind outside blew hail against the window and the room darkened as a squall passed up the lough.

Johnston moved around the table until he stood in front of her and she flinched as he loomed over her like some law-bringer from the testament of her youth, a visitant authorised to bring her before the seat of judgement.

'Leave me be,' she said.

'He's not going to hurt you,' Speers said.

'I should never have gone to the dance,' she said. 'I was told and I never listened.'

'It's not your fault,' Speers said. 'All we want to know is what you saw that night.'

'Who are you to talk to me of fault?'

'What was McGladdery wearing?' Johnston said. 'What was his attire? Was he wearing a light-coloured suit?'

'I paid no heed to his attire,' the girl said.

'Are you certain? A minute ago you were all eyes.'

'That's enough,' McCrink said, 'we're finished with you now, miss.'

The girl left, scurrying from the room, eyes downcast, as though released from some awful service to them. Johnston sat back in his chair and loosened his tunic.

'I felt like I just went three hours with some hell-and-brimstone boy baying from the pulpit,' Speers said.

'If she was that good-living then what was she doing at an occasion of sin? Same as the last boy.'

'They like being an outpost,' Speers said. 'Surrounded by unbelievers.'

'What do you think of the scabby bitch's story?' Johnston said. 'Never heard that Pearl was pulling McGladdery's chain.'

'You could put her in the witness box,' McCrink said. 'It's the first thing I've heard that goes towards motive. Pearl turned McGladdery down and he took his revenge.'

'There's motive enough in the way he left her,' Johnston said. 'What more motive does he need?'

McCrink returned to the Great Northern that evening with the file containing the transcripts of the previous day's interviews. A dinner dance was taking place in the hotel ballroom. There was a middle-European look to the dance crowd, men with hooded eyes and women in crinolines and satins, the strains of a waltz coming from the ballroom, an atmosphere of low-key intrigue running through the evening. McCrink crossed the carpet, people eyeing him, a shambling figure bringing with him the smell of the outlands. As he stood at the reception desk he felt someone touch his elbow. He recognised the man behind him from press photographs. Brian Faulkner, Minister for Home Affairs. Faulkner was wearing evening dress. McCrink was aware that there was mud on his shoes. He felt uncouth, tainted by contact with the case.

'Good evening, Inspector,' Faulkner said, 'let me congratulate you on your appointment.'

'Thank you, Minister.'

'You look tired. You must be putting in long hours on this dreadful Gamble business. A guilty verdict is assured, from what I hear.'

'We're collecting evidence, sir.'

'I have been told that an early resolution to the case is expected. That you can connect a man to the murder.'

'Connection is not conviction, with respect, sir.'

'You haven't worked on a murder case in the province before, have you, Detective?'

'No, my experience is confined to the Met.'

'Trust me. There will be a conviction. You do your job and I'll do mine. I must return to my company. But once again my warmest congratulations.'

McCrink looked after Faulkner. *You do your job and I'll do mine.* In the case of a death sentence appeals for clemency went through the Minister for Home Affairs. Faulkner was looking for a hanging.

He brought the file to the bedroom and sat down on the bed. The file already gathering history to itself, detectives' desks, grubby interview rooms, the cover handled and foxed. It looked as if it contained something fragile. He found himself thinking of scrolls, ancient papyrus at the edge of decipherment, containing all that there was to be known about lost times and dead races, the Aramaeans and Phoenicians, the out-of-reach languages and dialects. There was scope for awe here, he felt.

McCrink read until eleven o'clock then he closed the file and went down to the bar. He could hear waltz music from the ballroom. He ordered a whiskey and soda from a white-jacketed barman. There were men in black tie sitting in the lobby, melancholy, predatory figures. McCrink felt that he had found himself among some lost bourgeoisie. There was a between-the-wars atmosphere in the room.

He looked up to see the librarian approaching him. She was wearing a peasant-style blouse and skirt. She had taken off her shoes and was walking barefoot on the carpet. Her hair hung to her shoulders. Her fringe partly covered her eyes. He saw the wry twist to her mouth, an outgrown coquettishness in her manner. She'd been drinking. The gone-to-seed small-town beauty.

'Detective McCrink. Are you here on sport or business?'

'Business. I'm staying here.'

'Have you solved the slaying of poor dear Pearl yet?'

'We're working on it.'

'That's what you get when you tease a man. Lead him on.'

'Is that what Pearl did? Lead him on?'

'That's what they're whispering round the town. You want to know what they're whispering about me? There she is. Near forty and not a man to show for it. Neither chick nor child. They're whispering maybe broken engagement. Jilted or thrown over. Take your pick. You're the detective. Detect a broken heart for me.'

'I'd say it's more a matter of you breaking hearts.'

'That's what I like to hear, a bit of world-weary gallantry. There's precious little by the way of chivalry in these parts.'

The lines sounded false, committed to memory. McCrink knew he'd be able to pick her out in the drama society photographs in the Reporter, going back years. In among the grainy smudged faces. Working her way up through the chorus line. Playing the principal boy in the pantomime in her twenties. Wearing tights and a hat set at a jaunty angle, a pencilled-in moustache, bringing a brittle transgender element into play, the dames standing around in powdered wigs.

'Come out onto the terrace with me,' she said.

The dance had ended. People were making their way to cars parked on the pavement outside. They went out onto the terrace overlooking the lough. At the head of the lough he could see the lights of Newry reflected on the underside of the turbulent cloud. The sea was choppy, gusty northerlies blowing onshore.

'You'll never find out what happened that night,' she said. 'You can hang who you like. It's the town's business and the town will take care of it.'

'What was the word you used? The one that means thief?'

'Nyuk.' She screwed up her face to say it. Her shoulders hunched. It made her look momentarily like some shuffling felon beckoning from the shadows.

He knew she would come back to his bedroom. She went ahead of him down the corridor. She had a loping walk. In bed she was earnest, working into the moment with deft, artisanal touches, libidinous gestures with a planned feel to them. Put your hand. Wait. Leading towards the centre, the hand-pushes and gasped biddings. Piecing together the narrative in the dark.

When she was asleep McCrink got up and took the case file over to the dressing table. He turned on the light and read for an hour. Trying to tease the outlines of a suspect from the halting accounts of the dance. Most of the witnesses careful about how they described what they had seen that night, picking their way through the shadows of it. Buses coming in from the country to the Orange hall. The shadow of rural temperance societies.

He closed the file and went to the window. He stepped out onto a low balcony facing the sea. He could see shallow waves breaking on the shingle beach. McCrink knew the lough to be dangerous. There were tidal races and undertows, sand bars at the entrance, wind sheers and deadly squalls coming off the rock faces on the southern shores. There were stories of pleasure craft foundered, boats gone aground or lost, suicides swept out to sea, drunks lost overboard. Three or four deaths on the lough every year.

Six

Interview with Agnes McGladdery, Corry Square RUC Station, 2nd February 1961

My name is Agnes McGladdery. I am the mother of Robert McGladdery who was born out of wedlock on 18th October 1935. From the start he was a sickly baby who would not feed and the midwife made comment. Other woman have a loving other half to stand by them in such a time of ordeal but I have been on my own since the day and hour the child was took out of me.

As a boy he was always at something. He was fit to put the heart sideways in you. The day he took the mother-of-pearl box from the bedroom and left it all night in the rain. When I says what did you do that for he said that it was to catch a meteorite that would tumble from the sky at night. Such a notion that the stars would fall from the black vault of heaven at your command.

Other times he'd sit so still you'd scarce think he'd any breath left in him. There is talk of neglect in his upbringing but if there was any it was that I neglected to put the belt to him when he give back cheek. And the school attendance officer was at me night and day but what could you do when your offspring took to the road when he was meant to be in school? The word they used was absconding from school and by his behaviour he absconded from a mother's tender heart like his father before him.

It is my opinion as a mother that he came back from London changed. That he fell among perversion of some kind or other. God knows what creatures roam them streets at night. He took to working in places of ill repute. He wrote to me about women of low morals who frequented his workplace as if it was all a laugh and made no odds. He sees the odds he made for himself now. A son that would relate these matters to his mother. He told me about the friends he had but I think these were lies. He was always a boy to let a lie slip out when the truth would land him in trouble. There were stories about Russians and agents I never heard the like. He was always a child for reading and in my opinion he has his head filled.

Before he went away he was backward with women, he'd go tongue-tied if one looked sideways at him. Now it was all chat and how are you doing today girls.

Some of the newspapers said that he was good-looking. Handsome is as handsome does I says. They said the same thing about his father who was a dancer he'd take your breath away to look at. Your breath is not all he'd take away if you let him under your guard, they says to me at the time, but I paid no heed. In the first days it was always your eyes your hands your lips until he got what he wanted, then it was the cold shoulder in the street and words like brazen.

The time that Robert came back from London he was secretive in his habits. There was also literature he kept in his room I do not wish to describe except to say that to bring such matter into a house. He was all stories of London and swank clothes you could tell it had gone to his head. He was about the town all hours of the day and night acting the dude.

You wish me to address the night of the murder. Murder is a word to put in someone's mouth when flesh and blood is absolved. I mind he was out in the pubs and dives of the town all afternoon. He came home then with Will Copeland who was his friend from childhood to get ready to go out. He always had to be dressed to the nines. I says it's only an old hop you're going to. He says, you never know, my princess could be there. Princess my eye I says you'll end up with some old crow.

When Robert left this house he was wearing a black suit. I never seen what his pal Copeland was wearing.

Seven

Agnes McGladdery told everyone that Robert had suffered a blow to the head when he was small. She said that a babysitter had dropped him when she was putting him in the pram.

'She was a Mackie from the Brook,' Agnes said. 'One of them Millies.'

The mill girl who had dropped him on his head was referred to often when Robert was young. Attributes were added over the years until she became a fully formed character in his mind. The girl drank. She met men at the back of the markets. A Jezebel, Agnes called her. She bore children to foreign sailors. The pale clumsy girl who had dropped the baby grew into a bejewelled figure reeking of gin and malice, fixing the infant Robert with hooded slatternly eyes.

Your problems began with her, Agnes said. Your abnormal leanings.

Agnes's days were populated with these fictions. A gallery of lurkers and slouchers and lower-class hangers-on. Women with the night in their eyes.

Robert said afterwards that he was a textbook case. As a child he suffered from pains in the head. There were incidents in school. A boy was beaten in the playground. When Robert was in prison he asked the doctor to examine him for brain lesions, injuries to the frontal lobe.

'I get these headaches,' he said.

He told the doctor there were procedures that could be carried out. There were instruments for severing, for cauterising. He had seen them depicted in monochrome plates in medical textbooks that he got from Newry library. Objects in chromium and stainless steel.

Agnes said that it would have been best if he had stayed away from the library. She said that he had his head filled. Robert said that in another life he would have been a doctor of medicine. He said that he would have had a door with a brass plate on it. At home he did drawings of the female reproductive organs from memory. The hanging tree, the dark tugging weight.

There was a railway depot behind Edward Street Station in the town. Agnes told Robert to stay away from it. It was a haunt of slum children from the Marshes and tinker children from the encampment beside the derelict custom house on the quay. On his way home from school every day Robert passed the mesh fence at the rear of the depot. He could hear the children call to each other in hoarse street argots. They clambered. They swarmed. They had sores and cankers and limb deformities. One afternoon he could not see any of the children in the freight yards. It was July and there was a heatwave. There were old oil drums, rail paraphernalia everywhere. Old coaches from defunct rail companies, stacked sleepers weeping creosote in the sun, a tarry chemical tang hanging in the afternoon air.

He peered into the engine sheds, the massive girdered interior, feeling that he was getting a grasp on the interior matter of the town. The iron-joisted substance of it. Wreckage piled in corners of the buildings, broken-down freight stock looking small in the vast shedding.

He climbed the fence to reach the spur where the old rail stock was kept. Weeds grew up between the sleepers. The carriage windows were broken and the locomotives were rustbound. He got into a cab and tried to work the seized levers and stuck valves. He closed his eyes and imagined the firebox stoked, the train rushing through the dark, and saw himself borne away in the night.

When he opened his eyes there were five other children in the cab. There were three boys and two girls. One of the girls was led by the others for she had cataracts in both eyes. The other girl wore a filthy cotton dress. Robert looked at the blind girl. There was no clemency in her sightless, milky stare. He jumped off the side plate and rolled in under the locomotive wheel skirting where they couldn't reach him. He could hear them talking and laughing outside. Robert spending the afternoon there, getting lost in the boxed-in structures, axle-bearings encased in grease, the heavy flywheels. Robert finding the secret internal histories of things.

After an hour he peered out and saw the children's feet walking away. Their voices faded. He lifted the wheel skirting and crawled out. The girl with the dirty dress was sitting on the driver's footplate. She was older than he had thought. He could see the shape of her breasts against the thin cotton of the dress, the fabric pinked at the tip. He could see the wiry outline of her torso under the thin material, skinny, pubescent, her breastbone slick with sweat, the hipbone jut. She got him down on the ground and wrapped her legs around his neck. Her legs were strong and wiry. He could feel the fetid heat of her at his throat, a hot stink, the slum heat.

When Robert was in prison he said he would write a biography of his life. It would be a sorrowful tale of a man beset by adversity. It would be a story of great odds overcome but not enough in the end.

Once you left Newry and went south you were in the frontier country. Agnes thought of an untravelled territory, fear-stalked. Out there somewhere was the border, a place of unapproved crossings, ill-lit frontier posts. Agnes thought of night's militias roaming the low hills, baleful excise demanded.

The McGladderys had moved from Tinkers Hill to Damolly when Robert was ten. Their next-door neighbour, Mervyn Graham, had a Hornby train set in the garage. Mervyn belonged to a model aircraft club and subscribed to model railway magazines. At the weekends he attended conventions at disused aerodromes with other small intense men. They greeted each other with solemn nods. They regarded themselves as custodians of flight, willing their aircraft through tumultuous skies, alert to their frail qualities, adepts of yaw and tilt. Mervyn was later described at the trial as a 'force for good' in Robert's life. He had offered Robert an apprenticeship at his shoe-repair business in the town, and Robert had worked with him occasionally.

Mervyn allowed Robert to help him with the train set. Robert broke everything he ever touched, Agnes said, but Robert always said he never broke any part of the train set. There were yards of slotted-together track which had been laid out on a sheet of hardboard. Die-cast locomotives. Tiny freight trucks. Robert liked the magneto whirr as the trains

went round the track, the smell of iron filings from the trans-
former. When you put your hand on it you felt the heat and
the low-voltage hum. You peered at the tiny brass screws and
copper boiler fittings.

Robert helped make the foliage and bridgeworks. They
worked with balsa woods and spirit glues. Mervyn let Robert
cut out the balsa shapes with a modelling knife. There was a
finesse to the blade. Robert liked the way the blade moved
through the wood without resistance. He ran his fingers over
the cut ends of the wood to feel the interior texture, and spent
hours working the aero gloss into it, always aware of the heart
of the wood, the burnished grains.

Mervyn kept a newspaper archive on the subject of famous
murders. He would spread the cuttings out on the workbench. There were photographs of Patricia Curran, the judge's
daughter who had been stabbed to death in Whiteabbey in
1952. There were photographs of Elizabeth Short, the Black
Dahlia, whose mutilated body had been found in western Los
Angeles in January 1947.

'She was cut clean in two. The clothing was missing. He'd
cut the corners of the mouth. He put a smile on her face and
no mistake. The organs were removed no doubt for satanic
practices. The man was intent on the devil's work.'

'Did they ever find out who done it?'

'No man ever faced retribution,' Mervyn said, 'but the
finger of suspicion pointed at persons of Hollywood renown.
There were suggestions that gangland figures might have had
a hand.'

Robert thought he could see the murderer as if glimpsed
through an open door, a figure stooped over a workbench,

his tools to hand and his face turned to his work, a profane hobbyist. A figure recognisable to other enthusiasts.

Robert's eyes kept returning to the photograph of Patricia Curran. The same formal photograph of the nineteen-year-old had been used in all the newspapers. The mouth downturned, the eyes shadowed. The hooded, larcenous stare. Robert was eighteen when Iain Hay Gordon was tried for the murder of Patricia Curran and found not guilty by reason of insanity.

'I know what I'd do to a cur like that,' Mervyn said. 'I'd fucking hang for him so I would. A flat-out cur is all.'

'I don't know,' Robert said, 'people's brains can be damaged in childhood so they can. Sometimes they don't know what they're doing.' He had studied illustrations of the human brain in World of Wonder magazines. He had learned how the brain had a cortex, a stem. He would stand on the railings at the outdoor swimming baths in Warrenpoint and watch jellyfish floating in the sluices. That was how he imagined the cortex. The pulsing, jellied matter, a mauve weave that seemed to show higher intelligence, advanced life forms.

When you look at the photographs of Pearl Gamble and Elizabeth Short there are likenesses. Short had a pronounced gap between her front teeth. Her teeth were bad and she used to fashion fillings from pieces of wax. During the trial Robert would come to wonder if Pearl did the same. There was a wide gap between her two front teeth, and smaller gaps between the others, which gave the impression of missing teeth if you looked quickly.

*

Mervyn had worked in the Harland and Wolff shipyard in Belfast in the 1920s. Armies of men on the move in the dawn light. He told Robert about the boilermakers and toolmakers and riveters. Gracious fraternities of craftworkers. Men who set out to test themselves against the materials of their calling, the cast-iron plating and lead ballasts and rolled copper sheeting.

They were times of political flare-up, sect killings, whispered tales of pogrom.

'There was these two boys from the Falls Road took up employment as shipwrights. They had no call to be there. No mission. Thought they could just keep the head down. They thought they could labour unseen.'

'What happened to them?' Robert asked.

'Some of the bow crew got a hold of them and threw them into the wet dock. Every time one of the bucks swum to the edge of the dock some man put his boot on his hand and sent him back into the water. You don't be long getting tired. It was brave and cold. February. You'd be going at the stopcocks with picks, they were froze solid with ice. Must of been five hundred stood around that dock and not a word out of any man jack of them.'

The men in the water growing dispirited. The ranked masses gathered around the edge of the dock. Aware of the element of spectacle which had been introduced. Knowing what was expected of them. To sink into the long dark. The shipyard had many ghosts. Workers who fell from ship scaffolding or were sealed by accident in airtight hulls. The two men would not be out of place. They would join the throng of the dead and receive their commendation.

As they sank beneath the water the men stood around the

wet dock in caps and donkey jackets like a frieze of labour from some Soviet institution.

Mervyn's shoe-repair premises was on the cobblestone mall beside the river. Robert liked to go down there. There was integrity in the making and repair of shoes, Mervyn told him. To send a man out into the world shod, to have a say in the matter of his kinship to the ground he walked on.

'Banker or pauper, it makes no heed to me,' Mervyn said, 'they all got to have shoes on their feet.'

Mervyn named the parts of the shoe. The tongue and the welt. He showed him the hide and the wooden lasts upon which the shoe was constructed. Robert liked to play with two of them, setting them to dance on the tiled shop floor like dead feet, articulate and clattering.

There were hundreds of shoes that had not been collected on the shelving behind Mervyn's workplace. Some of them had been there for many years, the leather cracked and bent. Robert thought of them as waiting for their owners, that some halt, shuffling legion of the dead might claim them and be debouched into the night.

Mervyn taught Robert how to put on steel heel tips and to fit stiff rubber soles to worn-out shoes.

'I'm going to be a shoemaker when I leave school,' he told Agnes.

'Damn the shoemaker you'll be,' Agnes said, 'when you don't know the right hand from the left.'

Mervyn could name the ships that had been built during his time in the docks. The Nomadic. The Wessex. The Northumbria. He could recite their draught and tonnage and net displacement. Their epic sea voyages.

'You're wasting your time with the likes of Mervyn Graham,' Agnes told Robert. 'He'll learn you nothing.' But Robert had learned that men could turn their thoughts to the epic. They could contemplate long sea voyages to the world's end.

~

The decade brought gangs onto the streets. Nightmare cadres at large in the post-industrial landscapes. There were skin gangs, football ultras. Motorcycle gangs patrolling the great northern roads. There were increases in teen pregnancy and backstreet abortion. Newsreel footage from the time shows boys in drape coats and girls in bobby socks and flounce skirts. The boys kept sharpened combs in their back pockets and sewed razor blades into their velvet collars. They saw themselves as dapper disciples of grubby modernity. Footage of the time doesn't show the freshness you would expect, the sense of an old order revised. They are seen on piers and seafronts, outside football grounds. They have a ghostly quality enhanced by the degraded film stock and badly synchronised reel-to-reel footage.

It was an era of things gone wrong, of seedy and violent undertows. The Krays and others were abroad in the night-clubs of London. There were nights of spurious glamour, showbusiness figures mingling with underworld figures. Sex-crime blondes out on the tiles with Ronnie and Reggie. The heyday of rent boys and acid throwers and safe blaggers.

On Friday nights Robert would take the train from Edward Street Station to Warrenpoint. The train ran through the

Marshes and alongside the shallow tidal waters of the lough. The smell of locomotive diesel hung in the night air. Looking down the lough you could see the green and red navigation lights on the channel flickering and beyond them the frozen darkness of the mountains and the sea. The lough known for its shifting bars and treacherous currents.

There was a caravan site at Cranfield at the mouth of the lough. Agnes brought Robert there for weekends when she could borrow a caravan. The caravan site was on the apron of an abandoned wartime air base. There were weeds growing up through the concrete. The wind from the lough made the caravans rock and creak during the night. Robert lay awake listening to Radio Caroline. The Haulbowline lighthouse stood on a sandbar at the entrance to the channel. You heard the heavy marine diesels through the fog, through the offshore murks. He read articles on the benefits to mankind of nuclear power. How the Bomb had ended the war.

There was an abandoned Sherman tank on the sand dunes. It had shed its tracks. Sand had drifted around its armoured skirting. The turret decals were faded, abraded by the wind and sand, and the hatch bolts were solid with rust. Inside the bare metal was salt-pitted. Robert climbed down into the cracked leather seat. The breech had a metal spike driven into it. He handled the gun controls, the nubbed grips, looked through the gunsight. Lining up the target. The fine adjustments and knurled rangefinder. The way the landscape suddenly seemed to be full of forboding, death-haunted, like some salt-pan bomb-test site.

One summer evening the lough pilot took him out in the pilot boat. Robert listening to the VHF navigational chatter, the voices staticky and remote. You leaned into the radio to try to hear what was going on, trying to penetrate the shipping-lane argots.

There were daytrippers on the beach. Girls from Belfast and Portadown. They were wearing belted dresses and white socks. Their voices drifted up to the dunes. They were the yarn spinners and loom operators. Dupont girls. The odour of early plastics seemed to have seeped in through their skins. The girls' breath smelt of acetone and they spoke in nasal tones. The boys were aficionados of early street gang cultures. The backstreet looks. Flat-top haircuts. Drape coats. They carried open razors and flick knives.

Agnes was a fan of Gone with the Wind and said the long hair and coats to the knee gave them the look of some degenerate band ridden out on horseback from a southern plantation, a debased gentry.

'It'd be the better part of your play to stay away from that crew,' Agnes said, 'though I can tell right and well you'll be stuck in the middle of them.'

One Saturday Robert lifted some money from Agnes's purse and took the bus to Belfast. He asked the bus driver the way to the Markets.

'What's the like of you doing looking for the Markets?' the driver said. He was in his late forties with grey hair and a union pin in his lapel.

'I'm looking to find something for my ma,' Robert said.

'You're looking to find trouble,' the man said. 'I want no hand, act or part of you.'

In the Markets Robert found a stall selling army surplus

stock. There were crossbows and hunting knives on display. He bought a flick knife with a tortoiseshell handle and a pointed blade. He thumbed the catch and the blade sprang out. It made him move differently with the knife in his pocket. He worked on the blade with a file. He walked on the balls of his feet with a streetfighter's roll. He saw himself standing over a body on the street. He imagined knife fights in the rain. He saw himself alone, his back turned on amnesty or redemption, a man adrift on rain-soaked streets, indifferent to the world. When Agnes found the knife she threw it into the sea.

When Robert discovered what she had done, he 'flew into a tantrum', Agnes said, and 'started punching himself in the head, a thing he had done since early childhood'.

Mervyn ran an athletics and boxing club in a disused warehouse building on the canal bank. There were fight posters on the walls, the paper damp from moisture seeping through the mortar.

'Town's built on a black fen,' Mervyn said. 'They drove wood pilings down into the mud and stuck the town on top of it.'

Robert imagined the timbers sunk in the ooze. He thought about the town raised on this scaffold. The posters were of Rinty Monaghan in the King's Hall. Sonny Liston in Madison Square Gardens. The boxers crouched behind their gloves, chins tucked, streetwise and wary as they faced the camera. The gym smelt of liniment. There was the sound of fighters' boots scuffing in the ring and the pelt-slap of the boxing gloves against flesh. Robert liked to work the bags. He liked the dead weight of the big bag, the foxed leather holding the shape of the glove when he hit it, the way the punch jarred you right up to the shoulder.

Mervyn showed him how to skip, stepping in and out of the rope. It was important that the face stayed expressionless while the rope moved so fast it was almost strobing.

Mervyn did roadwork with Robert. Mervyn had a proper Sun racer with Sturmey Archer gears. He had been to the South of France with a cycle club in 1957 and told Robert about the Casino in Monaco and the Hôtel de Paris. You could see the roof of the football stadium for miles, the Sporting Club de Monaco. He told Robert about seeing one of the sprint stages of the Tour de France, the great names of the time tripping off the tongue. Summer-evening crowds gathering outside provincial velodromes with dust pulses coming from the flexed race boards as the cyclists sped around the banked trackway. Watching the sprint finishes. He showed Robert photographs of the great cyclists of the time. Men from the polders and North Sea saltmarshes.

'Look at them boys,' Mervyn said. Trying to point out to Robert the values of the clean-cut young men who raced in the Tour de France and other great races of the era. Look at the peloton streaming past in primary colours, the spoke-whirr of the tyres on tarmac and the soft talk of the racers to each other. Mervyn was trying to communicate something important to Robert, but he didn't have the words to do it. He wanted to explain what it was like to stand in the road after the cyclists were gone and stare after them, the landscape suddenly bereft of their bright and shining presence, the crouched racers, the crowd wanting to call them back as though they saw them as the shining representatives of a new and aspirational world.

Mervyn accepted that Robert wanted to bodybuild but he

wanted him to do it properly.

'You want meat, you can go to the butcher's,' Mervyn said. 'There's a craft and an art to bodybuilding.'

He tried to get Robert to see that there was a grandeur to it. He taught Robert about the great muscle groups, the pectorals and the gluteals, the weft of fibre and protein, the God-loomed knit of sinew.

'I'm not sure if I'm getting through to you, son,' Mervyn said. 'It's not about going down to Warrenpoint and showing off to women. It's something you do for yourself.'

Robert ordered Bodybuilder International from the news-agent. He bought a bullworker in Smith's Health and Fitness Gym on Merchants Quay. The bullworker was endorsed by world bodybuilding champion Charles Atlas. There was a photograph of Atlas on the box, hands clenched at his abdomen to show off the oiled muscles, the abdominals.

He did bench presses and dumb-bells, working on the abdominals and pectorals. It made Robert think of those anatomy posters you saw in the doctor's office, all the muscles on view, skinned torsos, blue-arteried, eyeballs bulging in a pitiless veined glare.

'Imagine the ride you'd get off one of them,' Will Copeland said, pointing to the female bodybuilders.

Robert wasn't sure about that. They looked like animated anatomy posters. They stalked his dreams, semi-nude and profane.

Will Copeland was Robert's best friend. He lived on Exchequer Hill. They'd go swimming at the baths in Warrenpoint. Robert would climb onto the high board and strike poses there. He would pretend he was one of the olympians you saw on the newsreel at the cinema. Foreign men in one-piece bathing costumes and swim caps.

'Come on Robbie, you fucking retard. I dare you.' Will was always referring to Robert as a retard, or a spastic. Making him feel like one of the children that were brought on excursions to Warrenpoint during the summer. Sitting on the front in wheelchairs. The children with their heads to one side.

'Like animals of the field,' Agnes said. She didn't know what to do when she saw the children. She looked at them as if they had wandered out of the reach of grace.

These were the times Robert would remember with Agnes. Buying cones from the Genoa. The sounds of people swimming from the outdoor baths, looking up from the promenade to see someone poised on the high board, the thrum of the sprung plank in the evening air and the diver gone as though snatched away. There was music from the bandstand in the park and men in whites playing tennis and these evenings were fixed in Robert's mind like some reverie of well-tempered living.

Will bought them cigarettes in the Mascot on Margaret Square, No. 6 and Embassy Regal. They were always looking for new places to smoke, finding the hidden places in the town. It felt like an apprenticeship in the clandestine. Scouting out the ill-lit areas. There were parts of the town which felt like empty quarters. The canal bank. The back of the coal stores. The lock gates. They went to the sheds at the back of the canal basin. The basin was no longer used, the water still and oily. There was talk of something monstrous in the depths.

Robert and Will didn't know what the sheds had been used for. Some long-gone trade had been plied there and was now unspoken of. The walls were corrugated iron with a bitumen roof. The windows were broken and there was graffiti everywhere. The interior was a shambles of old bottles, empty paint tins, battered gear housings. People stayed away from the place. During the day there was a bad-news feel to the sheds, an air of job losses, local industry on the slide.

At night it was different. Loose asbestos sheeting flapped on the roof. The wind moaned in the empty windowframes and Robert thought of the secret histories, the inter-generational exchanges, the ghost narratives, fragmentary, almost out of earshot. The phantom discourse of the town.

In school Robert listened to the older boys talking about girls. They would sit on the wall at the Stonebridge and watch the High School girls walking home. These girls wore shoes with a heel and nylons and lived in the houses on Windsor Hill and Drumalane. Houses that were named on the gate pillars. The Laurels. Sometimes on his way home Robert would stand looking up the driveways, wondering what secret life was hidden behind the carriage lamps, the wind-tossed shrubberies.

The High School had a tennis club behind the houses on Windsor Hill. There was a green-painted pavilion overlooking the courts. Robert and Will would watch the girls playing tennis from behind the pavilion.

'High School Lawn Tennis Club,' Will said, 'come the revolution they'll be lining up for a bit of Will Copeland. I'm the boy that'll give them what they want.'

It was Will who wanted to climb up and look in through the

windows of the changing room. The same way it was Will got Robert to draw cocks and cunts on the back of the toilet doors in school. Robert taking hours over it so that Will told him he was doing it wrong. The drawings that Robert did bearing no resemblance to the crudely drawn sexual organs in the other cubicles. Robert's inked-in hieroglyphs were painstakingly drawn, taken from anatomical plates from the books in the library.

Will would lie on his stomach on the embankment looking down on the girls playing tennis.

'Imagine the bush on that. The tits on that one.' The bush, the big headlights. Will was always crude.

Robert didn't know what to say. The smell of cut grass, girls' voices calling out to each other. Forty–love. Deuce. As though courtly languages were being spoken. Fleet figures in white running in the dusk.

It was Will started the watching. Going up the alleys behind the houses at Drumalane, hoping to see a woman undressing in a bedroom window. Peopling the world with lonely married women and other archetypes of small-town desire.

'The whole town's at it,' Will said, 'you heard it here first. Like you wouldn't believe.' Will trying to persuade Robert that the sexual undercurrents were out there, a persistent rustling and whispering. The silky underthings.

In October they would go out after dark. The smell of fireworks hung in the air, rank and sulphurous. Will wanted Robert to go into one of the houses, force open a window. Will at him all the time, egging him on. Will had a pry bar he had found in the sheds and he showed Robert how you forced it into the door jamb.

They picked a house at the end of an Edwardian terrace.

'You go in,' Will said, 'I'll keep dick.'

'What am I looking for?'

'Anything. Jewels. That kind of thing. Anything we can sell. There's this boy out near the reservoir, my da says he's a fence.' Will using the vocabulary of crime because he knew that Robert easily found himself adrift in underworld mystiques.

Robert used the pry bar on the back door of the house and felt the door jamb give. That was as far as he got. He heard a sound behind him. He turned to see a policeman by the name of Johnston standing behind him. Johnston was a heavy-set man who was feared in the town.

'What's an ill-bred pup of Agnes McGladdery's doing in Drumalane at night with a pry bar in his hand?'

Johnston took the bar off Robert and set about him with his torch. Johnston carried a torch with a rubber barrel and eight ounces of lead wrapped around the flange. The beating was accurate and brutal, Johnston concentrating on the fleshy areas, the shoulders, thighs and buttocks. Through his pain Robert knew that Johnston was concentrating on the musculature, working towards something lasting. Robert understood that there was a mechanics of pain, that you could work your way into the deep pathologies.

'You cross my path again, I'll fucking bury you, son,' Johnston said.

Mervyn gave him boxer's salve and wondered at the extent and coloration of the bruising.

'Thon Johnston's a bad hoor,' he said, 'even his own mother couldn't like him. There's a job here fixing shoes for you when you're ready, but the company you're keeping'll put you in Johnston's line of fire.'

Robert had no idea where Will had gone that night. Next time he saw him he acted as if it had never happened. He was full of the next idea. They should rob the bank on Hill Street, the Northern Bank. He told Robert he would meet him at the sheds. Robert waited for him until it was almost dark. He threw stones into the dark canal water, hoping to stir something loathsome from the depths.

Will brought nylon stockings he had found in his sister's drawer.

'We can use them for masks.'

'I'm not robbing no bank,' Robert said.

Will pulled one of the stockings over his head. Robert wanted to tell him to take it off. Will's features were compressed until he looked like some ill-born thing. There were overtones of deep genetic damage.

'Try it,' Will said, holding one of the stockings out. Robert thought about Will's sister. She was in her twenties and worked in the mill. He pulled the stocking over his head. The nylon worn and discarded, the retained scents, the residual girl-smell. Robert trying to think of the sister's name. Sharon or Heather. The seamed darkness under the nylon felt like a secret he had been let into. There was a rank, used odour.

He imagined her rolling the stocking up her leg, the fit to the limb, the deft economies that women brought to bear on themselves, the thrift in the matter of their person.

Will talked to him all the time about robbing a bank. He evoked a bandit life, bank doors dashed open, outlaw words employed. Hold-up. Getaway. Robert could see himself speeding away from a crime scene, words of defiance on his lips.

'You should be fit to kill for a friend,' Will said. 'Anybody laid a hand on you they'd have me after them. They'd be for the heavy dint.'

Will was always asking Robert what he would do for him. Would he dive into a raging torrent? Would he take a bullet? He said they should share things. They would share women. They were all slags and sluts so it didn't matter.

But women liked Robert. He knew how to make them laugh and compliments fell naturally from his mouth. He noticed when someone had their hair done. They looked after him and shook their heads and said what about that mother, it's a pity of him.

Will noticed this and was always telling him to stop talking to old dolls at shop counters.

'Come on, Mr fucking Popularity.' Will was always talking about going up the back field to the convent at night and getting girls out of the dorms. He wanted to know if Robert thought that the convent girls were lesbians. It was all nudges and half-asides and what do you think?

~

Robert would watch Agnes at her dressing table getting ready to go out. Half-dressed with the stuff of her underthings visible so that he looked away. Heading for the dockside bars. She would start in Newry and move on to Warrenpoint. Drinking in dockside bars, seen in the dance halls of Warrenpoint. Drawn into clandestine scenes with men in uniform. Robert shut his eyes and could see her in the aftermath, lighting a cigarette. He saw it on her clothes when she came home. The zips and fastenings strained at. A button missing. Fabric pulls and ladders in the stockings. The formal lines of her blurred. She seemed ruined in an epic way, smelling of gin and smoke, sitting on the edge of his bed, her mascara running down her face. She would stroke his face and murmur his name.

Eight

Johnston came into the room. He had removed his tunic and his shirt sleeves were rolled up.

'We got McGladdery's pal in. Took us a brave while to find the bold Mr Copeland. He's usually in Hollywood's or the British Legion. We run him to ground in the heel of the hunt. We might get a turn out of him.'

'You want to sit in?' Speers said.

Copeland was in a holding cell on the ground floor. McCrink opened the door a crack and looked in at him. Copeland gave no sign of being aware of McCrink's scrutiny. His blond hair was swept back into a duck's arse. He was smoking, the cigarette held between his knees. Straw-haired, insolent.

'I left him in there for a while,' Johnston said, 'give him a feel for the place.'

'He's not under arrest,' McCrink said.

'He doesn't know that.'

McCrink followed Speers in. McCrink sat on a wooden chair at the back of the interview room. Johnston stood by the door. Copeland was thin, wary, hostile.

'You're a shifty-looking piece of work,' Johnston said.

'I never done nothing.'

'Where were you on the night of 28th January?'

'At the dance same as all the rest.'

'Were you with McGladdery?'

'I was.'

'You were with Robert McGladdery all day?'

'We done some drinking. Then we went back to his place.'

'What did you do there?'

'I don't remember.'

'That's not good enough. Did he show you anything?'

'I don't recall.'

'Did he give you a go on any bodybuilding gear?' Speers was the senior officer but Johnston was leading the questioning, leaning against the wall in the shadow.

'He had this contraption with springs and stuff.'

'A bullworker.'

'That's it. Did anything happen with it?'

'I can't remember. It might have. I'd a lock of drink in me. He was going on about bodybuilding.'

'How come you went back to his place?' Speers said.

'We wanted to get changed for the dance.'

'Changed for the dance. Did you swap clothes or something?'

'A right pair of ladies,' Johnston said. 'What clothes was he wearing?' Johnston always coming back to what Robert was wearing. There was a shape to Johnston's questions, a steel-trap architecture. He would circle back to an original question which had seemed unimportant and you would find it suddenly hedged about with meaning.

'I don't remember. He always had these clothes he got in London. Fancy stuff.'

'So he thinks he's the big cheese in the glad rags from the

big city? Puts the moves on Miss Gamble. She shoots him down. Is that it?' Speers said.

'What was he wearing? A light-coloured suit?' Johnston said.

'Where were you for the past two days?' McCrink said. Speers turned in his chair to look at him. He could hear Johnston shift his weight at the back of the room.

'What?' Copeland said.

'Sergeant Johnston said you couldn't be found in your usual places. He mentioned the British Legion.'

'So what?'

'Less lip.' Johnston spoke softly. 'We can't have the like of you giving lip to visiting officers.'

'It's a simple question. Where were you?'

'Here and there. The ma's. Out walking the dogs. Up at the morgue for to see Pearl brung home.'

Copeland lifted his head for the first time and looked into McCrink's eyes. The eyes were pale and colourless. The eyes of a traveller in some infernal region. I know what journey you took this past few days, McCrink thought, I know what barren itinerary unfolded.

'We'll break for the day now,' Speers said. They left the cell. McCrink looked back as they reached the end of the corridor. He saw Johnston re-enter the interrogation room.

⁓

When McCrink came into Corry Square the next morning there were men everywhere. He found Speers in his office.

'What's happening?'

'Kennedy's orders. We're to impose total twenty-four-hour surveillance on McGladdery.'

'What class of police work is that?' McCrink said.

'Kennedy reckons it'll soften him up. He'll crack in the end. Lead us to the murder weapon.'

'Kennedy's a retard,' Johnston said. 'He'd be brave and thick to go anywhere near the murder weapon with a bunch of clod-hoppers on his tail. Still, I can use some of these extra men.'

The week-long surveillance of Robert attracted national media attention. Reporters from the London papers inter-viewed Robert. He was described as a 'bodybuilding fanatic', and complained of what he referred to as police harassment. He was photographed for the Daily Mail stripped to the waist and holding home-made dumb-bells made from lumps of concrete moulded onto a metal bar.

The photograph of Robert shows a good-looking young man, flexing his muscles. He looks like an old illustration of a bare-knuckle boxer, a daguerreotyped figure from another era in a stilted pose.

'He's working on his defence,' Speers said.

'How do you work that out?' McCrink said.

'He told us he got the scratches on his face from the bull-worker. If he makes himself out to be a heavy-duty body-builder, it puts bones on his statement.'

'I'm not sure if he's that smart.'

'You might be right. A smarter client wouldn't let the world see how much he's enjoying the attention he's getting. If somebody was looking at me for what was done to that girl, I'd hang the head and keep the mouth well shut.'

'The little bastard loves himself, no doubt about that.'

'I can't work him out.'

'If we had a polygraph.' Speers had studied the application

of technology and forensics to criminal investigation. The polygraph had a home-made look to it, the delicate arm and revolving cylinder had a spidery authority. He'd studied polygraph patterns in criminology books. The heart rate and secretions scientifically measured. The scribed guilt.

It remained a puzzle to McCrink, the way Robert had started to behave once he knew he was a suspect, the bravado. It was McCrink's experience that those who showed the most defiance and demonstrated no signs of breaking down were the ones who admitted their guilt in the end. But not Robert. Show-off. Fancy Dan.

Speers organised the local men into four squads of two men each. McGladdery was to be followed twenty-four hours a day. From the beginning Robert seemed to welcome them in a sly, knowing way. The whole town seemed to be in open intrigue. People came out of shops to watch the detectives trail Robert. They followed behind, slouching, resentful. Robert making them look stupid. They saw themselves in a world of shadowy pursuit, suspects trying to give them the slip, officers of the court on the trail of justice. Instead they were standing outside the labour exchange while Robert signed on, the queue of unemployed men giving them smartarse looks. Robert faking surprise when he came out of the building, playing it up for the spectators. There were photographers from the national press on the streets. Local people were photographed and interviewed.

'He's a cheeky little fucker,' Speers said.

'I suppose.' McCrink watched him in silence. He wanted to shake McGladdery. To tell him that the death of Pearl Gamble was not a backdrop against which Robert could act out his life.

It was a maw into which his existence would empty.

There was an outpost of the tinker camp by the disused coal bunkers on the south side of the basin. They lived under tarpaulins stretched over railway sleepers and in tents fabricated from creosoted rags. There were sundry ragpickers and scrap-metal dealers. Half-starved mastiffs roamed the camp and there were spavined piebalds tethered to night lines. The men drank ether on waste ground beside the market and stepped in and out of the campfire smoke as though ragged ceremonials were being enacted. The women wheeled old carpet and furniture through the town on broken-down pram bodies and begged in doorways. They did not look as if they belonged to the town or country. They looked like Eastern European émigrés, wandering bands, the head-scarved women, their lips moving as though they recounted Talmudic mysteries

The traveller children took to following McGladdery and his escort through the town. They shuffled when they walked, talked to each other in street argot, backhand language. Cant.

'This is a fucking shambles,' Speers said, 'him running through the town like the Pied Piper.'

'He's not behaving like any guilty man I ever seen. I seen them ate up with guilt and I seen them cocky, but I never came across the like of this.'

McCrink had seen them too. The remorseful and the publicity-seekers. The bewildered and the calculating. A night cadre of the guilty abroad in the court precincts and prison vans.

'Forensics will sort out if he's guilty or not,' Speers said.

'What forensics? He doesn't have the odour of it.'

'He has the odour of something not right, sir.'

'I wonder.' McCrink wondered who would pass appraisal in the scrutiny now being brought to bear on McGladdery. He thought that McGladdery did see himself as a figure from a story, a capering fool brought out from the pages of some plague-time medieval lore. During this period the town seemed to rise above itself, finding haunted milieux not apparent before. Gallows Hill. Chancellors Road. The cold was like a weight. The town seemed to have acquired the dark spaces of a larger place. The small churchyard on Kilmorey Street seemed like a haunted cathedral cloister. Solitary men walking home along the esplanade cast the shadows of sinister boulevardiers. Foreign boats docked every two or three days at the coal quay.

'You keep hearing snatches of strange languages,' Margaret said. 'You never know who you're going to see next. I keep waiting for pedlars and the like. You know, groups of wandering Jews emerging from the forest.'

'People see their surroundings differently when there's been a murder,' McCrink said; 'they stop trusting what's around them.'

'People round here never trusted anything around them,' she said. McCrink had been standing at the window of his hotel room when he saw the Renault pull up outside, Margaret glancing around her as she got out, then walking quickly across the car park with her head down, at ease with illicit transactions of the heart. She knocked quickly on his bedroom door. When he let her in she went straight to the bed where he had spread out the photographs of Pearl's possessions. Each photograph was numbered and had the place where it was found written across the bottom. McCrink was looking at a photo of a brown shoe with a low heel. Charles Ashe had found a brown shoe at Damolly Cross.

'The friend Ronnie Whitcroft says she had black slingbacks on for the dance,' McCrink said.

'She would have brought the brown shoes for walking home when the dance was over,' Margaret said.

In the stubble field between the crossroads and Weir's Rock they had found Pearl's bloodstained handkerchief. McCrink read from Johnston's notes. 'The handkerchief looked as if it had been soaked in a basin of blood. Her blouse and brassiere were in the stubble field along with the slingbacks she was wearing at the dance. Her skirt and underthings were at the top of the field.' *The rustle. The silky underthings.*

'What's that?' The last photograph was marked 'Stubble field'. It was of a plain tin bucket. Margaret's fingers traced the dire utilitarian outlines of the bucket.

'Johnston's idea. He dug up a bucketful of bloodstained earth from the stubble field. I'm not sure what was going through his head.'

The clank of the bucket handle being carried from the stubble field at nightfall. The dank, stained pail. Brimful.

'The laboratory haven't found any physical evidence so far. No prints. No skin under the fingernails. They're looking for hair on her clothing. If he didn't leave any evidence on her he must of left some on himself. She bled out, the pathologist said. The whole thing worries me.'

'Why?'

'The fact that he left no prints, no physical evidence.'

'Why does that worry you?'

81

'McGladdery lay in wait for her because she resisted him in the hall. He beat her, stripped her, then stabbed and strangled her. He carried her for almost half a mile. And he left no physical traces of himself on her or on the crime scene. It doesn't ring true.'

'Maybe he was just very careful.'

McCrink didn't answer. He remembered the Nude Murderer. The care that was taken with each victim. The way the murderer erased himself from the scene. He did not want to be caught but there was more to it than that. It was important that he did not intrude on the narrative he had created for them, stripped of the chaos of their lives and eased into the storied dark.

'You'll need to raid McGladdery's house,' McCrink said, 'get a hold of the clothes he was wearing that night.'

'Already done, sir,' Johnston said. 'We obtained a search warrant at a special sitting of Newry Magistrates' Court the day you were in the city.'

'I would expect to be told.'

'You didn't ask.'

'What did you get?'

'A black suit. McGladdery says he was wearing it at the dance. We know different. No murder weapon.'

'We found this in the house as well,' Speers said. He held up a small pile of books and magazines. The magazines were badly printed on cheap paper. Pornographic stories were interspersed with underexposed black-and-white photographs of glum nudes with 1950s hairstyles. The covers of the novels were line drawings of young women cowering in mock terror. Another had a woman facing outward. She was wearing a basque and thigh boots. Her look was downcast, unchaste.

'Get an eyeful, sir,' Johnston said, 'it's free. There's lots more where that came from. All part of the service. Never let it be said that the Newry police were behind the door when it come to nudity and perversion.'

'It's all pointing McGladdery's way. There's no doubt about that,' Speers said. 'If he didn't get what he was looking for that night by asking for it, he was going to take it one way or the other.'

'We talked to the lead singer of the band. He asked for a song called "It's Now or Never" before he danced with the girl. A girl he knew all his life. She wasn't keen on dancing with him. He was pawing her, hands all over the shop according to witnesses, and she wanted him to stop.'

'What about motive?'

'A sexual motive. As Sergeant Johnston says, he couldn't get what he wanted one way. He allowed his appetites to get the better of him. He waylaid the girl on her way home and attacked her.'

'There was no sexual assault.'

'She was stripped to the skin,' Johnston said. 'She was sent out of the world the way she come into it. If he went no further it was because he was disturbed or maybe he just wanted to see the goods without handling them. There's them is fond of that kind of thing too.'

Agnes McGladdery had opened the door to the policemen and was served with the warrant.

'I thought you were the lot with the prize bonds,' she said.

McCrink had met others in her position before. A good line delivered under pressure was the closest you'd get to rueful good grace. He gave her a grim nod and a tight smile in the spirit of hardscrabble etiquette then pushed past her into the house.

'Robert's out,' she said, 'but you boys already know that. He can't go to the toilet forby there's a peeler there ready to hold it for him.'

The house was unkempt. They searched Robert's room first. Robert had cut out illustrations from Bodybuilder International and sellotaped them to the wall above his bed. Glistening veined torsos that McCrink found it hard to look at. There was a full-length mirror on the back of the door. McCrink thought of Robert standing in front of it turning this way and that, trying to throw the muscle into relief, trying to make the mass jump, the tiny narcissistic twitches. A bullworker and home-made bar-bells were on the floor beside the door.

One night Robert went out to Mervyn's garage. He lit an old carbide lamp. There was a suitcase on top of the tool rack. The leatherbound case was old and its fittings corroded. He opened it and took out a stack of yellowed magazines, Penthouse and Carousel. The pages were yellowed with age, the prints badly developed. Pages of mute, lightstruck nudes. Girls that seemed dazed, caught in a seedy undertow.

Nine

That night Speers took McCrink out to the Gamble house. The house was to the north of the railway embankment. McCrink and Speers parked under the embankment and looked up to see the 18.10 Enterprise go past, the iron-flanked diesel locomotive, McCrink feeling the heavy bogeys trundling in the ground beneath his feet, northbound, working the gradient. He could see the passengers, carried through the dark. Speers stood watching as it passed into the night.

There were neighbours standing in the darkness and they stepped aside as the two detectives walked towards the house. No one spoke. McCrink could see the whites of Speers's eyes. He looked like a man come to some place of judgement. In the distance the train's hooter sounded as it slowed for Newry Station and McCrink felt Speers start beside him as the dismal klaxon sounded in the night, reaching them like some carrion shriek.

The onlookers closed ranks behind them. They were called upon. To gather wordlessly in the dark. They had taken it upon themselves to fulfil this dire office. Men stood to either side of the door to the council house, framing the plain wooden door with their bulk and authority. McCrink understood that death had transformed the semi-detached house. People speaking in whispers. The neat fence and gravel path.

The policemen entered the house. Doors lay open. There

were people sitting on the stairs. McCrink saw the mother first. She sat on the edge of a sofa in the living room. She had her daughter's slant eyes and small, pursed mouth. She kept her gaze averted as if she kept some private agony under scrutiny, as if she was afraid that if she stopped looking at it for an instant she wouldn't be able to find it again.

There were ornaments on the fireplace. China dogs and figurines. They looked like tomb gifts. Pearl's father sat opposite the mother, sitting back on the leatherette settee. A small man with slicked-back hair. McCrink could see oil under his fingernails. He was wearing blue mechanic's overalls. McCrink imagined him in a backstreet garage. A man good with his hands with a well-kept tow-truck backed up alongside. The racked tools. The epitome of roadside providence. He would be an adept of the world of crafted machine parts, fine tolerances. He looked at his hands as if they could shape the grief which consumed him, as if there were fine adjustments that could be made to loss itself. They were helpless in the face of dank calamity that pervaded the house.

McCrink was aware of movement in the hall, a stirring among the mourners. A figure in clerical black came into the room, a man with black hair combed back, a high-cheekboned face. He invited them to kneel and took a leatherbound Bible from his pocket. He read from Deuteronomy. He read from Isaiah. The books of the unforgiving God. He sought to bring the deity into the room, to place them in his lyric, vengeful presence. In the hallway someone moaned.

When he had concluded his breviary he walked from the room without speaking. Pearl's mother rose to her feet, her hand to her mouth, and left the room, moving with a diagonal gait as

86

though she was trying to get out of the way of a falling object.

They followed the minister outside. Sleet was blowing across the railway tracks. The minister walked towards a dark-coloured Ford Zephyr parked on the verge. His vestments were blown about him. He stood at the car without opening the door and seemed to find some source of reverie in the skeins of sleet being blown over the embankment over his head.

'Hope he doesn't start quoting the Bible at us,' Speers said under his breath.

'Excuse me, Reverend,' McCrink said. The man turned towards him. His shoulders and hair were coated in sleet. For a moment it looked like ermine worn in token of cold office.

'Gentlemen,' the cleric said. He looked from one man to another, as though he had already made a reckoning for this encounter, gaunt provision set aside in his chilly soul.

'It's a bad do, Reverend,' McCrink said, dropping into the colloquial. 'The loss of the comfort of a daughter is a frightening thing.'

'She is gone to the place prepared for her,' the priest said, getting into the car. 'I will take the funeral service when the body is released to the family. In that manner I fulfil the duties of my office towards her. I trust you will discharge your duties in equal manner.'

'We'll do our best,' Speers said. They watched the car drive off.

'He said she was going to the place prepared for her,' Speers said, 'but he never said which place.'

Ronnie Whitcroft had been under sedation since the night of the murder. It was Wednesday before she was considered fit to be interviewed. A uniformed constable brought her to the interview room and left her at the door. Johnston motioned to the empty chair. She sat down. She looked as if she hadn't slept. Her hair had been arranged in a beehive which was starting to come undone. Her slip was visible under the hem of her dress. Her eyes were red. Behind her back Johnston held his nose and turned up his eyes. Ronnie knew what was going through their minds. Thinking they knew where she was coming from. Thinking cheap scent and bad choices.

'Ronnie Whitcroft. DOB 15th April 1942,' McCrink read, 'friend to the deceased. You accompanied Miss Gamble to the dance at the Henry Thompson Memorial Orange Hall.' Ronnie was looking past the moment. Seeing herself photographed at the crime scene in years to come. Giving tearful interviews on the anniversary of her friend's death, older and wiser.

Speers held up a photograph of Ronnie and Pearl.

'It was found in her handbag,' he said.

Ronnie remembered it being taken at the photobooth machine at the fairground in Warrenpoint. In the single shot Ronnie is looking at the camera with a sombre, flat-eyed gaze. 'Fuck's sakes,' she had said at the time, 'we look like the deceased.'

'Don't say things like that,' Pearl had said, feeling the strip of photographs with her finger, the shellacked surface. There were four frames of the girls, heads together, laughing, Ronnie making faces. Ronnie slipping her sweater off her shoulder, Pearl looking at her in mock horror, knowing sidekicks in a seaside photo booth.

'When you went into the hall, did you see McGladdery?'

'No. He come in after. Everybody wanted to dance with him,' Ronnie told McCrink. 'He could dance like somebody from the films. Even the snobby lot, the tennis-club crew. But that was all they done with him. Dance.'

'Why was that?'

'He wasn't good enough for them. You could see the way them girls stepped out on the floor with him. They wouldn't touch him with a barge pole forby the dancing.'

'Did McGladdery dance with Pearl that night?'

'Two or three times,' Ronnie said. She straightened her back. 'I was with my beau.'

'McKnight?'

'Yes. And Pearl come along.'

'Cramped your style?'

'Two's company.'

'So you left Pearl to the tender mercies?'

'She wasn't complaining. Not at the start.'

'Something happened?'

'Nothing happened. McGladdery was dancing with her, then the other lot moved in. The tennis crowd. McGladdery was well took in by that crowd. They had a bit of a reputation.'

'Did they do much talking? Pearl and McGladdery?'

'They didn't know each other except to see. Pearl said she might have met him once or twice when she was small. I seen her laughing. He said something to her and she laughed.'

'Is that a fact,' Johnston said. 'So he knew Miss Gamble?'

'I wouldn't say that.'

'Sounds like it to me. What sort of a girl was she?'

'What class of a question is that?'

'I mean did she spend much time on her back?'

'You talk about her like a beast of the field. Pearl was a good girl.'

'Did she lead him on?'

'She wasn't the type to lead anybody on.' Ronnie didn't look at them. She had had a fight with Pearl a few months previously after a dance in Warrenpoint Town Hall. Pearl hadn't been feeling well and McKnight had offered to bring her home.

A mile from Warrenpoint McKnight started trying it on, driving alongside the tidal mudflats in the neck of the lough. Rain falling on the windscreen. The car filling with McKnight's aftershave, dusky man-scents. Telling Pearl how beautiful she looked, how the white linen dress nipped in at the waist with a leather belt became her. Pulling into a layby and putting his arm around her shoulder. There were other cars parked in the layby. Shapes moving in the windows in the faint illumination from the port lights, ghostly shiftings behind the laminate glass. This part of the lough had a reputation for hauntings, stirrings in the pine woods. There was talk of a white lady, a dead minstrel, occult personas adrift in the psychic spume.

'Stop it,' Pearl said. McKnight touching her knee, leaning into her. Telling her she wasn't like Ronnie. That she had class. That she was a lady. Pearl found herself looking beyond the moment, McKnight's breath against her ear, his hands working at her. She had that ability. To step back from the moment. She had read about people who left their bodies during operations. You floated to the ceiling and looked down on the team of surgeons and nurses labouring over your body like anatomists from an old book. She could see the red and green channel markers, ships in passage riding out the night beyond the sandbars.

McKnight stopped touching her. He sat back in his seat and lit a cigarette.

'Ronnie was right about you,' he said, 'you're like a fucking iceberg.'

Pearl hadn't said anything to Ronnie about the incident, but the following Saturday McKnight had told Ronnie that Pearl had wanted to kiss him that night, but that he 'hadn't been up for it'.

Ronnie met Pearl that night in the toilets of the Town Hall. The toilets full of girls putting Silvikrin in their hair, fixing the big eye make-up in fly-specked mirrors. Girls you went to school with. All the bitch talk, the girl-spite, the jostling cattiness. The girl hierarchies coming across in scathing top-to-toe looks, leaving remarks trailing in their wakes. There was always someone being sick. There was always someone weeping in a cubicle, mascara running down her face, memory-fixed in her clownishness, woebegone, a boy's name repeated.

'What do you think you're doing trying to get your mitts on my man?' Ronnie said.

'I never,' Pearl said, 'it was him pulled into the layby. I wouldn't, Ronnie, I swear.'

'I suppose you're too good for him now?'

'Don't, Ronnie. Please.'

'He's fit for the likes of me, is that it?'

'Is that what you think?' Pearl said. 'Maybe next time I'll let him, then you won't be able to say stuff like that to me.'

Pearl started to walk away but Ronnie called her back and they made up. Ronnie was sometimes jealous of Pearl. There was this look she had in unguarded moments. 'If you could bottle it, you could have sold it,' Ronnie said. Pearl looked foreign, as if from some far-flung republic. She looked like one of those Japanese women you saw on the newsreels, scurrying, kimonoed, eyes downcast.

Johnston questioned Ronnie about leaving the hall. She told him that Pearl had gone up Church Avenue with a man called Joseph Clydesdale for about ten minutes. Ronnie had spent the time with McKnight.

'Had a good time to yourself then, Ronnie?' Johnston said, winking, complicit.

A different look in Ronnie's eyes this time, a shifty, in-heat look, Ronnie caught up in something blatant and interior, a sensual introspection. McCrink had seen the look on a suspect's face before when it meant a husband betrayed, a lover jilted. It was a heavy-lidded look that betokened illicit couplings, underhand pleasures, lingered over and unregretted.

'We know you drove home with Pearl, Rae Boyd, Derek Chambers and Evelyn Gamble in Billy Morton's car,' McCrink said. 'Did you see anyone on the way up to Damolly Cross?'

'No,' Ronnie said, 'but there was a car going up when we were coming down after we dropped Pearl off.'

There were no more witnesses to be questioned that day. Pearl was to be buried after a service at the Presbyterian church. McCrink sat at the back of the church, the service barely audible. He kept his head down as the coffin was carried past then looked up to see Speers following the cortège, his head bent. McCrink stood up as the last person passed and followed the cortège out into the shadows under the yew trees.

92

The cortège went ahead of him through the mausoleums and tilted headstones under yew trees, a hemmed-in processional.

McCrink left the graveyard and returned to Corry Square. At five he left the station and crossed the canal by the metal bridge. The girder bridge had been designed to swivel but it had not been used for years, its mechanisms seized. He crossed Soho car park onto the Mall. He went into Mervyn Graham's shoe-repair shop. The shop smelt of leather and rubber, dense organic odours. He could hear a lathe in the back room. The cubicles behind the counter contained dozens of matched shoes and underneath that hundreds of old, uncollected shoes, laceless, cracked and welted. He remembered that Speers had sent all Robert's shoes to the forensics lab to have the matter adhering to the soles analysed. They were doing blood ESDA tests, looking for muds and sediments.

The lathe stopped turning and Mervyn came out of the back.

'There's a rumour going about the town. You're looking for Robert's suit.'

'We're looking for evidence leading to a conviction,' McCrink said. Mervyn picked a woman's shoe from the countertop and ran his fingers along the instep.

'Woman's the devil for broke heels, torn stitching,' he said. 'There's nothing they won't wear out.'

'You're not fond of the women then.'

'I'm fond enough of them except when it comes to bad treatment of footwear.'

'Does Robert like women?'

'His early life wouldn't point in that direction, but there's many the mother lifted a hand to her son for no cause.

Women are blew this way and that by their own discontents and woe betide the man who gets in their road.'

'You mean he's afraid of women? That he might lash out?'

'You're putting words in my mouth, Mr McCrink. You wouldn't be the first policeman to put words in a man's mouth.'

'What do you mean by that?'

'The man who got convicted for the killing of Judge Curran's daughter. They say the detective in charge told him what to say and held his hand to put his signature to it.'

'And how would he have got him to do that?'

'The detective, Capstick, said he'd tell his mother that he was a homo. He was that scared of the mother he confessed to murder instead.'

'If you're that big an expert on murder, maybe you'd tell me who killed Pearl?'

'You needn't come to me looking to put a rope around McGladdery's neck. No one seen him do anything. You made up your mind who done it and you never looked at anyone else.'

'Did he have any girlfriends?'

'Not that I know of. The women's fond of him though. He's a good dancer, has a way about him. Maybe when he was in London.'

Ten

Ronnie used to tell Pearl that the gap between her front teeth was attractive in the manner of film stars with an imperfection or quirk in their looks. Ronnie took her to the pictures at the Aurora and laughed at Pearl when she wondered at the size of everything. At cowboys mounted on great dream-horses riding across the screen and actresses accepting giant kisses on their flawless lips.

Ronnie brought Pearl into the library. They looked up words in the French dictionary. Vierge meaning virgin. Ronnie said the French teacher was a ride. Un rideau. That's not French, you twit, Pearl said. Le mort, Ronnie said. That's the word for death.

Ronnie and Pearl would go down town after school. The boys from the Abbey and the High School waited for buses at the Stonebridge and at the Mall. The mass of boys frightened Pearl, the sense of mob about them, everything seeming on the edge of control, the boys keeping it like that, the milling bodies, massed in the narrow walkways. Ronnie would walk through the middle of them, gathering their attention to her. Relishing the jostle, the half-understood innuendos. The way the boys wanted to handle you, pull your bra strap, snatch the grip from your hair. Pearl wanted to tell her not to. Terrible longings were being brought to bear.

'It wouldn't be the cubs I'd be afraid of,' Ronnie said drily, 'it'd be them that sired them.'

'They don't know themselves,' Pearl told her, 'they don't know what class of a thing they can do.'

As if Pearl foresaw the boys' fates, the coming-of-age dramas that were to befall them, the way that they could be engulfed by malefaction. Dark spirits of teenage suicide, of accidental drownings, of pranks going wrong, slumped over the wheel in a ditch at 2 a.m. The insults and dirty talk were the chanted elegies of their age. 'They know what's up ahead,' Ronnie said. 'They know the odds.'

'Boys are thick as planks,' Ronnie told Pearl, 'girls aren't like that. At least I'm not. I'm an old-fashioned girl at heart. You're different, Pearl. People look at you different to me. Give the likes of me ten years I'll be dragging a pram down Hill Street with some ne'er-do-well husband hanging out of me. Girl's got to enjoy herself while she can.'

Ronnie seeing Pearl in a homely light. Picking out soft furnishings in Foster Newell's home department. A Housing Executive semi-detached in the Meadow. The longed-for verities of a well-kept home.

In the evenings they would drink coffee in Falloni's or the Satellite. They would read through the entertainment pages of the Belfast Telegraph and imagine themselves pulling up outside music venues in the city, the Boom Boom Room, or the Maritime Hotel or the Orchid Blue.

'You'll get to them places, Pearl,' Ronnie would say, 'one of these days.'

Ronnie's mother bought True Crime magazine and Ronnie would bring it into school to show it to Pearl. Terrible depravities

were hinted at. Fraudsters who worked their way into the heart
of a family the better to satisfy their monstrous urges. A variety
of post-industrial locations were evoked. Laybys. Motorway rest
stops. Malefactors seemed to have access to forests and moors.
There were dismemberments and mutilations. There were tales
of dogged police work and lucky breaks.

Ronnie said that Pearl was a loner. Pearl would take the bus
to the Point in wintertime. Like Robert she was drawn to the
seawater baths. Like a lot of people from the Newry area she
had learned to swim there. The baths were closed for the winter and the wind drove waves over the walls. Weed hung in
swags from the railings, and seawater gathered on the cracked
tiles. The baths were filled by tidal sluices. She had always
been afraid to swim in the deep end.

She liked to read about Brigitte Bardot and sometimes when
she walked along the front at Warrenpoint she imagined herself in the South of France. The towns of Monaco and Nice.
Le Promenade des Anglais. She always thought of it as being
wintertime when the towns were sparsely populated, the tour-
ists gone home until the following year. Chairs stacked in the
seafront cafes. She imagined that she stood on a faraway harbour
wall listening to a cold mistral driving sand across the bathing
beaches, the breakwaters and empty lidos.

At the weekends cars lined up in the square in front of the
amusements in Warrenpoint. The Hillmans and Sunbeams and
Cortinas. Men combing their hair in the wing mirrors. The
Newry girls walked up and down in front of them. Pearl liked to
watch them from a distance. You got the gleam of T-cut panels
and chrome trim, deep lustres in the turbulent night. The men
going for the GI cuts. Going to the barber's on Saturday morning

to get quiffs, southbacks, looking for the strut that would come with the haircut and the Sta-prest trousers.

Pearl would take the last train from Warrenpoint to Newry and walk home through the graveyard in Kilmorey Street. Glass jars stood on graves with wilted flowers in them. She stayed away from the old part. There was a sense of rigid Calvinists there, her wintry forebears. She paused in front of the graves of infants. It brought a tear to your eye to think of them alone in the dark and sometimes their mothers left toys or brightly coloured clothing there. She thought of small white coffins with toys on top of them. She imagined her own melancholic funeral and who would be there and who would shed a tear at her passing, a tear unnoticed by all save one. A secret lover for ever true. Pearl liked to give herself up to ravaging sentiment. She would read out magazine stories to Ronnie of odds defied, of young love's triumph.

At fifteen Pearl went to Newry Technical College to study bookkeeping. After her death Ronnie said that there was a side to her that she did not know. Pearl began to join the boys who smoked behind the chemistry block at breaks. They stood at the gable wall underneath the fume vent for the chemistry lab. On still days sulphurous clouds hung in the air and they went back to class smelling of the wreathing vapours. Pearl smoking the cigarette down to the maker's crest. On winter evenings after school they would smoke in a derelict house on the street while they waited for the bus, the evenings draw-ing in and the nights giving way to small-town gothic. Pearl's voice was starting to acquire a throaty tone. She admitted to Ronnie that she practised it in the bathroom mirror at night, forming her lips, looking for the voguish overtones.

On her own in the Tech library Pearl continued to take down the Oxford French dictionary and pick out sexual terms. Using her forefinger to underline the words. Vierge meaning virgin. Froideur meaning frigid. It was a word that she kept hearing. Ronnie said that boys only said it because they were scared of her. Pearl had a way of withdrawing into herself. There was a stillness that seemed to emphasise a growing exoticism in her features. Her Chink look, Ronnie called it. It was imperious, almost haughty. Don't be looking down your big long beak at me, Ronnie would say, and the look would disappear as Pearl started to laugh.

At school it was Ronnie brought the long pleated brown skirt to Pearl who pinned it up for her. Ronnie making sure she wore her skirt shorter than any other girl in the school. Other girls made arch remarks to her in the corridors but Ronnie didn't care. She had a way of walking down the corridors. Sashaying, she called it. I'm just going to sashay down to the cloakroom. If there were remarks about Pearl then Ronnie would speak up for her.

'Never mind them saucy bitches, pay them no heed,' Ronnie said.

Pearl went out with Davy Higgins from the Meadow. He took her up Shannon's Avenue.

'She's a prick tease,' he said, 'all over you and then nothing. Sits up right in the middle of everything and says she's going home.'

The town had a tradition of musical theatre. Pearl wanted to join and asked Ronnie to come with her.

'I bet there's plenty of talent,' Pearl said.

99

'Full of homos as far as I can see,' Ronnie said. But she agreed to come to rehearsals with the Newpoint players.

Pearl liked the Town Hall theatre. An ornate red-brick building that straddled the river on three arches. There was a sense of provincial civics at work, the well-off of the town gathered in the midwinter, local grandees in the ornate boxes, plump and venal, the mill owners and shipping agents. Middle-aged men looking you up and down, the idea of provincial masqued balls, people gathering from the outlands bringing with them the feeling that somewhere just out of sight another unimagined life was being carried on, a sexual guile in the glances that followed you around the theatre. Going onstage to do the show tunes, the comic operas, works that carried some sad and sinister charge under the glib lyrics. Something afoot in the backstage hush, the dusty storage rooms and rehearsal space.

Pearl wanted to join the chorus but found that it did not suit her. The director of the drama group, Mrs Hollywood, understood.

'Ronnie is the outgoing one,' Pearl said.

'Outgoing is one word for it,' Mrs Hollywood said. 'With your expertise you'll be able to help with the make-up. We're the backroom girls.' Mrs Hollywood made it feel like some cheery wartime service. Mrs Hollywood wore too much foundation, its grains gathered in the roots of her hair. She smelled of Parma violets.

She'd wink at Pearl when the performers panicked or became tearful. She tutored Pearl in theatrical traditions and superstitions. Touching wood and not speaking the name of the Scottish play. Mrs Hollywood referred to Pearl as her 'right-hand woman', and Pearl was content to be part of the backstage crew. Ronnie started off full of enthusiasm but after a few weeks she stopped turning up.

Pearl told Ronnie she would like to go far, far away some day. Pearl told Ronnie she would go up to the railway line on her own at night. She used to watch the trains going past on the viaduct. She wondered who the travellers were. Their presence on the train seemed to remove them to a different order of existence. They had different concerns. The lit carriages in lyric passage through the night.

~

When she left school Pearl got a job behind the beauty counter in Foster Newell's department store on Hill Street. The era of shortages was just coming to an end, the time of rationing. The utility years stretched out behind them, the cheerless post-war decade. She had a mirrored counter with fluorescent lights overhead. She sold Rimmel and Givenchy products. These were forerunners of the years to come, the largesse starting to build.

The ladies coming in to her. The wives and daughters of the merchant families of the town. There was something ravaged about them, an air of fortunes in decline. Pearl would write down their orders using their married names. Their husbands initials were included in the names. Mrs J. A. Graham. Mrs D. B. Stapleton. Pearl thought it gave the names a metropolitan weight. It sounded as if they were being announced at the top of a marble staircase before sweeping down into the glittering night below. Pearl longed to be like them. She imagined herself standing outside the Orchid Blue wearing a pillbox hat with a veil and long gloves. She wanted the complex look the women had. The appearance of being weighed down by melancholy burdens.

The cosmetics counter looked out onto Hill Street. Evening time. Pearl would lean on the counter looking out onto the darkening and rainblown street outside. Traffic was sparse. Pedestrians walking quickly. There were grave matters to be weighed in her own heart and this always felt like the time to do it. Pearl subject to an edge-of-life feeling. Of things going on without her.

They barely looked at Pearl. She held a hand mirror for them so that they could sample the lipsticks. She handed tissues to them so that they could wipe off the excess, pressing their lips to it and leaving the imprint on the tissue. Pearl wondered if you could identify them from the tissue afterwards, pick out the whorls and ridges like policemen did with fingerprints.

'There's men in this town would pull the whole face off you, never mind the lips,' Ronnie said, 'and the fingernails is never that clean either.'

It was said afterwards that the ladies liked Pearl. She was chatty and literal. Pearl told Ronnie that she would like to be like one of the married ladies. She told Ronnie she liked the way they used their husbands' initials as part of their names. Mrs D. G. Waring. Ronnie had started to work as a waitress in the Golf Club.

'You think so,' Ronnie said, 'you want to be around the husbands so you do. All hands when they think nobody's looking. Mr A. D. Grope. Mr X. B. Bumgrab.'

It didn't stop Ronnie from going off in a car with one of the club members, a bank official called McKnight with a house on the Mall. Pearl rarely saw Ronnie at the weekends unless it was in the bank official's Humber.

'He keeps a Frenchie in his wallet,' Ronnie said. 'He showed it to me. "Be prepared, that's my motto," says he. He can prepare all he likes, says I. If he's looking for a girl like that he can go up to the Mill. I'm not doing the deed with the likes of that. He'll put no bun in this oven.'

Pearl suspected that Ronnie had started to do the deed with McKnight. McKnight made her nervous, the way he looked her up and down. He had a moustache and wore suits from Burton or C&A. He was spivish and knowing. Ronnie would meet him in the Satellite cafe after work and she got Pearl to come along.

'He's always late,' Ronnie said, 'and I don't want to be sitting there on my tod with a big head on me waiting for the likes of that.'

The Satellite cafe was a chip shop on the corner of Kilmorey Street. A satellite had been painted on the gable wall, a Sputnik. Ronnie thought it was sinister. Pearl wanted to know the science. She had read articles about space exploration. Soyuz rockets blasting off from Siberia. She liked its sinister aerialled look, carrying some deep-space payload. She thought how alone it must be, out there beyond the asteroid belts, among the spiral nebulae. When she mentioned this Ronnie laughed.

'There's plenty of lonely to go around down here, never mind outer space.'

But Pearl kept her mind on the science of it. She remembered reading about Marie Curie. The discoverer of radium. How the radioactivity had eaten away at her bones, working into the deep cell structures, but the Frenchwoman had kept working to the end, her features bathed in sickly luminescence.

Pearl could see herself like that. Beautiful and doomed.

McKnight was half an hour late. Ronnie kept looking at the door. They sat in leatherette banquettes and drank coffee with steamed milk. When McKnight came in he sat between Pearl and Ronnie. He put his arm around Ronnie. Pearl could smell Old Spice. He kept on at Ronnie about the way she dressed, about hemlines, the shade of her lipstick, how much cleavage she showed, the freckled expanse that she thought of as being open to appraisal. There was a kind of sensuous aplomb about her that men liked.

Pearl kept feeling his thigh against hers. He had a way of inching towards you. Ronnie was no help. She was too busy smoking McKnight's Lambert and Butlers. Pearl noticed that Ronnie had love bites on her neck just under the collar of her blouse. It made her look wounded and imperilled like some bruised princess. To get away from him she kept getting up and going to the Wurlitzer. She liked Elvis Presley. How he sounded, the stately chords. She kept playing 'It's Now or Never' over and over. McKnight laughing at her.

She saw Robert and Will come in. They sat down at the table in the window. She knew Robert to see but he was seven years older than her and she had never spoken to him. He had been in England for a while and she knew that he had been in trouble with the law. He stood out because of the way he dressed. He wore drainpipe trousers and suede shoes and combed his hair back in a quiff.

'Them McGladderys,' her mother said, 'they were neither reared nor let alone.'

Robert had mitched school. He had burgled a house in Drumalane. He hung around the pool halls and bars of the town with others. It was a small-town thing. Once you acquired the delinquent reputation, the truant shadow, it never left you.

Will noticed that Pearl was uncomfortable with McKnight and kept getting up to go to the jukebox.

'That boy McKnight's trying to feel up the Gamble girl, you heard it here first,' Will said. 'Why don't you have a go at her yourself. See if she'll come up the Avenue with you. Bet you'd get the lot.'

It was part of Will's narrative. Going up the Avenue with girls, getting the lot. The tit. The bush. The box.

The next time Pearl went to the jukebox Will was there first.

'Don't think much of the company you're keeping. He's bad news that chap.'

'Hark who's talking,' Pearl said back, pert as you like, she told Ronnie afterwards.

'Put the knife back in the drawer, Miss Sharp,' Will said. 'You like Elvis?'

'What's it to you anyhow?'

'That's for me to know and you to find out.'

They watched the jukebox, its gimcrack mechanisms like something from early robotics selecting the 45.

'I worked as a jukebox engineer in London.'

'I bet you never.'

'Swear to God. I can fix anything.'

They listened to Elvis. Deferring to the darkness in the voice, the picked-out chords and backroad harmonics. The drawn-out delinquent vowels.

'Me and you could run away together,' Will said, 'take to the highway. Leave this lot behind. A girl like you.'

Pearl looked at him, wondering if he was joking. She

hadn't come across the road-dream that the Yanks had, the myth of the highway, the American road-lore. They watched the vinyl 45 dropping into place in the jukebox and the jittery arm coming across.

'In Alaska they got one road goes for a thousand miles, straight as a die. You never seen the like of it. They got trains that go on so far they take a day to pass.'

'The only one's going on around here is you,' Pearl said, pleased with herself, feeling she was getting the banter right, setting the texture of the moment. Trying to think of herself as a town girl, a lippy street type. Giving him the backchat.

'You're a right little miss, aren't you?' Will said. Smiling at her. Letting her know that Pearl had got his number, a small-town charmer on the make. Pearl thinking there was no harm in it.

'Any chance you'd take a walk with me?' Will said.

'I don't go walking with boys I don't know,' she said.

'Do you do anything else with them?' Will said, leaning into her, Pearl's face going blank, backing away from him, waiting for the response, the hissed-out word. Frigid.

'No,' she said. 'I'm going back to my friends.'

'Go on,' he said, 'I don't go out with yellow people anyhow.'

When she got back to the table Ronnie was sniffy. She didn't think much of Pearl's choice of companion. She said Will was a perv, that McGladdery was a show-off. A fancy Dan.

You're some girl to be talking, Pearl thought. Pot kettle black, she said in her own head.

'McKnight says he's going to leave his wife,' Ronnie told Pearl afterwards. If you believe that, Pearl thought.

Will wouldn't stop talking about Pearl when they left the cafe.

'Did you see the way she looked at me, the slanty-eyed bitch?

106

She was dying for it. The Japs and the Chinks, the women are built different. The hole's the other way around.'

~

Around that time Will started to go into Foster Newell's. Pretending not to look at the lingerie section. The wire-framed brassiere displays. The synthetic legs with tights rolled on, and the breathy vocabularies of the underthings. Flesh-coloured, opaque. Sneaking looks at the seamed nylon and at the women with their heads bowed on the front of the cellophane-wrapped packs. All the secret fastenings, the hooks and buttons and poppers. The gathered-in lore of dress.

'He came right up to the make-up counter to talk to me,' Pearl told Ronnie. 'I didn't know what way to look. All the other assistants were sniggering. I was afraid the manager would come.'

Will asked Pearl about the make-up. She wasn't sure if he was making fun of her. He asked her about the brushes and compacts. How the make-up went on and what it was for. Putting the foundation on and building on it, the artifice involved.

'Please go away,' she said, 'this counter is ladies only.'

'It's a free country,' Will said.

So Will watched her from a distance. She was painting a young woman's nails, the two women's heads bent over the counter in an intent companionable way, as though they had something of goodwill to share between them. When Pearl wasn't looking he put a bottle of Rimmel nail varnish and several lipsticks in his pocket. It was something he had been in the habit of doing. He shoplifted things and then gave them to Robert. He liked the sense of outlaw largesse that it gave him.

'She give me loads of stuff,' Will said. 'She said she'd meet me down on the towpath some night.'

Robert gave the lipstick and nail varnish to Mervyn.

'You could use them in the train layouts,' he said. 'If you want to do something in pink.'

'I seen a brave many trains,' Mervyn said, 'but I never seen a pink one.'

~

Later that year Robert had gone to England, taking the mail boat from Warrenpoint to Liverpool.

'He had this thing about going to England,' Will said afterwards, 'he was always going on about it, saying you could make it big over there.' Robert had cut out pictures from Bodybuilder International of the world championships in Earls Court and stuck them on his wall. He imagined himself on the stage with Charles Atlas and other world-champion bodybuilders. Rows of men with muscles bunched and oiled, a fellowship with shared memories of pre-dawn gyms, working with the weights and bar-bells, doing the chin-ups and squats, all the grind you needed to do to add to the tissue mass, hearing the sound of the Earls Court crowd in your ears. Robert could see himself in the high-cut trunks, getting admiring glances from the other competitors. He told Mervyn he would bring him over to act as his trainer so that he could stand in the wings, looking grave with all the other sage elders of the bodybuilding business.

'Watch what gyms you go to,' Mervyn told him. 'It's not just about putting on muscle. Any fool can do that. It's about the tone. You have to get up on the balls of your feet, be supple. Forget all this stuff with calipers and measuring. You win a body-building contest in here,' Mervyn said, tapping the middle of his forehead. 'You don't want them to see your big pecs or your big girly clenched arse. You want them to see your heart.'

Mervyn lent Robert £20 for the boat fare from Warrenpoint to Liverpool. Robert took the night mail train from Liverpool to London. He sent a postcard from London showing Big Ben with a red Routemaster bus in the foreground. Mervyn had given him the addresses of several boarding houses on the Holloway Road. 'It's like Canal Street!' Robert wrote home to Mervyn. There was the smell of drains. There were Hasidic Jews on the street, men in skullcaps and turbans. But there were the same smoky gothics of Canal Street, the feeling of having been stranded in some turreted Eastern European capital. It made you think of graveyards and things coming at you out of wreathing mists.

There were several Russians staying in the boarding house. They were small men with moustaches. Robert had never come across people like them before. Gloomy, heavy-accented, semi-alcoholic. They went out in the evening and returned late at night. Robert could hear their footsteps going past outside his room, their heavy, dragging gait weighed down with Slavic woes. They spent the daytime in their rooms with the curtains drawn.

Mrs Pieloski, the landlady, was a small thin woman who smoked Embassy Reds. There were cigarette coupons and Green Shield stamps in the vase in the kitchen. She had been brought up on Marrowbone Lane and spoke in a street trader's guttural, a spat-out Whitechapel cant.

'Them Russkies is up to no good. Them and their fucking bomb. Spies is what I think.'

Robert started off working for tips as a busboy, barely able to afford his rent. He was subject to all the sensations of the city newcomer, the crushing anonymity, the gaping stance in public places. When he had no money he would ride the tube. He liked being underneath the city, seeing the exposed pipes and brickwork, feeling himself among the workings of the city, the tunnelled-out doings of the place. He liked it when the carriages built up speed, careening through the dark, blue flashes thrown up from the rail, a sense of unseen forces at work.

Robert worked hard on sounding as if he belonged. Picking up the Greek Street patois. He started talking about toms and ponces.

The London papers were full of spy cases. George Blake. The M21 Lonsdale spying case. Robert saw himself as undercover in Soho, felt the night around him alive with plotters, stealthy figures with Eastern European accents.

Robert got a job as a waiter in a restaurant on Berwick Street. The owner of the restaurant was a Frenchman. He had a board behind the till where he had pinned kitchen chits, each with a lipstick imprint of a woman's mouth on it and a signature underneath.

The owner would get the girls to do a lip imprint on a chit for him, then he would buy them a drink. Between shifts Robert would stand at the back door to take in the air. Couples would go into the alley behind the restaurant. You could barely see them in the dark, men and women labouring in the shadows. In the morning there would be used condoms on the ground.

The restaurant was popular with minor showbusiness figures who worked in the theatres on Shaftesbury Avenue. It was also frequented by girls from the Raymond Revuebar where semi-nude shows were performed. The Revuebar was subject to closures and prosecutions under obscenity laws. Robert felt at home with the performers. Many were runaways. There were tales of harsh provincial upbringings, sexual violence in the home. Robert told them he would write their stories of hardship cheerily overcome, of odds defied. He offered them a tale of gritty romance. Something to set against the desolation that assailed them from within.

But at some stage of the night they would let themselves down. They would slip off into the night with one of the male clientele, a night cadre of grifters and ponces.

'It's like they want to be treated like dirt,' Robert said, watching them walk into the night. The other girls would go quiet. For all Robert's talk, somebody else was writing their story. They recognised the tawdry landmarks of its narrative in each other. The wrong men. The unpaid rents and backstreet abortions. They showed Robert how to hide a bruise or a cut with face powder, how to mask a black eye with a surgical eyepatch so that it looked as if you had been to the doctor. They had convictions for soliciting and shoplifting. They were unreliable, lightfingered, guileful in ways that Robert couldn't even imagine.

There were shops on Berwick Street which sold Titbits and other titillating magazines over the counter. Once they got to know you other publications were produced from under the counter in brown paper bags. The shop owners leered, hinted at unspeakable depravities. Robert bought several without seeing the contents. The magazines consisted of a series of poor-quality photographs of minor fetishes. Robert also frequented bookshops in the backstreets behind King's Cross Station, buying books with titles such as Souvenirs from a Boarding School and My Secret Life. It was these materials that were found when the Newry police raided Robert's house, leading to the rumours that swept the town concerning Robert's sexual preferences.

The girls who worked in the restaurant saw Robert as prone to unworldliness. They covered up for him when he was late or didn't hear the bell to pick up orders from the kitchen. He told them that Russian agents had tried to recruit him at a gym on Tottenham Court Road. He hinted at previous employment on secret government programmes. He told them his head was full of dangerous knowledge. He dreamed of U2 spy planes borne aloft, floating through the ionosphere as though they might drift off the edge of the known landmass. He sat through newsreel footage of Cold War flare-ups, Soviet divisions massing. He immersed himself in the literature of moles and infiltrators.

Robert didn't work Mondays and Tuesdays. He would take the train into the countryside to see the spy station at Menwith Hill, the tracking complexes. But it was the nuclear missiles that drew him, the bunkers and silos. Their silvered, enthralling fuselages inching from bases in the United States. He imagined them tracked into the atmosphere, the parabolic flightpaths aimed towards the Soviet centres of populations, the secret tundra cities.

He took the train to Greenham Common and stole a bicycle from the train station. He cycled around the outside of the base, watching the B52s take off and land, the afterburn roar as they lifted slowly into the air. He made the trip several times. The second time he was arrested by members of the Military Police and taken to Greenham police station where he was questioned before being released. A Minolta camera and a spiral reporter's notebook where he had recorded the take-off and landing times of B52 flights were confiscated.

It is not known whether Robert's detention and trial on capital murder charges became known to those he had worked with in London. He was featured in several London dailies before his arrest, but the working population of Soho was transient. People drifted on without leaving forwarding addresses. For most of them Soho was something they were glad to leave behind. Its backstreet sex barkers and rip-off clubs and strip joints, its louche camaraderies good for a year or two only.

Robert spent ten months in London but he missed Newry and its gloomy, elegant malls and end-of-the-line mills. He missed the town centre and the empty halls and crumbling mansions of the industrialists on the canal bank. He pictured the town empty like some plague-swept city of olden times with charnel mists drifting in the streets, the seabirds' lone hootings in the fogbound bents at the head of the lough.

When he got a letter from Mervyn reminding him about his offer of an apprenticeship in shoemaking he went back to Newry.

The first person he met when he got back was Will. Robert

was wearing a black drape suit he had bought just before he had left London.

'I hardly knew you, you big spastic,' Will said, 'in that fancy London get-up.'

'How's the town?' Robert said.

'Town never changes,' Will said, 'which is more than can be said for you, you big girl's blouse.'

Eleven

McCrink had left his car at the courthouse. He walked back towards it. As he got close he could see that the front door of the Robert Thompson Memorial Hall was open. He looked at the faded board frontage of the Orange hall with Bible texts inscribed on placards. He stepped inside. The walls were hung with silk banners and tattered Orange collarettes. There were Masonic devices fixed to the wall above the stage, flute band insignia on the rear wall of the stage. Rising Sons of the Valley. True Blues.

He had arranged to meet Margaret at the bandstand in Warrenpoint Park. She was late and he stood at the tennis courts watching a mixed doubles match. When Margaret came she linked her arm through his.

'What is it about tennis matches?' she said. 'They always seem to be taking place in the past.'

'There's always an Edwardian look to them,' he said. 'Makes you think about a lost generation. Young men in tennis flannels sent to face the German guns. I used to spend hours watching the hockey players when I worked in the central library. The Malone hockey club. You'd go down and watch them through the fence. Playing hockey in short skirts, the daughters of the big houses.'

It was the epitome of nostalgia. Grammar-school girls playing hockey on summer evenings, willowy and fleet. Malone
girls and svelte Wesleyans. Well-bred voices ringing out over
the hockey fields, playing on as the light fell, learning qualities of earnestness, how to set tight margins on a life and
stay between them, their long, expressive faces bent to the
game, the evening wind brushing the top of the cropped
grass. Sometimes you would see one of the girls standing on
their own, looking downcast, unnamed longings assailing
her, leaving her marooned in the temperate parklands.

'There's an innocence about these things when you look
back on them.'

Margaret said that the hockey girls knew more of the world
than they let on. 'That's your problem,' she said. 'You idealise
those people.'

It was true. He had trouble seeing misfortune's dark hand
at work in the merchant quarters of the city, ill intent abroad
in the laurel shrubberies on the outskirts of town.

'Patricia Curran was one of your hockey girls. Look what
happened to her.'

Stabbed thirty-seven times on her own driveway. So many
stab wounds the first doctor to see her thought that she had
been struck with a shotgun blast.

'You know about that?'

'Everyone here knows about that.'

'It's not the same thing as what happened to the girls in
London.'

'What girls?'

'The last case I worked on. The Nude Murders. Prostitutes.'

'You think any of those girls feels it's different when they're walking home on their own at night and they hear footsteps in the dark behind them? Doesn't matter what size of a house they go home to, when a man wants something and he doesn't get it, it all ends the same way.'

'Maybe. What happens when a woman doesn't get what she wants?'

'You sound like you're talking from experience.'

'My ex-wife.'

McCrink remembered the night that his ex-wife had told him about her infidelity. She called it an affair, letting the word hang in the air between them in all its tawdry meaning.

'If you'd paid more attention to me you would have noticed what was going on.'

'So now it's my own fault.' She didn't reply. She stood in the doorway, inferences of bags packed in hallways.

It had started when he was at police college and had carried on through their marriage. She told him how she had met Ronnie Speers at a police function in Belfast.

'You were trying to lick up to the Chief Constable,' she said.

She told him how she had gone with Speers to a borrowed flat in a tower block in Larne, seventeen miles east of Belfast. She described the rooms, the wallpaper, curtains blowing across open windows, rainspatter. The textures of deceit. Working their way towards the melancholia that they both knew was the lasting thing they would have as lovers. Looking down on the ferryport. Hearing the ships loading at night. The clang of gantries. Containers being stacked. Anne always had to work around the details. The delved-into particulars of love. She named the cafes they had eaten in. She said that she had walked the promenade with Speers every evening. She was scrupulous in her account. It was important to them both that the extent of her treachery be brought into the open. Every aspect of their life together had to be undermined, ambiguities and hidden meanings unearthed. The trips back to Belfast, the late-night phone calls. They spent weeks uncovering new layers of deceit. The betrayed husband. He employed a cunning he didn't know he possessed to find out more. She recounted narrow escapes, sex in borrowed bedrooms, coupling in a stairwell outside McCrink's apartment in Belfast. They both understood that they had to tend to McCrink's hurt, that it was a dense textured thing with its own internal structure, plots and digressions.

'Ronnie Speers,' Margaret said, taking his arm. 'You're working with him now.'

'I know.'

For a while the knowledge of her cheating had excited them. They had uncovered an erotics of loathing. They pushed each other into acting out vile cravings. She sent him to buy cheap porn from a newsagent in the town. Glum nudes, badly photographed. She liked to get on top of him while he told her stories, obscenity-laced narratives of encounters with sailors, Negros copulating. He moved out into a cheap flat in Kilburn. There was an odour of urine in the lifts, cisterns flushing in other flats, the smell of drains. It all became part of their encounters. In the end she left one morning. The last he had heard of her she was living in Blackpool, drinking heavily, transients passing through her flat on a weekly basis.

'What will you do?'

'I don't know. I put money in our account every month. It comes out.'

She took his arm. They stood with their backs to the court looking out onto the dark lough waters.

~

On the fourth day of the total surveillance of McGladdery Special Constable John Morris was posted to Damolly village. He saw Robert leave his house by the front door and cross several fields until he reached the Clanrye river. Constable Morris described how McGladdery looked around him before plunging into the swollen river. With the water reaching to his chest McGladdery crossed the river. He then crossed several more fields until he reached the footbridge across the canal. Crossing the canal, he went into a semi-derelict house and remained there for several minutes.

When he came out he was lost to view behind Damolly Factory but was seen several minutes later walking along the Belfast road by Sergeant Johnston who was driving towards the town. Observing that McGladdery was soaked Johnston stated that he invited McGladdery to come down to the Corry Square barracks to 'get dry clothes'. According to Johnston he 'stayed there until he was dry'.

The evidence of the two policemen was never properly explained. Was Robert already under surveillance on the morning following the murder? An obvious inference may be drawn that Robert intended to destroy evidence or to interfere with it in some way. Following the murder the town was in an uproar. Volunteers were combing the countryside looking for evidence. No evidence was given as to whether the semi-derelict house was searched following Robert's reported visit to it. There are other difficulties associated with the policemen's statements. What did Johnston mean by saying that Robert stayed at the barracks until 'he was dry'?

The police statements implied that Robert had been behaving furtively in the days following the murder. That he had paused on the bank of the river before fording it, 'looking up and down for a minute or two'.

As in much of the evidence there are other subtle under-tones in the policemen's statement which the prosecution would have been aware of. The fact that Robert had gone to a 'semi-derelict house'. The semi-derelict house on the edge of town was something that had worked its way into the pop-ular imagination. The dimlit interiors, the rubbish-strewn rooms and faded wallpaper. People felt that some old magic was at work in them, a watchfulness. Places that were home to half-remembered happenings, folkloric terrors. Children populated the locations with an array of dark agencies and people. The red woman. The one-armed man. The aban-doned rooms and windblown curtains. Robert made himself part of an eerie throng by going to the deserted house.

~

Robert McGladdery was arrested at his home at Damolly Villas at 7.45 on the morning of 22nd February 1961 on the orders of Chief Constable Kennedy.

They had prepared the warrant for McGladdery's arrest in Corry Square. McCrink and Johnston drove to Damolly in Speers's car with two uniformed officers coming behind in a marked squad car. They had given no notice of their inten-tion. There was no one on the street as they stopped in front of the house in Damolly. McCrink and Speers went to the door and rang the bell. Agnes McGladdery opened the door. They could hear a transistor radio in the living room. Agnes was wearing a housecoat. Her hair hung around her face. Her look was slovenly, defiant. Speers held up the warrant. Agnes turned back into the house and spoke into the darkness.

'Them policemen is here. By the look of them I'd pack a bag. You won't set eyes on this house for manys a day.'

Robert came out of the living room. He was wearing an open shirt with the sleeves rolled up and he was carrying an open copy of the Daily Mirror. It was the picture of Robert that McCrink would carry with him. Like a man just come from work, tolerant, at home with his limits, his face changing when he saw the policemen, frowning at the untoward thing they'd brought to his door. He seemed to straighten his shoulders then, ready to put his mind to the damning perplexities that were looming up in front of him.

'Will you pack a bag for me, Ma?'

'I'd pack ten if I thought it'd put you on the high road out of here for good.'

'You're a pal, Ma. Trouble is, there's nothing to pack. The peelers already took most of my clothes.'

'Watch out, Sergeant. He'll have the shirt off your back.'

'You hear my ma, Mr McCrink? She's all heart. You know what the maternal instinct is? You won't find too much of it round this house.'

'No,' Agnes said, 'but you'll find plenty of out all night drinking and not giving any of your dole to your upkeep. That's what you'll find.'

McCrink felt the deep-seated familial rage at work. There were unhealthy undercurrents in the sphere of mothers and sons, a degenerate badinage between the two which left him with a bad taste in his mouth. He could see Speers looking from one to the other. He knew that Speers had worked on several murder cases involving extended families living in remote coastal communities. He understood the blood mechanics of families sunk in generational rancours, the red-eyed feud territories.

'Robert John McGladdery, I arrest you for the murder of Pearl Gamble on the 29th January of this year.'

'Do I get the cuffs,' Robert said.

'Get into the fucking car, McGladdery,' Johnston said.

At 8.45 that morning he was brought to Corry Square RUC Station where he was charged with the murder of Pearl Gamble at Damolly between the hours of 1 a.m. and 9 a.m. on 29th January 1961. When charged he replied, 'Definitely not guilty. I am an innocent man.'

There had been a single photographer from the Newry Reporter present when McGladdery was arrested. Neighbours stood at their doors as Robert was led out. He had an in-the-know look on his face, as if he had some sardonic aside prepared for this moment, a shirt-sleeved malefactor stepping out under a desperado moon.

At Corry Square Station there were reporters and photographers from the city and national press. They knew Robert by name and called out to him. The charges were read to Robert. He was asked if he wanted a solicitor. He replied that he did and Luke Curran, a solicitor with an office in Trevor Hill, was summoned. Johnston asked him why he had chosen Curran.

'Because he has the same name as the judge whose daughter was murdered.'

'I'd say you wouldn't want to get Judge Curran for your trial.'

'I wouldn't mind. I'd say he'd have to be seen to be fair.'

'Now you've picked the judge would you like to pick the jury and all?'

'You're a comic sergeant.'

'I'm not the comedian around here, McGladdery.'

'If I got to pick my own jury who would I put on it? You think my ma would go on the jury?'

'She wouldn't be let.'

'No, she'd be too keen to put me in the ground.'

The solicitor, Curran, who was in fact no relation to Judge Curran, arrived at around 10.15 p.m. He spent half an hour alone with his client. He emerged to say that McGladdery would be pleading not guilty to all counts and that he vehemently denied any involvement in the murder of Pearl Gamble.

On 22nd February 1961 Robert McGladdery was charged with the murder of Pearl Gamble at Weir's Rock, Upper Damolly, at a time unknown on 29th January that year. He was brought before a special sitting of Newry Magistrates' Court and was remanded in custody to appear at Downpatrick Crown Court on 4th April following. Detective Inspector Speers told the court he believed he could connect the accused to the murder. He further believed that McGladdery posed a flight risk.

The court adjourned. The windowless prison van carrying McGladdery left from the back of the courthouse, its tail lights fading, dark come early in the bitter February cold. There had been other cases in the court that day concerning smuggling and border fraud. The sundry defendants left the precincts of the court to return to their homes, dark figures hunched against the cold, and it didn't take much, McCrink thought, to have them armed and departed upon some frontier brigandage.

'They'd smuggle corpses if there was a pound in it, them lot,' Speers said. 'They'd smuggle bags of cats.'

It was raining when McCrink and Speers left the courthouse. There were press men from the national papers on the courthouse steps. McCrink and Speers kept their heads down, pushing through the reporters. They knew what the photographs in the next day's paper would be. Provincial detectives – dour, trenchcoated men. A sullen and resentful local populace. McCrink had heard Brian Faulkner on the radio that morning telling the presenter that they didn't need Scotland Yard. Faulkner telling the man they didn't need any help. They could hang their own.

McCrink, Johnston and Speers crossed the road and went into the Copper Grill. The restaurant was full. McCrink recognised policemen, solicitors, barristers. McGladdery's case brooding on top of the felonious list.

Several national papers would describe the accused man's demeanour in court. He smiled. He acknowledged friends in the public gallery.

'Does thon buck understand what's going on here?' Johnston said.

'Doesn't look much like it,' McCrink said.

'If he keeps on going like that, he'll be ate alive,' Johnston said. 'The yellow press is baying for blood as it is.'

'Let them bay.'

'Let them bay?' Johnston looked at McCrink. 'It's well seeing it's not your blood, sir.'

'He'll be tried according to the rule of law.'

'Rule of law my hole. The time he gets to Crown Court every man jack in the room'll know what the job is.'

'We haven't got enough to convict.'

'We'll find enough,' Speers said.

'Connect him to the charge my arse,' Johnston said. 'All we got is circumstantial, pretty weak circumstantial at that.'

'We got the fact that he was at the dance and got up with Pearl, and that no one seen him after he left. We've got the scratches on his face,' Speers said.

'He's got no alibi.'

'We need something more to convict him. We need the clothing, that suit he was supposed to be wearing.'

'Do you know something about the suit, Sergeant?' McCrink said. 'You keep asking about it.'

'I don't know any more than you, sir.'

They went over the witnesses who claimed to have noticed McGladdery at the dance. Of those witnesses the majority had said he had been wearing a light-coloured suit, although they disagreed as to the colour.

'What if McGladdery was telling the truth? What if he wasn't wearing the light suit that night?' McCrink said.

'That means the witnesses are all lying,' Speers said.

'Or mistaken. They can't agree what colour it was. The dance floor was dark enough. A mistake is possible,' McCrink said.

'Could be. They're all born-again merchants up that way. Blinded by the light. Tell them the canal was the River Jordan they'd believe you. Mind you, they done tests on witnesses in the states. The FBI. People don't see the things they think they see. The mind plays tricks. McGladdery's the main suspect. He's enjoying the attention, pretending to be the big murderer. Next minute he has everybody else convinced he done it.'

'We need to have a chat with our friend McGladdery, a proper interview,' McCrink said.

'You won't get anything out of him, sir,' Johnston said.

'Why do you say that, Sergeant? Have you talked to him already?'

'Only when we took him in to dry him out.'

'That's the first I heard of McGladdery darkening the door of this station.'

'He was acting suspicious. He walked across the river. Two policemen took him back here to dry out his clothes. That's all.'

'That's it?'

'Cross my heart.'

'I want to be told about these things.'

'Yes sir.'

McCrink left the restaurant and walked across town. It was a frosty night, arctic air crossing the country. 'From Siberia,' Margaret said the evening before Robert's arrest. Low pressure systems moving silently down from the steppe, the permafrost regions. The whole town was chilled. Water froze in taps. The canal was iced over. The water in the basin turned milky. At the dockside workers spread sand and salt over the roadway.

Dull fires burning in the tinkers' camp. McCrink could see dark figures in front of the fire, moving restlessly to and fro. Sometimes one would stand still, seeming to look towards the town, others joining him, stark unmoving compositions in the night, a troubled frieze.

McCrink had been offered offices in the larger barracks on the Belfast Road but he had decided to stay at Corry Square Station in the centre of the town. The square hemmed in by red-brick terracing and a sense of commerce in decline, weeds growing through the sleepers on the rail spur across the street. There was a convent on the hill above the barracks. Across the other side of the town the Abbey. They were built on the high ground. There was a looming, a gothic clinging to the side of hills.

The canal was less than a hundred yards away. Warehousing ran down from the backs of the houses on Corry Square to the river. The stone-built warehouses were no longer used for goods transported by rail or canal. They had been taken over by a network of small garages and workshops.

He passed the duty sergeant and went to the incident room. He stood in the doorway.

There was Pearl's death and this was the book of it, her epistle and that of Robert's guilt or innocence. The amassed witness statements. The halting accounts. The Remington clatter in the typing pool now silent. There was a psychic clutter here, the spilled-over A4 sheets reeking of copying fluid. The pored-over transcripts. Each one a witness. Each at the centre of their own tale, subject to encroaching fictions. They were like spies abroad in the night, skulking, untrustworthy.

McCrink took the file of crime-scene photographs back to his office and spread them out on the table. The location of

Pearl's clothes numbered and indexed, the crumpled body just visible where it had been dragged and partially hidden behind the rocks. He ran his eyes down the index. A stocking in American tan, laddered, torn. White Ladybird slip, soiled. White brassiere, clasp broken. The garments sized and inventoried, the intimate apparel they called it.

Beaten. Strangled. Stabbed.

McCrink could not escape the feeling that the murder of Pearl Gamble shared a quality with the Nude Murders he had investigated in London. There was an arch, scripted feel to those murders, an air of knowing asides to the audience. In the Nude Murders all of the girls had been stripped and strangled. In each case the body had been kept for a couple of days before being dumped. The investigators kept coming back to the detail. Why keep the body for forty-eight hours? They consulted psychiatrists and criminologists but they were unable to supply an explanation. McCrink was tasked with reading through the criminal casebooks to see if similar crimes had been committed in the past. He was given an office in Chiswick CID headquarters. He spent days alone with the files, working his way through the photostatted pages. *Last seen getting into blue Ford Prefect.* The way their lives seemed to seep backwards from their last moments like dank contrails.

He worked his way through the close-typed A4 pages for weeks. The crime scenes. The autopsies. The bare text.

He read the victims' names aloud to himself. Elizabeth Figg also known as Ann Phillips. Gwynneth Rees also known as Tina Smart. Hannah Tailford also known as Terry Lynch. The recitation of the names settling into the pure rhythm of a chant. That was his job. To interrogate them. To make the dead account for themselves. He had found himself revisiting the places where the bodies had been dumped. Locations that had received an eerie charge from the presence of the murdered girls, the fact that the murderer had been there, a mystic force. He could feel the structure of each murder. The dark grammar of it.

There was a stillness at the heart of the London murders as there was a stillness at the heart of Pearl's death. Stripped but left undefiled. Beaten, strangled and stabbed in an apparently uncontrolled attack, yet the killer had left no trace of himself at the scene. It pointed to a planned killing, a patient and methodical approach. The killer had taken care not only to hide the body, but to remove the murder weapons – the stabbing instrument and whatever cord had been used to strangle Pearl.

~

The first formal interview with McGladdery took place the following day. Present were Detective Sergeant Johnston, Detective Inspector Speers and Inspector of Constabulary McCrink. From the start McGladdery denied that he had anything to do with the murder of Pearl Gamble. Johnston took the lead in the questioning.

'Why did you kill Miss Gamble?'

'I never killed her.'

'Maybe you don't remember. Maybe you done her in in the grip of a mental illness.'

'I never touched a hair on Pearl's head. All I done was dance with her.'

'The evidence says different.'

'The evidence is that you decided I done it at the start and you haven't bothered your arse looking at nobody else. The real murderer's out there getting away.'

'Everybody at the dance says you were bothering Miss Gamble.

'Then they're lying. Or drunk.' Robert laughed. 'Not much chance of them being drunk in that place, is there, Mr Speers? They're a good-living lot up there. Not like me and you.'

'There's no me and you here, son.'

'Come on, Mr Speers. When you catch the right man, me and you'll have a laugh about this. I could help you find him. I'm no stranger to the science of detection.'

'Give it a rest, McGladdery,' Speers said.

'Motive, opportunity, means, isn't that what they say? Give me long enough I'll work it out for you.'

'We found books in your house. Perverted literature. Magazines. Disgusting stuff. We know what sort you are.'

'I got an interest in anatomy is all.'

'I'd say you got an interest in anatomy. How do you think that filthy stuff would go down with a jury? What was your relationship with the deceased?'

'Me and the deceased never had no relationship.'

'Witnesses say you were bothering her at the dance.'

'Show me them witnesses. If I was bothering her then why did she dance with me three times? Tell us that, Mr Policeman?'

'You're a bit of a show-off, aren't you, McGladdery? Coming back here with your fancy London suits. So where's the suit you were wearing that night?'

'You got the suit. The dark suit.'

'Everybody at the dance says you were wearing a light-coloured suit and a shortie fawn jacket. Where's the jacket?'

'Suppose I had a shortie coat,' Robert said, 'I'm not saying

I had. If I was given thirty-six hours on my own I would ring you and tell you where to find the shortie coat.'

Robert leaned forward in his chair. He was smiling at Johnston. McCrink wondered what was going through his head, the way he looked detached, finding ironies in the situation that no one else was aware of.

'What are you playing at?' Johnston said. 'Where is the coat and suit?'

'You didn't get what you wanted so you stole the bicycle, cycled to Damolly Cross and waited for her, then you attacked her.'

'I never. I went home and I went to bed.'

The witnesses' assertions that he had been wearing a light-coloured suit were put to him but he shrugged and said that the witnesses were either mistaken or lying. There was a childish quality about his accusation of lying, a tell-tale note to his voice. You could hear the playground chant.

'Did you ever see a man hanged, McGladdery?' Speers said. 'Did you ever hear the crack of the trapdoor open under his feet? I seen Evans hanged in Cardiff Gaol for the murder of Rachel the Washerwoman. You should have heard him squeal. He tried to say he was innocent but they all squeal in the heel of the hunt. Tell the truth and shame the devil. You don't want to end up gasping for breath at the end of a rope.'

'You don't gasp for breath. The knot snaps the neck vertebra. Severs the spinal cord. Death is instantaneous,' Robert said, 'I read it.'

'I'll make sure you gasp, McGladdery,' Johnston said. 'I'll talk to the hangman special about it.'

PART TWO

Robert was examined by a prison doctor in Crumlin Road. The doctor made him take off his clothes and get on the scales. It reminded him of swimming at Warrenpoint baths. The white tiles and the chlorine smell hanging in the air. Men stripped naked and padding between the wooden benches. Robert was weighed and measured. The doctor looked into his eyes and ears. He held Robert's testicles in a gloved hand. Robert watched himself in the mirror above the sink.

'I'm working on the physique,' Robert told the doctor. 'I'm doing one hundred chin-ups in the cell before breakfast.'

The most chin-ups Robert had ever managed was twenty-five. He thought it was important to convey the right impression. To say to the world, here is a man who is not prepared to go to seed despite an unjust incarceration. He started to scratch the days of his confinement on the cell wall. He fed pigeons between the bars. He had read about men who had spent many years in prison. In the Mickey Spillane books he had read about the importance of doing your time. Hard time. Easy time. He had read about the Birdman of Alcatraz. He thought about a man in a dusty cell, the lonely years stretching out. He wished that he had been put in a place like Alcatraz. He appreciated the lonely grandeur of it, the island prison surrounded by deadly shifting sea currents, the fogbanks closing.

'I suffered a head injury when I was an infant,' Robert told the doctor.

'There's nothing in your records to indicate a cranial injury,' the doctor said. He was a small man with a dissatisfied

135

look. Robert wondered how you ended up being a doctor in a prison. He thought it must be because you weren't allowed to work anywhere else. Robert looked at the man's hair, dyed and slicked back. The doctor told Robert that excessive masturbation was an indicator of sexual deviance.

'I'm not a pervert,' Robert said. The doctor measured Robert's skull with a set of brass dividers then wrote in a spiral-bound notebook.

'If they hang me can I leave my body to medical science?' Robert said. 'There's things could be learned by examining the like of me.' He imagined an eminent doctor bent over the corpse, an eyebrow raised in surprise and wonder.

'The corpse of the executed man is the property of Her Majesty,' the doctor said, without looking at Robert. 'Post mortem the body is interred in the grounds of the prison. No record is kept of the body's location.'

Robert couldn't stop telling the other prisoners about what happened to the executed man. He was impressed by the sweeping heartlessness of it, the body denied to the family. One of the warders told him that quicklime was poured on the body in the grave to ensure that it was erased from the earth. He could see, when he closed his eyes, the body incandescent in the dark earth.

'The prison doctor looks like a Nazi on the run,' he told Mervyn at visiting time. He had that Josef Mengele look to him. Robert had read about the ratlines, Nazis spirited out of Germany.

'South America. Chile and the like. That's where you find Nazis,' Mervyn said. 'Wearing panama hats in the jungle.' Robert wasn't convinced. He watched the doctor as he went about his surgery. Robert thought he looked evil. There was an air of vile experiments about him.

Mervyn was interested in how the prison worked, the timetabled mealtimes and slopping out, men in procession through the exercise yard.

'I'm just keeping me head down, doing my time. The screws isn't too bad.' Letting the prison phrases hang in the air between them. He knew that they were wasted on Mervyn. He wasn't able to focus through the prison noise, the clang of iron doors and keys rattling, raised voices, the whole arduous hubbub of prison life. Iron and stone. Robert knew that Will would appreciate it. The prison argot. Cons and lags. He waited for Will to come and see him but he didn't. All he had was Mervyn, white-faced and tongue-tied.

Legal documents were served on him every day, the story of his life opening out into new dimensions. Robert felt as if he had access to whole new languages. His solicitor brought him affidavits and writs, laid them out on the bare prison table. You thought of them as being written on archaic materials, parchments and vellums, the scribed wisdom of ages. Robert loved the sound of the Latin terms in his mouth. Habeas corpus. He hadn't thought that the bare events of that night could be retold in such a way. That you did with malice aforethought. He read the documents late into the night. The warders who checked on him through the spyhole saw him as scholarly, hunched over.

∼

After an initial period in a cell on his own Robert was put into a cell with a young prisoner called Hughes. Hughes had been an apprentice in the Belfast Telegraph print room. He was thin with tattoos on both arms and an inked-in teardrop below his right eye. He had tried to tattoo letters on his own fingers and on the backs of his hands but the ink had leaked under the skin so that his hands looked like he had been conducting some narrative of self in a lost tongue.

'What are you in for?' Robert asked.

'Interfering,' Hughes said.

The prison psychiatrist found Robert to be of average intelligence. He seemed to bear some hostility towards his mother. He was described as boastful and arrogant although these qualities may have masked low self-esteem. He was prone to flights of fancy, for instance ambitions to be the world bodybuilding champion. He also referred to an alleged approach from Russian intelligence during his time in London. Robert had a rudimentary knowledge of psychiatry that he had acquired from books in the library and had a tendency to use medical terms out of context. He asked the psychiatrist about blackouts caused by blows to the head. He spoke about aneurysms and tried to engage the psychiatrist on the subject of schizophrenia and of phantom voices urging you to wrong. Robert was found fit for trial, although emotional immaturity was noted. A mild anti-depressant was also prescribed.

～

Agnes thought that being the mother of a criminal would lead to shunning but that was not the case. Of course there were certain women in the town who put their big noses in the air when Agnes walked past although Agnes knew for a fact that they were more dragged up than reared themselves. In fact Agnes found at first that she was granted more respect than had ever been shown to her. For the first time people knew what a heartbreak Robert had been and not from laxness on her part. She was sympathised with in the street though when she saw the Gambles and them ones from Upper Damolly she looked the other way. The man from the Daily Mail took her to the Shelbourne and she was taken also to the Great Northern Hotel by other gentlemen of the press and also to the Crown Hotel in Warrenpoint by a man from the Press Association who bought her Courvoisier in a balloon glass all night. He was after more than a story that one well she had news for him.

Agnes was a Scorpio, kind but also passionate. She read her stars every day. There were often mysterious references to a burden she would be called upon to bear in her life, which she took to mean Robert, but also there was romance just around the corner.

Twelve

On 19th March 1961 twenty-two-year-old George Bratty was arrested and charged with the murder of twenty-year-old Josephine Fitzsimmons. Fitzsimmons's body had been found under a hedge near Hillsborough, twenty-five miles from Newry, on the night of 17th March. The body was discovered by Constable Robert Hodge. There was a ligature around the girl's neck, pulled so tight that he could not get his fingers under it. Hodge observed a bicycle lying on the ground six yards away, and a pair of lady's black underpants on the ground beside the body.

At the pre-trial arraignment Bratty's solicitor described him as a weak and immature individual who had wet the bed until the age of twenty. He had known the murdered girl all his life, but had no memory of the attack on her. The solicitor told the court that his client was not in his right mind at the time of the killing. He intended to plead not guilty by reason of insanity. He was first remanded to Crumlin Road, where Robert was being held, then to the Downshire Mental Hospital. He was held in a different wing from Robert, who saw Bratty only once, as he was being led to the prison van for transfer to the mental institution. He was a pale, big-boned youth with a shuffling walk. Robert followed the case closely and discussed it with Hughes.

'He looks mental to me,' Hughes said.

'Could be putting it on. He was cute enough to get the knickers off her anyhow.'

'He'll get the rope is my opinion.'

'I reckon he'll go the same way as Gordon. Not guilty by reason of insanity.'

Robert had reason for saying this. He had read Iain Hay Gordon's statement in which he told Chief Inspector Capstick that he had murdered Patricia Curran and that 'it was solely due to a blackout'. Robert wondered if Bratty was aware that the claim to have suffered a blackout, if accepted by a jury, would be sufficient to ensure a verdict of guilty but insane under the Defence of Lunatics Act. Bratty did subsequently tell police that 'a blackness came over me'.

'Cute as foxes some of these boys,' Hughes said.

'A blackness isn't the same as saying you got a blackout,' Robert said, but he thought he knew what Bratty was about when he said 'a blackness came over me'. He wasn't talking about some state of mind where he was unaware of what he was doing. He was talking about being overcome by evil, consumed in the esoteric dark.

'You could go for it yourself,' Hughes said, 'not guilty by reason of insanity.'

'Wouldn't fit me,' Robert said, 'it only works if you actually done the killing and I never touched Pearl.'

'He'll never get away with it. All this old chat about wetting the bed.'

'It says here he was saved. "I asked the Lord to save my life," says he.'

Bratty had told the court that he had experienced a religious conversion prior to the death of Josephine Fitzsimmons. He said he had taken to reading scripture but when challenged as to the nature of his reading he said, 'These were mainly words I could not understand so I studied them out.'

'They'll hang thon bastard high,' Hughes said. 'If they hang him they won't hang you and vice versa.'

'They won't hang me because I never done it.'

'Then prove it.'

'I'll prove it where it counts, in a court of law. I'll have my day.'

Robert was always acting as if there was some big secret about Pearl's murder that only he knew. Hughes said it got on his nerves. It was all secret smiles and that's for me to know and you to find out. He didn't tell Robert that there was a book going in the prison that Robert would hang by Christmas.

In his role as Inspector of Constabulary McCrink had been given an office in the Commercial Buildings opposite the City Hall in Belfast. There were others in the building but he rarely saw them. He felt as if he was at the centre of some ghost administration. The building was full of long corridors, gloomy civil-service vistas. His secretary was a tall woman in her forties, elegantly dressed, with the air of an abandoned mistress. She had a tight-lipped, distrustful look. When he came in she looked him up and down, a sensual assay, cool and disinterested. McCrink suspected she reported back to Harry West.

He began to carry out inspections of city police stations. He visited North Queen Street RUC Station where he inspected the new interrogation suite. They had developed a system of pin-boarding that day's calls. While reading through the recorded incidents he saw a reference to *the Glen, Whiteabbey (Curran)*.

He remembered that Patricia Curran's body had been found in the grounds of the family home, the Glen.

'What does this mean?' he asked. The duty constable said that a Constable Rutherford had requested permission to inspect the Glen on foot of a call from the contractor who was now working on the house.

Constable Rutherford had answered Judge Curran's phone call to Whiteabbey RUC Station on the night of Patricia Curran's murder nine years previously. He had cycled up to the Curran house to find Patricia's body being removed by Desmond Curran and his father in the family solicitor's car. Desmond maintained that she was still breathing although Rutherford had seen that rigor mortis had already set in. The corpse, he said, was as stiff as a plank.

Rutherford was sitting in the CID wardroom. He was a heavy-set man in his mid-fifties. His manner was formal and he referred to his notebook. He said that Judge Curran had left Whiteabbey following the sectioning of his wife. The Glen had been on the market for a long time before it sold. The new owners intended to use it as a hotel and had started to renovate. The previous day they had halted renovations and called Whiteabbey RUC Station.

They drove to Whiteabbey in McCrink's car. They walked up the driveway to the Glen and Rutherford pointed to the spot where Patricia's body had been found. The grass on the verge was rutted and unkempt. Rutherford related the events of 13th November 1952, the night scenes. The trees lining the drive were bare of leaves, with rooks' nests in the upper branches. McCrink was reminded of London. You felt you were being watched. You imagined an artificer in the shadows. The house rose out of the trees with scaffolding built up around it and building materials piled on the lawn, the plasterwork stripped and guttering removed.

Rutherford opened the front door and went in. The house was cold and bare. There were light patches on the walls where paintings had been removed. There were dead bluebottles on windowsills.

'The house got run down since Mrs Curran got took to the floating hotel,' Rutherford said, 'though it was always a brave and cold place to my mind.'

He followed Rutherford up the stairs to the landing. Cloud swept in from the sea, and the house darkened. McCrink tried one of the light switches but the electricity had been turned off. McCrink feeling he was following a servant to the night, a shuffling retainer in bond to the shadows of the house. McCrink saw his own shadow on the wall, a crabbed figure. The floorboards on the landing had been lifted so they had to step from joist to joist over the exposed pipework and cabling. He followed Rutherford to the end of the landing and into the Currans' bedroom. Most of the furnishings had been removed from the room. The sprung base of a mattress leaned against the wall. The carpet had been rolled back exposing a large dark stain on the floor beneath.

'The workmen found it,' Rutherford said. 'One of them used to work in the Shambles in the city. He said it was blood by the smell of it.'

McCrink knelt down beside the stain. He touched it with his fingertips, feeling the dust and grain of the plank flooring. Rutherford held up his cigarette lighter. The stain covered the centre of the room.

'Could be anything,' McCrink said.

'The man who found it was a butcher, I told you,' Rutherford said, 'blood was his trade.'

In the flickering matchlight Rutherford had gained an authority that he hadn't possessed before. He looked capable of menacing pronouncements. He looked as if augury might come unbidden to him.

'There are things you can do,' McCrink said. 'Hydrogen peroxide will cause blood to bubble. At least it will tell us that it isn't any other substance. They're developing techniques to test for blood groups in old stains.'

'To what end?' Rutherford said. 'To what proof?'

'To prove whose blood it is,' McCrink said.

'The judge said she was murdered outside,' Rutherford said, 'and the accused Gordon was condemned for a lunatic. A conviction carried out in the eyes of the world.'

~

Margaret said she didn't like coming to his hotel. She sought out boarding houses and off-season hotels. The day after he had been to the Glen they met in the Grand Hotel in Bangor, driving up past millennial texts painted on barn walls. She had taken to cutting her hair short, wearing red berets and blue serge jackets. She looked like a young communist pioneer. He booked a bedroom and they went upstairs. The bedding was damp and there was a smell of drains. Rain beat against the window. She wanted him to make her ashamed, force minor abasements on her. Looking for dingy backdrops to remind him of how unworthy they both were. The damp mattresses and unheated dining rooms. He knew what she wanted. He would turn up unshaven, surly, stains on his shirt.

'I'm going to look into the Curran case.'

'Are you sure that's wise?'

'No. But there's something wrong about it.'

'Do you think Mrs Curran was mad?'

'It's starting to look that way. But who knows what the loss of a child can do?'

'I wouldn't know. Being barren. Barren of my loins, isn't that what they say? There's a kind of biblical ring to it. Maybe I could become a prophetess. I could be wild-haired, speak in tongues of flame.'

'Don't.'

'There's something insane about the Gamble case. The frenzied attack. How far was the body dragged?'

'Half a mile.'

'There you go. Superhuman strength. A frenzied attack and superhuman strength. They always go together, don't they?'

'You think that's funny.'

'I'm not being funny. People can be delusional. In the clinical sense. They can believe that someone is the devil.'

'You think the devil was up at Weir's Rock the night that Pearl was killed?'

'No. But there's plenty around that town who do.'

'I don't believe in the devil. And I don't think someone with superhuman strength dragged her up there.'

'What else then?'

'A car. Someone in a car is the logical answer. Either she got into it or she was dragged into it. Probably dragged, since one of her shoes was lying at the Cross.'

'Nobody saw a car.'

'Ronnie did. Ronnie said she saw a car when they were coming down the road after leaving Pearl at the Cross.'

McCrink got up and went to the window, looked down over the esplanade. The closed amusements and salt-pitted railings. He knew why she was drawn to these seafront towns. There was an air of disappointment about them, of sinking away into small consolations, windswept boating ponds, unlit bingo halls. There were lone walkers on the pier, solitary figures, besotted with the town's post-Victorian gloom.

'Stick to McGladdery,' Margaret said, 'stay away from the Currans.'

~

That Monday McCrink drove out to Special Branch headquarters in Castlereagh where he put in a requisition for Lance Curran's file. He went down to the file room, closing the fireproof doors behind him, massive asbestos-lined vault doors. The place felt like a nuclear bunker, something afoot in its walkways and long troubling vistas. Everything was functional. The unpainted concrete floors and exposed steel handrails. Fluorescent strips affixed to the ceiling. There was nothing to draw your eye away from the contents of the files.

He noticed the size of the file room and wondered how many people had files open. The clerk returned with Curran's file and he sat down at a Formica-topped table. Each intelligence report was typed out on foolscap, dated and numbered and stamped 'Confidential' at the top. The same typewriter seemed to have been used throughout, but there was no way of knowing if the same author had compiled the whole file.

In the first few pages the tone was uncertain. 'Place of

Birth Unknown'. After 'DOB 1900' there was a question mark. The year of Curran's studies at the Bar was given. There was an early photograph from an election night. Curran was standing outside a count centre handing out leaflets. The man beside him was identified as his election agent, Harry Ferguson. Ferguson looked low-key and purposeful, the archetypal political fixer. It was snowing in the photograph, snow blowing across the lens and emphasising the blackness behind the two men. Curran looked reserved, cold, bent on some amoral husting of his own.

There was an incompleteness to the early years. Whole periods were left out. The judge's political affiliations were not what McCrink expected. There were associations with marginal figures, gospellers, street-corner evangelists, Orange agitators. The figure of Ferguson always beside him during his ascent, MP, Chairman of the Bar Council, Attorney General.

The years of his marriage to Doris. The children. Patricia. Desmond. Desmond's religious convictions were outlined. His attachment to moral rearmament and other right-wing causes. The reference to Patricia was brief. Her reputed promiscuity was not explicitly mentioned but McCrink felt as if he had seen it in the papers. That there had been a nuanced aside.

Again Curran's gambling was not brought up directly. There was mention of his nights in the Reform Club, the trips to the Isle of Man. He was reported to 'have been seen in the company' of 'a Roman Catholic bookmaker'. Difficulties with his wife were alluded to. The file covering this period seemed to be laced with arch references.

The pages for 1952 were different. You had the impression

that the intelligence officer had lost control of his material. Reports of Patricia's murder and of the investigation were filed out of sequence. Newspaper cuttings were stained and torn. Whole areas of the investigation had been blacked out. Sheets were missing. Names were struck out at random. McCrink moved backwards and forwards from the murder to the trial. The text seemed to be full of implication, hidden meanings just out of reach. There were reports from Doris Curran's GP ('Extreme distress'). Random eye-witness reports. 'Patricia was seen being threatened several times by a man with a scar. She appeared frightened.' A memo from Chief Inspector Capstick, the officer in charge of the investigation, stating that he had 'got' the accused man 'on masturbation' before the accused had confessed. Illegible notes had been added in the margins in biro. McCrink found his lips moving as he read. A dire office recited.

At the back of the file McCrink found a carbon copy of the order committing Doris Curran to Holywell Mental Hospital at Her Majesty's pleasure. There were newspaper cuttings concerning the conviction of Iain Hay Gordon for the murder of Patricia Curran. The unsaid on the margins.

After that the reports were sparse and neatly typed. There was a falling away, the momentum lost. Judge Curran's ambitions to become a privy councillor were brought up. It was noted with surprise that he had attended his son's ordination as a priest in Rome.

McCrink noticed that the election agent Ferguson's name was mentioned with less frequency once the subject of Patricia Curran's murder arose. In the end it was absent. McCrink began to wonder if Ferguson was the author of the report. If he had decided to erase himself from the file. There was a careful slipping away. An affinity with backgrounds.

~

On the Monday prior to McGladdery's first remand hearing Speers phoned to update McCrink. He had pieced together the events in the dance hall. McGladdery and Copeland had arrived together. They had been drinking that day in Newry but had gone home to change.

'Drinking, but not drunk,' Speers said.

'Not falling about the shop anyhow.'

'Still and all, McGladdery was making a nuisance of himself by all accounts.'

'Acting the smartarse. It's not a crime.'

'He dances with the deceased. More than once, according to witnesses.'

'He says he danced with her two or three times.'

'There's something about that, about Pearl. You don't dance three times with somebody you don't like.'

'That's true.'

The following day he had another call from Speers. He drove down to Newry. Speers had received the pathologist's report. The wounds on Pearl's body corresponded to the shape of a hexagonal shoemaker's file.

'The same kind that McGladdery was seen buying in Woolworths the day before the murder,' Speers said. 'We have a case.'

'It's still not enough. McGladdery bought a shoemaker's file. The girl was stabbed with a similar weapon. There's no direct connection unless we find the weapon and connect it to McGladdery.'

'It's close enough. The scratches he had on his face. A jury likes a scratched face. They like the idea of a victim who fights back. They can picture the scene. A spirited defence. The victim's cries getting fainter. There's only the sound of the killer's breathing at the end.'

McCrink pictured the scene. The killer looking down on the body. Crouched, bestial. He could see how a jury would take to it.

They went back to McGladdery's house to look for the murder weapon. The finding that the wounds appeared to be caused by a shoemaker's file brought a new urgency to proceedings. It was a plain, artisanal object which evoked old-fashioned virtues. Something you could picture on a rack in a workshop, coated with oil against rust. Belonging to the world of things that are carefully tooled, made to last. There was a sense that whole value systems were under threat.

There was a fury about the way McGladdery's house was searched this time. Floorboards were torn up, wall cavities breached. McCrink found himself crawling through the roof space with a torch in his hand. There was something more fundamental than police work going on. The garden was dug up. The cistern was drained and searched. Policemen in blue overalls dismantled the shed at the back of the house and opened up its foundations.

It became known in the town that the murder weapon was being looked for and members of the public began to arrive at Corry Square with agricultural implements and pieces of metal they'd found in the open. Rusted hinges and old spanners, lain forgotten for years gathering a stature and authenticity to themselves, jagged, rusted. There was a longing to be part of the story, the gathering force.

The canal and the basin were dragged. People walked the mud of the river at low tide. McCrink received a letter from a medium saying that the file would be found near water. The medium's handwriting was scratchy, difficult to decipher. She spoke of guidance from the spirit world. She implied difficulties, impediments in the psychic channels.

As in the Patricia Curran case the weapon was never found. In the Curran case, the convicted Iain Hay Gordon stated in his retracted confession that he had 'probably' used his service knife and had thrown it into the sea. McGladdery admitted having bought two shoemaker's files as indicated by the testimony of policewoman Margaret McCance who had seen him buy them in Woolworths.

McCrink was still unhappy with the quality of the evidence against Robert.

'Put him in the witness box and the silk will take him apart,' Speers said.

'There's no guarantee that the defence will put McGladdery on the stand,' McCrink said, 'and if he doesn't then we only have circumstantial evidence.'

'We need to stay on the case in hand,' Speers said. 'Kennedy has the press lined up for a public appeal in the morning.'

'Who's talking to them?'

'Me and you.'

'We can't make an appeal for McGladdery's suit. It'd point the finger right at him.'

'If we got what he was wearing that night.'

'Might do the trick.'

'I'll find that suit. I'll sink the slippery little fucker,' Johnston said. 'I'll get the rope around his neck.'

'Even if we can't prove a case?'

'The way it is, sir, the criminals I get in here, I'd hang them all.'

McCrink met Margaret at Ballyedmond Castle, a castellated and turreted sandstone hotel on the northern side of the lough. Before dark she took him for a walk in the forest between the hotel and the shore. There were tumbledown boathouses in the woods beyond the building, dry fountains with trees grown through them. They stumbled on broken statuary, found themselves in overgrown pleasure grounds.

'What the fuck is it with these people around here and their fairy-tale castles? Everything has turrets.'

'It's the cruelty in the fairy tales that appeals to them. Mirror, mirror on the wall.'

'They'd string McGladdery up from the nearest tree given half a chance and damn the trial.'

'The poisonings with deathly apples, fingers pricked on spindles, eyes torn out with thorns. Rapunzel, Rapunzel, let down your hair, that's the kind of fairy tale they like. I've joined the campaign against the death penalty.'

'I wondered how long it would take you.'

'Don't lecture me.'

They went into the dining room. There was oak panelling and suits of armour in the corners of the room, chandeliers hanging from the ceiling. A log fire burned in a vast fireplace.

They were the only people in the room. A woman in a black pinafore with a white apron served them. They sat on into the night, Margaret looking pale and drained, swamped in the fake baronial gloom.

~

The press conference was carried on the front page of the Belfast Telegraph and on the inside pages of the national press. The report is still available in the newspaper archive in the central library in Belfast. The original archive has been copied onto microfiche. The microfiche viewer has the feel of out-dated technologies. The finger-marked plastic casing and badly proportioned controls. When it is used the mechanisms are flimsy, the filmstock rushes past in a manic way, always on the verge of coming unspooled. The newsprint is photographed from above, badly lit, so that sometimes it is illegible.

You can go back to the original archive, stored in a back office. There is an authoritative heft to the bound volumes of back issues. The paper is yellowed and brittle. The pages are torn in places. There are water stains and moulds. The archived papers are authentic in a way that the microfiche is not. Taken down in shorthand and transcribed into dense inky columns, the accounts seem verified by the age of the paper and the ornate fonts.

The photograph of the press conference has a smudged, out-of-focus look, heavily pixellated. McCrink is wearing heavy-framed black glasses. He has a cigarette in his right hand and in the other he holds a sheet of A4 paper. The glasses make him look like a scientist, a white-coated physicist. He is answering a question from the press and there is an abstracted, boffinish air about him. Speers is beside him looking pale and ill. Johnston is sitting among the reporters wearing a leather sports coat and a no-nonsense expression. Out of uniform he looks like a member of a flying squad, a legendary police unit subject to allegations of brutality and corruption.

The report is straplined 'Inspector of Constabulary McCrink and Detective Inspector Speers: appeal'. The report goes on to say that they are 'seeking an item of apparel which may be of assistance to their enquiries'. They ask for the help of members of the public who are asked to 'be vigilant'.

Chief Constable Kennedy sits to the right of McCrink and Speers. Members of the London press asked Kennedy about the death penalty and whether he favoured it. Kennedy replied that he was a public servant bound to enforce the law as it stood. Legislation was a matter for parliament. Although in his case he wished to see the streets free of violent sexual criminals.

'Might as well of said string McGladdery up and be damned. He near winked at the journalists when he come out with that line about the streets being free of violent sexual crim-inals,' Johnston said. 'We're away on a fucking hack.'

'Item of apparel my eye,' Speers said, 'we'll have the whole laundry basket flung at us now. They'll be bringing in every bit of rag they find lying in a ditch.'

'You've been interviewing people about McGladdery's suit for weeks now. The whole country knows what item of apparel we're looking for,' McCrink said.

The London journalists were queuing in the reception to phone in their copy. One or two of them nodded at McCrink. Len Barrett of the Express was talking to Kennedy. He called

McCrink over. Barrett wore an Aquascutum coat and a pork-pie hat. McCrink had run into him in Bow Street and the Old Bailey before the Nude Murders. Barrett had been seen in the Black Cat and the Top Hat in the wake of the Kray twins and Jack McVitie. He scattered his conversation with what he imagined to be West End thieves' argot. Talking about heists and safe blags. However McCrink remembered that Barrett had been despatched to report on the murder scene at Dukes Meadows and had thrown up when he'd set eyes on the body of Elizabeth Figg, stripped to the waist, her eyes open, fixing them with her cold, hexed stare.

'You're off your beat,' McCrink said.

'The editor wants a capital murder angle. Vile sex murder of innocent shop girl. Let Harry Allen get his mitts on the perv murderer. Looks like you got a lucky break, McCrink. Deployed to the provinces and a plum falls into your lap. A full-blown Black Dahlia with national interest. The London boys are going mad for something like this – gives them an angle to campaign on for the death penalty.'

McCrink walked away. Barrett turned to the man beside him.

'Eddie McCrink. Couldn't catch the Nude Murderer and now he's looking to us to catch his country cousin.'

~

The next day McCrink drove to Holywell Mental Hospital. The hospital grounds were well tended, the lines of the red-brick building softened with shrubs. Unsupervised patients tended flower beds. You were meant to see the place as kindly, ordered. There were corridors leading off long existential vistas. There were nurses in old-fashioned starched uniforms, habits and wimples like medieval nuns, bringers of succour, enclosed and mendicant.

McCrink had arranged an appointment with the warden, Malcolm Hume. Hume was a small man with a neatly trimmed beard. He wore a tweed jacket with leather patches on the elbows and leather sandals. It was what you expected from mental-health professionals. An unconventional air. They had ventured into the sombre infrastructures of the self and had not come back untouched.

The warden confirmed that Iain Hay Gordon had been released the previous December.

'It is my opinion that Gordon has never suffered from any psychiatric condition whatsoever. I said it at the time he was committed. And as such he had no place in this hospital.'

'Yet he was found not guilty of the murder by reason of insanity.'

'That's beyond my competence, Mr McCrink.'

Hume sat back in his chair, legs crossed. McCrink felt as if he was being observed, that professional detachment was being brought to bear. He was being watched for tics and spasms, tiny neural lapses.

'Do you know what's happened to him?'

'He was told to return to Scotland and to change his name. I believe a job was found for him with a publishing firm. But we weren't given a forwarding address.'

McCrink wondered why Gordon had been told to change his name and where the instruction had come from. The subterfuge of changing his name seemed unneccessary on a practical level. It didn't matter if anyone recognised Gordon and connected him to the case. The use of the alias seemed to perform a different function. It added ornamentation to a narrative already replete with gothic detail.

'I'd like to speak to Doris Curran,' McCrink said.

'Mrs Curran is heavily medicated. It keeps her stable but sometimes her mind drifts.'

'I understand.'

Hume brought McCrink to the long-term wards at the back of the hospital. The atmosphere grew more muted as they penetrated the deeper parts of the building. He no longer saw anyone in ordinary clothes. People were gowned, padding silently on static-free flooring. The unlocking and locking of doors was done in silence. The psychiatrist was greeted with grave nods by fellow staff members, the air of sanctum acknowledged. The outside world fell away. Occasionally a window would look out onto the garden outside, each glimpse of the plants appearing as a formal composition designed to direct the mind inward.

'I sometimes wonder if a medical environment works against our patients becoming well,' Hume said, 'if they would be better off in familiar surroundings. Although in fact Holywell should be familiar to Mrs Curran, in a way.'

'Why's that?'

'Strange as it may seem, her father was superintendent of Broadmoor Hospital for the Criminally Insane. She was brought up in the warden's house there.' It was the kind of detail that kept emerging when the Curran case was concerned. There was an added-on feel to it. Broadmoor made you think about the wind howling down from the desolate moors, the building looming out of the fog. There was a piling-on of texture. It felt like a place where the mad were elevated. Where they were seen as close to the godhead, given to flashes of blinding insight.

Doris Curran's room was on a small windowless corridor. Hume unlocked the corridor and they entered the deep medicated silence.

'Mrs Curran may or may not speak to you. Her illness is suppressed by a combination of drugs, anti-psychotics, but there are moments of lucidity. She has good days and bad days.'

'Anti-psychotics? I thought that Mrs Curran had suffered a breakdown of some description.'

'Mrs Curran suffers from paranoid schizophrenia. Sometimes she thinks she is someone else, a figure from history. There are certain historical figures that the sick mind seems to light on – the Tsarina, Amelia Earhart, people like that.'

Doris sat alone beside a steel-framed bed. She was wearing glasses and a dressing gown. The room was bare. McCrink thinking of penitential spaces.

'I've brought a visitor,' Hume said, 'Mr McCrink. Mr McCrink is Her Majesty's Inspector of Constabulary.'

Doris Curran looked frail. She was cautious in the way she moved. There was a husbanding of resources. McCrink found he had prepared himself to face the devices of the mad, the reputed cunning, the delusional episodes interspersed with outbreaks of hauteur and wrath. But Doris looked as if she had been shaken out of a kindly reverie. Her hands moved continuously on the bedspread. Her eyes moved around the room to the observation window in the door, the table attached to the floor. There was nothing sharp in the room, and all the furniture was bolted down. She was wearing slippers and the belt of her dressing gown had been removed.

'Mr McCrink. It's very good of you to come. Please sit

down.' Doris appeared anxious, easy to please. She looked about worriedly and McCrink wished that there was some plain domestic task to hand that she could be given. He sat down on the edge of the bed.

'I heard about the girl on the wireless,' she said. 'What was her name?'

'Pearl Gamble,' McCrink said.

'Her poor parents. What age was she?'

'Nineteen, Mrs Curran. Pearl was nineteen.'

'Nineteen-year-old girls are wilful, don't you think?'

'They have the culprit under arrest.'

'Do they? Lance will take the trial.'

'Do you think so?'

'Yes. He will want to. And my husband always gets what he wants.' Her voice was flat. It was easy to feel that Doris wasn't living up to her role. She had been haunted by murder and insanity. McCrink felt that more was required. There should be rocking backwards and forwards. There should be disembodied voices issuing deranged instructions.

'Why would he want to take the trial?

'Because of Patricia. He would have wanted someone to hang for Patricia. Desmond will want to know. Have you met my son Desmond?'

'No I haven't.'

'He has become a Roman Catholic, you know.'

McCrink was aware that following the murder Desmond had joined the Catholic Church and taken holy orders. He had joined a missionary order and been sent to South Africa. *My son a papist priest, my wife committed to an asylum, my daughter in her grave nine years.*

Doris talked about the early years of her marriage. In the early days Doris and Lance had played bridge with the Lord Chief Justice and his wife. Doris served tea in Minton china. There was talk of motoring holidays in Scotland. New car models were admired. The judge discussed the possibility of building a tennis court at the rear of the Glen. 'Gracious living' was a phrase that Doris admired.

'Do you know who I am?' Doris said.

'Of course, Mrs Curran.'

'Yes,' she said, 'but do you know who I really am? I'm quite famous, you know.' McCrink could feel psychosis flood the room, the misfiring selfhood. Who was she? Amelia Earhart?

'Who are you?' he asked. She gave him an arch look and winked.

'The answer is in the blood,' she said, 'the answer is always in the blood.'

Thirteen

During the winter months Judge Curran would travel every third week to the Isle of Man where gambling was permitted, flying from Aldergrove, the British Airways DC-10 with an air of evacuation about it, the last plane from a beset city, the engine note rising and falling, hitting the low pressure systems swept down from Greenland, rain squalls blowing across the landing lights at Douglas airport.

Lance Curran would play bezique at the Colony Rooms in Douglas early in the evening, moving on to roulette at the Vogue Casino.

In late February following the arraignment of McGladdery Ferguson travelled with Judge Curran. He had never been to the island before but as a young man he had raced motorcycles at Nutts Corner and Tyrella and he wanted to see the Isle of Man TT course. All he had ever wanted to know was there, expressed in terms of speed and transcendence. Ray Amm and Mike Hailwood crouched behind the fibreglass fairing, dropping down the gears for Ballaugh Bridge. In 1955 Ray Amm was flung from his MV Augusta and killed at Imola. Hailwood was to die in the rain outside Birmingham. Ferguson remembered cutting out photographs of them on the winners' podium and pasting them into a scrapbook. Sombre, garlanded figures.

Ferguson joined Judge Curran for a drink in the bar of the Grand Hotel. There were other men from the Bar library present. Queen's Counsel and solicitors nodding to Ferguson as he made his way through the tables.

He saw Isaac Hanna, a QC from Antrim town. Ferguson had heard that Hanna had given land recently for the building of a fundamentalist chapel.

'You know Hay Gordon was released? The buck that murdered Curran's daughter?'

'No. When did this happen?'

'You're not on the ball at all, Ferguson. The murderer was released eighteen months ago, sent back to Scotland and told to keep the beak shut if he knew what was good for him.'

'On what grounds?'

'On the grounds that he probably never killed Patricia Curran at all. You'd of thought that Curran would of told you.'

'He knows?'

'What do you think? For all he keeps his nose stuck in the air, the judge knows what's going on. He's keeping you in the dark, Ferguson.'

'Why would he do that, Isaac?'

'It was Brian Faulkner who ordered the release of Gordon. Maybe Curran put the word in his ear. Maybe Mr Justice Curran knows rightly who killed his daughter. Anyway. Water under the bridge. What's more to the fore is the question of whether or not the judge is going to disqualify himself from the McGladdery case. It's the talk of the Bar library.'

'The judge takes his own counsel.'

'That's a fact. I hope he takes you along with him when he goes to the House of Lords.'

'Why would he go to the House of Lords?'

'There's an opening for a Lord Justice of Appeal coming up. Did he not tell you that either? Our Lance is vain enough to fancy himself in the old ermine, don't you think, Ferguson? A lord's fur collar'd be a snug enough fit around thon crafty old bird's neck.'

Ferguson saw Curran at the bar and walked towards him. Curran had in fact spoken to him about the possibility of a seat in the House of Lords, but Ferguson had not been told about the release of Iain Hay Gordon.

The barman had put two Black and Whites on the bar, with a soda siphon beside them.

'Patricia used to like to do this, do you remember, Ferguson?' It was the first time since his daughter's death that her name had been spoken between them.

When Patricia was young, Ferguson remembered, she used to ask to fill their glasses with the soda. He remembered the look of concentration on her face as she hefted the siphon, the lab-flask feel to it, the valve-hiss, the wreathing vapours in the glass.

'I didn't know that Gordon had been released,' Ferguson said.

'Released,' the judge said, 'released, renamed and consigned to some wretched Glasgow tenement.'

'Doesn't seem right in the light of the damage that he did.'

'No,' the judge said, 'considering the damage that he did. If she had lived Patricia would have been twenty-eight years old now. Would you set odds as to the likelihood of Gordon's guilt, Ferguson?'

Ferguson looked down into his drink. Who would run a book on his child's death? What would be the stake in such a wager, and on whom would fall the burden of paying?

'I don't think it would be a right thing to do,' Ferguson said. The judge ignored him.

'I would put it at eight to one, perhaps. No higher.'

'This is not appropriate, judge.'

'And if the odds are set so high against the convicted man, then what odds could be ventured against others, Mr Ferguson? Do you think I am unaware of what is whispered around the Bar library? My son a papist priest, my wife committed to an asylum, my daughter in her grave nine years. You use the word appropriate, Ferguson.'

Ferguson was aware of traffic passing in the rain on the esplanade outside. Laughter from the lounge bar. He wondered what had brought him to this place. He looked around the faces in the lounge. Dark-suited artful men, leaning towards each other. They would be recounting anecdotes of the Bar. Ferguson had often called to the Bar library in the evening on constituency business when Judge Curran had been a QC. The silks preparing the following day's casework, taking down the case records. The All England Law Reports. The Criminal Law Review. Setting themselves to the dusty interlinking narratives. The hanging fluorescent tubes were switched off, the library lit by desk lights here and there. There were murmured conversations. Men passing in the shadows under a dim devotional light. You thought of objects that were handed on from generation to generation. A lighting which evoked the volumes held sacred. The books of the law.

Curran had followed Ferguson's eyes.

'Don't waste yourself on them. They are the corrupt servants of a corrupt province. Not one of them was man enough to defend Gordon. They are linked by family, school and profession. They passed his defence to a scholarship boy.'

'They didn't want to offend you. Or your office.'

'I heard the other rumours as well. I know that Gordon changed his defence team. I know that it is said that he admitted his guilt in private and that the original defence team could no longer represent him on that basis.'

'It would be unethical for them to assert his innocence when they were aware of his guilt.'

'Yes. But what if that wasn't the case? What if this admission of guilt had not in fact happened? What if the whole story was a fabrication to conceal the fact that they were too craven to offend their superior? What if someone deliberately created the story, simply to protect themselves?'

It is also said that your daughter did not die where she was found. That she was killed in the house and her body carried out onto the driveway. There were thirty-seven stab wounds and yet there was no blood on the ground around her.

'I'm not sure what you're trying to say.'

'I'm saying their blood is befouled with cynicism, Ferguson. Tell me this, if I did not sit on the bench for the McGladdery case, would one of them serve? Would one of them be judge in this cause?'

'It would have to be a local man, all right.'

'And would they hang McGladdery to please me? Their superior whose own daughter was murdered? Would they see fit to take my vengeance for me, since Gordon escaped the gallows?'

'You wouldn't put it past them.'

'So by taking the case myself, I am perhaps giving McGladdery a better chance of a fair trial than otherwise.'

'And that's why you're taking the case. To ensure a fair trial for McGladdery.'

You must think I was born yesterday, Ferguson thought. Sleet driven down from the north channel rattled on the glass skylight over their head as though some manic thing sought entry. They both glanced upwards.

'It is wintertime,' the judge said.

'It is that all right.'

'There is a coldness in men's hearts that cannot be gainsaid by any judgement that I might or might not pass down. To equate law with equity is a mistake. Justice is a by-product of our system of law, not an end.'

Ferguson thought of two nineteen-year-old girls killed and left in the open and wondered if they too were a by-product.

'Shall we go?' the judge said. 'I feel that fortune is on my side tonight.'

He stood to go. The sleet beat insistently on the skylight above them. Ferguson sat for a moment, his unseeing eyes fixed on the window, and on the wintry bight beyond.

~

Thirty-six hours after the appeal for the missing item of apparel a letter was delivered to Corry Square. The anonymous letter was addressed to McCrink and had been typed on a single sheet of A4 paper. The detectives were told to search a septic tank which they would find two hundred yards to the rear of the McGladdery house.

The detectives had received dozens of anonymous letters in the weeks since the murder. Some referred to the Lord's judgement being delivered on Pearl. Others pointed to the suspicious behaviour of various local men. The canal bank and the public toilets on the Mall were reported as homosexual meeting places. This kind of correspondence seemed a necessary part of a murder inquiry. The detectives were reminded that there were other contexts to their investigation. It was felt that the detectives needed access to the psychic undertow of the town. Apparitions were reported, spirit worlds invoked. They received articles clipped out of the local press with key words ringed in biro.

Speers read the letter first. The directions were careful. The writer seemed to have gone to the trouble of measuring, or at least pacing out, the distances involved. Unlike the other letters, the prose was unadorned. Speers examined the typeface with a magnifying glass, looking for damage to the metalling of the keys that would identify the typewriter. Under the magnifying glass each letter looked monumental, flawed. McCrink envisaged a sparsely furnished room with a typewriter on a bare table, a Remington in gun-metal grey.

'This one's worth a follow-up,' Speers said, 'this one's definitely got legs.'

'Round up some of the local uniforms. We'll have a look first thing in the morning.'

Speers was enthusiastic about the letter. There was a textual sparseness to it that appealed to him. A sense that the writer was picking up clear narrative threads, identifying and developing themes. Ordered progress was possible. McCrink was less sure. The letter-writer wasn't acting out of a sense of civic duty. He felt more at home with the inherent fearfulness of the other anonymous letter-writers, their sense that unseen forces were at work.

They left Corry Square at dawn on the 24th. Johnston had called up members of the Special Constabulary. He liked the drama of it, the intimations of a repressive state apparatus, uniformed policemen clambering into unmarked vans in the pre-dawn chill. It made you think of front doors smashed down, booted feet on the stairs.

They drove in convoy to the Belfast Road. They parked on the hard shoulder. Technicians from the Belfast laboratory unpacked rudimentary forensic kits. They moved across the fields in a fanned-out formation. The septic tank was found within minutes. The technicians examined the concrete lid which was then photographed. When they lifted the lid they found a bundle of filthy clothing suspended from a length of cord. The bundle was partly submerged in the contents of the septic tank.

McCrink and Speers accompanied the technicians back to the forensic laboratory in Belfast. The laboratory was situated in a complex in a residential area close to the university. The laboratories were housed in nondescript red-brick buildings. McCrink could see that the scientists preferred it that way. They liked the atmosphere of scientific advances in low-key surroundings. The scientists were white-coated, aloof. They moved silently in pairs along the corridors in a way that suggested inwardness. Wall-mounted posters depicted the Periodic Table and the structure of the atom. There was a hushed monastic atmosphere in the public spaces.

The bundle of clothing had been taken to a laboratory upstairs. When McCrink and Speers arrived technicians were opening the bundle with tweezers, taking samples as they went. One of the technicians pointed to the Burton label.

When the bundle was opened out, Speers shook his head.

'We'll never get any forensics out of that lot.' The bundle consisted of a shortie jacket wrapped around a pair of black shoes and a red-and-black tie. The fawn colour of the jacket was barely detectable under the sodden matter adhering to it from the septic tank. McCrink didn't speak. He had seen the bodies of those who had met violent death but the still bodies, the faces expressionless, vacated, lacked the power of these ravaged garments, the jacket crumpled, reeking of organic matter. The jacket seemed to do justice to the events of 28th January, the crime done by night, filling the room with its corpse stink. The shoulders were stiff and hunched and the elbows crooked. It implied the existence of a perpetrator equal to its uncanny shapes, a murderer by night, shambling, fiendish. McCrink found himself thinking about the writer of the anonymous letter, the double-spaced lettering.

The detectives waited until the technicians had established that the jacket pockets were empty. Speers kept pointing to stains, talking knowledgeably about decomposition rates and blood spatter.

It was almost night before they were back in Newry. Uniformed policemen had been left at the septic tank. As they passed by on the Belfast Road they could see a light in the fields and men standing around. McCrink thought they looked like travellers, lamplit, sent from afar.

'You can smell it the car,' Speers said.

'What?'

'McGladdery's suit. The stench of that soakpit from it. It's like something you'll never be rid of.'

Fourteen

McCrink was awakened by the phone. In London you steeled yourself for the call-out. Death abroad in the stricken night. The dawn crime scenes. Men standing around a body smoking, their coats dripping rain, saturated with unbidden evil and the sweet corpse dew. Men given to laconic asides, crime-scene braggadocio and other wry permissions vested in them by virtue of their calling.

'McCrink.'

'Harry West here, McCrink.'

'What can I do for you, Mr West?'

'What I want to know is what you were doing at the Curran house.'

'The Glen?'

'You went up there and interrogated a member of the local constabulary about a case that was closed eight years ago.'

'Interrogated? There was no interrogating going on. Constable Rutherford accompanied me to the house.'

'How did you come to be at the Glen?'

'A report came in about a bloodstain on the floor. Rutherford went to investigate as a routine matter. I accompanied him.'

'There will be no attempt to re-investigate the murder of Patricia Curran. Have you any idea what you are meddling with? Judge Curran is in line to be a privy councillor.'

'It was a routine call-out.'

'Lance Curran will be the judge in the McGladdery case. The Inspector of Constabulary, a man involved in the McGladdery investigation, is seen to interfere in a closed investigation into the murder of that judge's daughter. If I could do it without drawing attention to you, I'd have you pulled from the McGladdery case here and now and packed off back to your backstreet murder beat. Dead tramps and spivs is more your line of work. You're here to get McGladdery where he belongs. Stood on a trapdoor with a rope around his neck. Stick to the case in hand, McCrink. Don't think you can re-try the Curran case.'

West hung up. McCrink found himself holding the heavy black receiver listening to the dial tone. Feeling like a functionary in some far-flung corner of empire. Orders coming through from the capital. You imagined hundreds of miles of telephone lines. Crossing the forests, the still-frozen tundras.

He got dressed and drove to Newry. There was no one moving on the streets of Warrenpoint. Lovers had parked their cars in the shadow of the castle at Narrow Water. He thought of them as being gentle, considerate. Of this being a place where they gathered to offer consolation to each other.

On the way into Newry fires burned in the traveller camp. He could see moonlight through the timbers of the buildings on the site. The assay office and counting house. There were figures moving among the buildings as though some night-time guild were summoned amid the ruins. *Nyuk*. The old languages invoked.

He found Speers in the Bridge bar. Speers was sitting at a corner of the bar on his own.

'That's why policemen drink in their own bars,' McCrink

said, taking the stool beside him. 'People don't want to sit next to them. There's an edging away.'

'More running than edging, but I get your drift.'

'Did you hear who was going to try the case?'

'No. Not yet.'

'I heard it was going to be Judge Curran. He has the eye on the Privy Council apparently.'

'A hanging won't do him any harm in that bid. Might wipe out the dead slut daughter, the mad wife and the priest son. I'd say McGladdery's well and truly fucked whether he done it or not.'

'I went up to the Curran house. There's a massive bloodstain on the bedroom floor.'

'Leave it alone, McCrink. It won't do you any good.'

'Patricia Curran had bled out. There were no bloodstains on the ground around her body.'

'Gordon done it and even if he didn't there's no mileage in going after it. Do you think they'll re-open the case because you found a bloodstain in the house?'

'We'll see. Any news on the jacket?'

'Like we thought. Too soiled for any forensics on it.'

'Doesn't matter. It was hid behind his house. The jury will lap it up.'

'I'm not happy without a confession.'

'You won't get it from McGladdery.'

'You know what we're looking at here if McGladdery didn't do it? Along with them bloodstains in the bedroom?'

'What are we looking at?'

'A guilty man hanging an innocent man.'

~

That summer, in the build-up to the trial, Robert's name became the subject of schoolyard chants and threats. McGladdery's going to get you. He was seen as a long-legged, malevolent figure, a night stalker who preyed on women and children. Young children claimed to have seen him at the back of the gasworks, on the towpath, in all the haunted post-industrial spaces. He reached for you with long, strangling fingers. Youths from the town went out to Damolly at night and threw stones at the windows of the McGladdery house. Agnes chased them in her nightdress. One night she followed them through Damolly as far as the Belfast Road. She looked like a madwoman escaped from the Downshire. Her hair stood out from her head. She looked like a woman assailed by dreams and visions.

McCrink rented a caravan for the summer months at Cranfield. Margaret would stay there with him at the weekends. The apron filled around them. Caravans towed in from distant industrial belts. Motorcycle gangs from the city idling along the beachfront path. People came equipped. Thermos flasks, bitumen stoves and collapsible furniture. They took long walks along the beach in the rain wearing oilskins. They brought their dogs with them – hardy, outdoor breeds. They liked to be seen as resilient, capable of improvised habitations on the move. They felt there was something of the Voortrekker spirit to their excursions. Their destination located at the mouth of the lough. With the east wind funnelled down towards the exposed caravan site there was a highveldt harshness to the weather.

She made excuses so that she didn't have to travel down during the week.

'You're always at me when I'm in that caravan.' It was true. She didn't like the caravan park, or the muffled sex in the cramped quarters. There was an eyes-screwed, putting-up-with-it quality to her responses that he couldn't resist.

'What are they saying about McGladdery in Newry?'

'That he's a sex maniac. There's talk about the things found in the house. Books, whips and things. They say there's a dungeon in the basement. People say they've heard screams in the night.'

Margaret liked to be direct when sex came up in conversation. She used the correct anatomical terms. She spoke about cunnilingus. She said the word penis out loud. She used stripped-down clinical vocabularies.

'I feel like I'm in a VD clinic sometimes,' he said.

'It's the librarian in me,' she said. 'I know the language. I look up the words.'

'Do women do that?'

'What?'

'Go through the dictionary. Looking for the dirty words.'

'There's no such thing as dirty words,' she said. But he knew that there were such things. Words that had a deep, hurting timbre. He looked at the photographs of Elizabeth Figg and Patricia Curran and Pearl Gamble and knew they had heard the harming vocabularies breathed in the dark. Spoken, whispered, blurted-out, the shadows gathering. Their killers reaching inside themselves for the occult phrase.

'What's wrong?'

'I read through McGladdery's interview transcripts yesterday.'

'You say that like you went to visit someone in hospital. Some ageing relative who's so delighted to see you that you feel guilty for not going more often.'

'It feels like that. He keeps talking about the killer. Was he excited at the time? He says, "I wonder if the killer stood over the body, the slow horror of what he had done slowly dawning on him." He says to me, "Do you think the killer is racked with remorse now at what he done to that young girl?"'

'You said he reads crime novels in prison.'

'Paperbacks.'

'Sounds like it.'

'He says he's writing a story.' Writing a story. The dialogue racing through Robert's head. 'In the transcripts he keeps asking about forensic details from the body of the victim. Microscopic traces he's looking for.'

'Microscopic traces of what?'

'I don't know.' Robert getting lost in the dazzling technologies of crime. Imagining himself peering into a microscope eyepiece, drawing on the minutiae, the arcana.

'Does he think he can solve the murder?'

'Looks like it.'

'What happens if he finds out that he did it himself?'

On Sundays they drove to Warrenpoint, the town filled with trippers from Newry, the place already awash with yearning, its heyday always in the past, people picking up postcards and memorabilia of better days. There were cards of men in whiskers, the women in crinolines and parasols, their faces serious with the knowledge of what was being disbursed to them, that they were held to be keepers of the past, embody

nostalgias, hold the line against the mill girls and dye workers coming off the train at hourly intervals. Ghost custodians
caught in the noon glare of far-off eras.

McCrink saw Agnes McGladdery several times, playing the penny machines in the fairground, coming out of
the Crown or Victoria, talking loudly, drawing attention to
herself, aware of the whispering that travelled ahead of her.
McGladdery's mother.

'She seems to have no bother with the men friends,'
Margaret said, slipping back into the Newry accent, the harsh
salt estuary idiom. *Nyuk.*

'She's no addition to him anyhow. It's a good thing they're
not picking a jury around here. They'd dig a hole for him and
fire her right into it after him if they could.'

'What chance did he have with that rearing him?' Agnes
made her way through the fairground crowd. Loudmouthed,
reeking of gin. People looking at her as some exemplar of
monstrous womanhood.

The men in frock coats and the women in crinolines could
have told them what was happening, McCrink thought. Carried
in their knowing eyes. That this was the reason they came to
the fairground. Looking for the old-time carney exhibit in the
tent that opened after nightfall. Shuffling forwards to cast your
eyes on the whimpering grotesque in the straw.

~

Everywhere she went Agnes heard different stories. What
Robert done to Pearl when he got her alone. People asking her
brazen as you like or saying it's a wonder you stayed in the house
with him, what he might have done to you his own mother.

You'd put nothing past a monster like that. They'd come up to you in the street looking for news of the trial without shame.

Or saying that Judge Curran would try him and what about his own daughter stabbed to death. If Robert went looking for mercy there he'd be going the wrong road. There were times the town did not seem like the town she grew up in but some other place, strange, you'd never seen before, the people like foreigners. Like a story you would be told about a town in another place. Agnes kept turning corners in the town and finding herself in places she'd never been before, the workshops at the back of Sands Mill or the Abbey Yard, so that she had to ask herself what town is this?

She knew right what people were saying was that she was skulking at home with her head bowed with shame, so to defy them she'd go to Warrenpoint on a Sunday and be seen brazen as you like.

There was the night she awoke with a fearful narration in the street. A noise fit to put the heart sideways in you. She looked out of the window and saw the pups of the town gathered there and shouts directed at her in tones of mockery and gibe. Agnes lit out after them forthwith and they scattered to the four corners but weekend nights they'd come back. Sometimes they'd stand in silence and one morning she came out to find a scaffold drawn on her door. It was well for Robert sat in Belfast with the eyes of the world on him, delighted with himself. He always loved attention and well she knew it would be his downfall. He was always in a state about books and stories and now he was in the middle of a story of his own and had dragged her into it too.

There was talk that she did not go to Crumlin Road

prison to visit her own son in his cell but if there was one good thing to Robert he wrote to her to say not to visit him. You wouldn't like it here, he said, the smell would choke you and many of the other women on visits are coarse. The other prisoners tell me of contraband tobacco and the like concealed you wouldn't want to guess where, Ma! At the same time he had to be crude, he always had a bad tongue in his head. So in answer to those who accused her of neglect she said I do not neglect my son's stated wish.

He also said the food is bad here. It makes me feel at home for cooking was never your strong point! The letters arrived with censors' stamps on them and it would have been the best part of the censors' play to edit out wounding comments to a woman left on her own.

Many's the time she wondered about the difference if Robert's father had given her a daughter. He didn't even have the apparatus to do that. A daughter would be an aid to her mother to shop, to talk long into the night with confidences exchanged. There would be knowing looks between them at the remarks of the other ladies in the town. A daughter to know them for the vipers they were. A daughter to come home perhaps with feminine gifts instead of a son fallen among thieves. So she could ask did you ever find yourself walking to the shops and feeling yourself abroad, perhaps in a great city of Bible times, people walking past giving you strange looks?

How does a mother take a son to her breast, Agnes asked herself, a man with the born features of his father? How could such a thing be fruit of her body? A son is an awkward ill-fitting thing.

~

Record temperatures were recorded that August. High pressure systems coming in from the Azores. The front at Warrenpoint was crowded every night. Trains bringing crowds from Portadown, Belfast, Craigavon. Rudimentary gang cultures forming. Teddy boys and suedeheads on the beach at Cranfield. Orangemen gathering at rural halls in the evening heat. Airmen and troops billeted at Ballykinlar were trucked into the resorts in the evening. There were knife fights in the square in Kilkeel, sectarian attacks in isolated country areas. McCrink had a sense of militias abroad under cover of dark, confederacies of unknown origin. Graffiti about McGladdery and the murder was scrawled in public toilets, detailed accounts of the crime. It was important that the obscene thing be written down, that the darkest imaginings of the town be put on record.

McCrink thought there were more people than before in the traveller camp. Children swam in the basin. The traveller women roamed the town wrapped in blankets. People expected mumbled snatches of wisdom, gifts of fortune-telling. They were expected to have the ability to invoke old curses, make gestures of warding and deflecting of evil. Margaret showed him marks they had scratched on gateposts and doorframes. Angular, runic symbols.

'It's information for the next ones coming along,' Margaret said, 'if it's a good place to be at, what the people are like. They're supposed to be able to make the sign against the evil eye. I always wonder what the sign against the evil eye is.'

McCrink put his finger on the symbol gouged on a shop doorframe, feeling there was more to it than a description of the inhabitants. There was a sense of warnings on a deeper level, meaning freighted through the ages. He felt a sense of far-off chants and invocations, the gateposts and doorframes made into psychic wayposts.

'The gypsies are treated worse than animals,' Margaret said. 'The child mortality rates are like something you'd find in Africa.'

She sought to understand things by turning them into causes. She took him back to her flat and showed him pamphlets about the Windscale nuclear plant forty miles away. Raising her voice to something like reverence as she turned over the pages. Magnox, fusion, discharges, intoning the tech words, the futurist vocabularies that had gathered round the domed containment structures raised on the shale coastline.

Afterwards they went up to her bedroom. The window was open, the room hot. McCrink could hear people passing on the street outside, late-night conversations drifting upwards. She liked the idea of being just out of sight, keeping their voices down. She would put his hand on her breast when they were driving through the town. She would reach for him under the table in restaurants. She spread a towel over her lap when they were sitting on the front at Warrenpoint and directed his hand under it.

McCrink started to wonder if there was an ethos of snatched sexual contact in the town, if they were all at it, the gropes and covert delvings.

She would lead him, telling him what she wanted him to do next, instructions detailed in a series of breathy asides. Put your hand there. Slower. She had been working towards unspoken things, the sighs and mewings and wordless pleadings and barely uttered parleys on the fringes of love. Afterwards she took a packet of cigarettes from the bedside table. Gitanes. It went with the ethnic hangings and Indian throw in her bedroom. The small-town bohemian look. The smoke hung in the warm night air, a rank Gallic odour.

'Do you think McGladdery killed Pearl?'

'Probably.'

'Why would a man do something like that?'

'I don't know. I seen plenty of it and I still don't know.'

'Poor Pearl. She was perfect in that shop. She was all buttons and bows like a china doll. Pearl was the right name for her.'

'I just realised. I never asked you if you knew McGladdery.'

'Course I knew him. He was never out of the library.' McCrink raised himself up on one elbow. He thought he heard a rumble of thunder over the mountains. Two men passed beneath the window, talking in lowered voices, passing beneath the mock-Venetian frontage of Thompson's Mill on Canal Street. A night of forboding. Secrets afoot in the torrid air. The masculine reek of the cigarettes hanging in the room.

'How come you never told me?'

'You never asked.' Falling into the town accent, the marsh-town guttural. He sat up in bed and looked down at her. Beginning to grasp the town, the frontier place. The people and their infiltrated hearts. The way that information was never offered. You had to go looking for it, the way they worked off the undeclared and the withheld. He had noticed that people in the town answered the phone without speaking. You found yourself babbling into the void.

'Did you talk to him?'

'Sometimes. When he was taking books out.'

'Is there some sort of librarian's professional confidence here?

Can a librarian plead privilege? Like a doctor or something?'

'He was always very polite. Called me Miss.'

'Am I allowed to ask what kind of books he was taking out, or does that fall under privilege?'

'All sorts of things. He used to tell me he had an "enquiring mind". Different things all the time. Bodybuilding. Crime fiction.'

'I can't believe you didn't tell me this.'

'The whole thing feels like a story,' Margaret said, 'the terrible murder. Librarian falls for brooding big-city detective.'

'I don't brood. And I'm not big-city.'

'Not any more anyway.'

'What does that mean?'

'You never talk about yourself. When you were in London.'

'There's nothing to say.'

'People talk about it. How come he left the job in London if he was such a hot shot? They're saying McGladdery might get off.'

'Is that what they're saying?'

'Why did you leave London?'

'I got tired of it.' Tired of the murder squad. The gangland killings, corpses dumped in motorway pilings. The steady rain of domestic murders, husbands and boyfriends, the inner-city gang fights in the West End. The Nude Murders.

'And anatomy.'

'What?'

'Anatomy books. McGladdery was always taking them out.'

Crime fiction and anatomy. A figure crouched over Pearl in the night, the dark imagined criminal of a novel, McCrink thought.

Fifteen

During Robert's second remand hearing in Newry court-house the court stenographer used a manual typewriter. The Belfast Telegraph reported that 'the accused seemed to be agitated and objected to the sound of the typewriter'. Robert may have been reacting to the noise of the typewriter, the cutler's blade-sharpening slither of the key arms and the end-stop click of key on paper. Or he may have become agitated by the sense of a narrative being driven forwards, themes developing, the story spreading outwards and gathering material to itself.

When people in Newry talk about the case they always refer to it as McGladdery and Pearl Gamble. Pearl gets her full name. McGladdery's surname is used. An intimacy is implied by the use of both names although the fact is that, according to the court record, the only relationship between the two is that McGladdery murdered Pearl. Nevertheless people put their names together. Going through the archive you come across the wedding photographs in the social pages. The bride and groom smiling at the camera with their fifty-year-old smiles. Looking into the flash as though dazzled by the promise of the life to come. Robert and Pearl the sombre reverse of that promise. Fixed in the ghoul-light of murder.

*

McCrink found himself spending more time in the two rooms at the top of the Corry Square Station. Speers had been recalled to Belfast to work on the Bratty case. Instructions coming through from Harry West, from Brian Faulkner. They wanted daily updates. They wanted to be informed immediately of developments. McCrink went over his casenotes again and again. The scratches on McGladdery's face which he said were caused by the bullworker. His unexplained behaviour in the days following the murder. The suit concealed in the septic tank. The wounds on his hands and the star-shaped wounds on Pearl's body.

Among the pathology papers he found a statement that he had not read before. The statement had been given by one of the mill workers who had met Robert at a dance in Warrenpoint three weeks before the murder. She described how Robert had walked her along the front. They got as far as the park, the girl ready to be backed up against the wall of the public toilets, ready for the body pressed up against hers, the encroaching hands, the small-town ceremonials of desire. Instead Robert put his hands to his temples and shook his head from side to side as though denying an insistent inner voice and she found herself aware that they were completely alone, Robert like some Hammer Horror villain in the throes of transformation into a loping were-creature.

'What is it? What's wrong?' she said.

'A headache,' he said. 'O Jesus the lights.'

It was ten minutes before Robert was well enough to walk back to the bus stop for the late-night bus to Newry. He was pale and shaking and did not speak. She let him get on the bus first and sat several seats behind him. He fell asleep on the bus and the driver had to wake him when they reached the terminus in Newry. McCrink wondered if the statement had been deliberately hidden among the pathology reports or whether it had been misfiled.

McCrink's room seemed to be filled with the clutter of a long-ago investigation, a dusty case room sealed-up, a criminal affair brought to a melancholy conclusion. The crime-scene photographs on the wall curled up at the edges, case papers yellowing. The photograph of Pearl an elegiac thing, freighted out of an era of long-forgotten elegance.

He assembled the autopsy, crime-scene and crime-lab reports and went through them again. There were injuries to the hands indicating she had tried to fight off her attacker. The lips were swollen. The face and throat bruised. There was a puncture wound behind the ear. The right ventricle chamber of the heart had been pierced. The wounds were not the cause of death. The cause of death was strangulation.

He was in the room late one Wednesday afternoon when Speers came in. He had a telegram in his hand.

'The jury's come in,' he said, 'Bratty's for the rope.' McCrink was surprised. There had been an expectation that Bratty would be found not guilty by reason of insanity. McCrink had watched him in court, a tall, white-faced figure who spoke in what the Evening Standard described as a 'low calm tone which never varied'. A Doctor Kurt Sax employed by the defence had suggested that he suffered from psychomotor epilepsy.

'The date of the execution is fixed pending appeal,' Speers said. 'With any luck we'll see two of them swing this year.'

~

All that summer McCrink returned to visit Doris Curran. The superintendent told him that she had no other visitors. The judge did not come and Desmond had taken up his parish in Soweto where he was to become known for his bravery in opposition to apartheid. Sometimes Doris was lucid. Sometimes there were long drugged silences. McCrink said little, allowing Doris to talk. It was something he had learned from Newry. You kept your mouth shut. You invited people into the silence.

When she was little Doris had wanted to be a nurse. She had a picture in her head of Florence Nightingale and other kindly figures in history. She would be an instrument of hygiene and morality and also of comfort to dying men. This tale was the bare bones of a joke in light of her current life which was incarceration at the behest of her husband Mr Justice Lance Curran in Holywell Mental Hospital. On grounds of mental diminishment. He had judged, condemned and sentenced her in an assize of his own devising.

She knew that she was pointed out often in the wing. There goes the mother of Patricia Curran who was murdered. The judge's wife. The judge put her away after the daughter was done in. They had no idea who she really was or the secrets that lay concealed within her breast.

The day and hour she heard about the murder of Pearl Gamble she knew that Lance would be there dressed in robes to partake of vengeance. Lance Curran was no stranger to icy thought.

The other patients referred to Holywell as the floating hotel but Doris did not understand why it would be floating and besides a hotel was a place of resort and leisure. Holywell was a hospital and place of rest.

She hears them talking. They think she doesn't hear them but she does. His long white judge body. His long black judge robes. His black judge mind. Come to me in the darkness of my mind, your worship. Doris minded what Patricia was like when she was little and that was wilful like the shadows in this hospital are wilful and will not do as they are bid.

They had put her on Haloparidol and other anti-psychotics. The medical staff at Holywell were surprised by her knowledge of drugs and procedures. In fact she felt obliged to inform them that she had been brought up in the grounds of Broadmoor Hospital for the Criminally Insane where her father had been superintendent and she understood them perfectly and all their little tricks.

Doris liked to discuss the difference between procedures as she had observed them in Broadmoor and the medical practices she observed at Holywell. At Holywell the staff were well-mannered and respectful. There were nurses dressed in white. In Broadmoor sometimes you would have wondered who were the staff and who the patients.

The doctors think she does not know the effects of the meds but she does. She knows the doses and contraindications and the difference between tranquillisers and anti-psychotics. They were given to her in a stainless-steel kidney bowl and she had to swallow them and then drink a plastic cup of liquid medication. Broadmoor was full of murderers not in their right mind. She used to see them at work in the gardens but each one seemed distant to her like a traveller seen from afar.

Once her father took her to the laundry in the women's

section. The women did not look at her and afterwards she imagined them in their cells left to think about their lonely crimes of infanticide and poisoning.

At ten she had a vocabulary of slop-outs and remands and lockdowns not known to other girls of her age and class. She knew that the shape could go out of the world. She could not make that clear to her daughter Patricia. She could not get it into her head.

Her father had learned discussions with her about the origin and causes of madness. He wished her to go equipped in the world with strange knowledge. He had a bakelite skull which he kept on his desk and he would point out the ridges and protuberances, the contours and outcrops which indicated the criminally insane.

There were days when Doris's mind was clear and she remembered the Glen. Patricia would try to get her to go to the pictures. She said that she should go to see Bette Davis. She said that the Glen where they lived in Whiteabbey was like a house from the pictures with something prowling in the shrubbery. Patricia laughed and said that she could see Doris alone in a big house, pale and ghostly sitting by the fire. 'I imagine you alone in the murderous night, Mother,' Patricia said.

When she was seventeen Patricia took a job driving a builders' lorry, an act she did in defiance of Doris. Even now Doris nearly chokes on the word 'lorry'. She wonders sometimes if the doctors who visit her know about Patricia and the builders' lorry, had she told them about that fact which changed everything? Patricia wore a donkey jacket and went about the country with bricks on a lorry. Doris spoke to Patricia's employer on the telephone but he was a crude man and only laughed so Doris barred her door to Patricia. Patricia wept in the night and said 'Let me in Mother,' but she would not.

Desmond her son was a different matter. Although she put up no defence of what her husband called popery and superstition it was a matter of great pride to her that he had taken holy orders although she was not at liberty to attend his ordination. Desmond was at present in South Africa and she could not imagine the conditions and the people he had sacrificed himself to, the burning sun, the unholy practices. It broke her heart to think of it.

The others never saw the way Patricia would look at you, the wilful stare, and the pert ways she had and a tongue in her head. Doris would reprimand her then it would be a case of through the house slamming doors and objects flung at her backside.

She told McCrink about her coming-out in London. Doris was a sight to see abroad in London with Lance. All the great hotels. The Ritz. The Majestic. Doris wearing a dress she had made from a Vogue magazine pattern. Doris floating through the ballrooms in the arms of young men of good means.

Her father drove a Humber and Doris remembered the smell of leather from the seat. Doris thought of the shoes polished and lined up on a Saturday night for service on Sunday. On Saturday evenings her father would send her to the storeman for Guardsman shoe polish. She would be sent down between the shelves of soaps and washing powders and disinfectants. The Daz and Sunlight bars and Jeyes fluid. The storeman Mr Roberts kept the poisons on the top shelves. The warfarin and paraquat and sodium chlorate.

Mr Roberts would tell her about people who had ingested

poison. Children drinking warfarin from unmarked lemon-ade bottles. How they died. Black-lipped, heaving.

She told McCrink that they were not allowed to use the telephone in Holywell. She kept coming back to it, that they were not permitted to use the telephone, saying that you would not have thought there was so much harm in a telephone and in hearing other voices. Every time she talked about the telephone she had a sly look on her face. McCrink thinking it was like the delusions of high birth, one more empty secret.

~

At Corry Square McCrink had the feeling that the McGladdery investigation was going on without him. Johnston was rarely seen in the station. Many of the papers had been transferred to the Crown Prosecution Service. He travelled to Belfast several times a week, but the office there seemed to run itself. He started to spend time in Newry library. He could see local people looking at him then looking at Margaret, exchanging knowing glances, but she ignored him when she was at work. She signed out books to him with eyes lowered.

He found himself going through old maps of the town, poring over records, poor-law valuations, lists of rate-payers and electors. He felt that there was some kind of murmuring in the town about the murder of Pearl Gamble, that an interior dialogue was taking place to which he was not admitted.

He had started to order books on mental illness. Margaret asked him if he thought McGladdery was mad.

'I thought the psychiatrist examined him in hospital and found him of sound mind.'

Of sound mind. The tolled-out word, formal and archaic.

McCrink didn't tell her that he wasn't taking out the books because of McGladdery. He applied himself to the symptoms of paranoid schizophrenia.

Delusions of persecution, of exalted birth or special mission, bodily changes. Hallucinatory voices that threaten or give commands. Auditory hallucinations. Hallucinations of smell or taste or of sexual or other bodily sensations. Visual hallucinations may occur but rarely predominate.

There were case histories of patients who had attacked and killed loved ones believing them to be the devil. These were the tales of the bewildered, the chronicles of bedlam.

Sixteen

Following Robert's arrest Agnes often saw Ronnie on Hill Street. Gone were the low-cut tops and the short skirts. There was a girl who knew which side her bread was buttered. She saw the way people came up to Ronnie and put these big faces on as if to say isn't this is a heartbreak but you'll get through it. And Ronnie would look back at them with this big soft head on her as though to say yes I am full of sorrow. Agnes knew the only sorrow that had come to her door was the sorrow of not luring a married man from his lawful bed. If Agnes had the right of it then McKnight ran a mile in fear of questioning. Where were you on the night of the 14th of this month? On the night of the 15th of this month?

Agnes could swear it was all the books and reading that got Robert into trouble. He took grand notions about himself until she cried out in her heart there is no grandeur for the likes of you and me in this vale, only scorn.

She knew from the start that she lived in a cruel town but how cruel she had not realised. A place where men thought they had a right to her person and women looked at her in seaside tea rooms as though she was muck. There was a Mrs McDonald whose husband was a solicitor and a Mrs Keenan whose husband was a doctor would stick their big heads in the air any time they seen Agnes. Their faces wrinkled up so that you'd think they had shit on the ends of their noses so that one day Agnes marches right up to them and says to them take that snoot off your faces or I'll take it off for you.

~

Robert was reported to have settled in well to prison life. The prison MO, James Newell, examined him on 21st May. He said, 'McGladdery presents a cheerful and well-adjusted exterior. He has expressed the wish to "make the most" of his situation and says he is confident that the "truth will out".'

Newell's medical exam concluded that Robert was in 'reasonable' health although there was some evidence of malnutrition in infancy. His torso showed evidence of bodybuilding. His blood pressure was normal. The lesions on his face had healed. It was recommended that McGladdery attend the prison dentist as he exhibited extensive dental caries.

The inmate complained of wheeziness. This appeared to be some impairment of lung function which merited further investigation.

'Unless he gets fucking typhoid,' the chief prison officer, McBride, said, 'let it lie.'

Hughes told Robert not to go near the prison dentist.

'He's half-cut or hungover most of the time. He'll rip the jaw off you and leave you lying in your own blood. Save yourself the agony, my son. You'll not be needing teeth if Allen gets his mitts on you anyhow.'

Robert told Hughes that it was something he had in common with Pearl. They both had unusually shaped teeth.

'For fuck's sakes would you quit that?' Hughes said. 'The girl's dead and buried. You'll have that in common too if you keep on about having the same teeth.'

Robert read volumes on self-improvement which he took from the prison library. He told Hughes about the importance of being 'up' no matter what. 'The upbeat personality will always prosper,' he said, 'while the more "down" type of character will struggle to perform the simplest tasks.'

After lock-up Robert continued with his writing. He wrote by hand on sheets of unlined foolscap. He was amazed to learn that paper had weights, and that it came in reams and quartos and folios. There was a whole mechanics to the process that he had never known about. Papers that were embossed and offset. It seemed to give his words more weight on the page. He began to worry about his spelling and his grammar. He thought about master craftsmen, the trans-European guilds. There was a whole dimension to the business of writing things down that he hadn't thought about. He imagined the craft-workers gathering, aproned freemen.

He wanted to tell his story but elements of it had started to get away from him. There were things that he had taken for granted.

Hughes said that Robert did not appear alarmed by the guilty verdict in the Bratty case.

'Bratty won't swing,' he said confidentially, 'the weight of public opinion is against hanging mental defectives.' Hughes wasn't so sure.

'The weight of public opinion would be as happy swinging off Bratty's ankles on the scaffold to make sure his neck's good and broke.'

Robert's solicitors had engaged a Belfast QC, James Brown, to represent him. Brown had the reputation of never having lost a man to the gallows. Brown took the brief on the day of the Bratty verdict. He went to Crumlin Road prison the following day accompanied by an elderly solicitor's clerk from the Newry office. A warder led him through ill-lit passageways and anterooms. He unlocked doors with keys carried on the chain at his waist. The clerk walked at his side, aware of the theatrics of the place, the doom-laden clanking of doors and the purposeful movement in secure spaces, the architecture designed to address the transgressive self. The brick walls and barred windows and ornate ironwork carried in doleful spans across the empty central hall. The inmates' pale faces glimpsed in the penal gloom.

'I know what I'd do to a man who would be fit to do the likes of that to a girl,' the warder said. The warder had the look of a lay preacher. 'He's for the rope anyhow,' the clerk said, 'that'll drive the devil out of him.'

'He says he never done it.'

'They all say that till they see the scaffold,' the warder said. The two men talked all the way to Robert's cell.

'You have him up on B wing,' the clerk said, 'high security.'

'He's on the sex offenders' wing,' the warder said, 'for fear the other prisoners will do the hangman's job for him.'

The two men seemed to regard lugubrious dialogue as part of their office, that Brown would feel let down if they were not there to exchange grim drolleries in the shadow of the gallows.

The warder opened the door to McGladdery's cell and Brown saw him for the first time. The image stayed with him for many years. McGladdery looking like a lone charismatic, pale-faced, seeing himself as beset on every side.

The warder and clerk stepped aside. Brown stepped into the

cell. McGladdery was sitting on his bed. Brown always found something devotional in these spaces. The window placed high in the wall so that light streamed down. The prisoner's pale face picked out like a supplicant in some medieval illumination, looking upwards, bathed in the god light.

McGladdery was sitting on the bed. There were books lying on the blankets, novels with cracked spines, the covers foxed and the corners turned up. Brown had defended those facing the death sentence in several jurisdictions. There were those who seemed to be lost in their own murderous transcendence but McGladdery was different, boyish and involved.

'I want to tell my story, Mr Brown. I'm going to write it down so people understand.'

'I'm sure you do, Robert.' Brown had met gaolhouse writers before. Sex criminals usually, bespectacled men who uncovered psychologically complex narratives in themselves. They believed themselves lost in the lonely mechanics of desire. Their writings reeked of self-justification.

'Just don't admit anything.'

'I don't have nothing to admit to. I never laid a hand on her.'

'The Crown have a lot of circumstantial evidence.'

'The Crown's got damn-all if I never done it. When people get to read about me they can make up their own minds.'

'There are a fair few who have already made up their mind, Robert. That's the problem. Perhaps you would tell me what happened on the 29th January?'

'I'll start with the day. There was a fair slap of drink on board.'

'Who were you drinking with?'

'Me and Will Copeland. We were in Hollywood's. Then we went down to the Legion. We laid a few bets in Hughes.'

The winter Saturday afternoon. The races coming through on the bookmaker's tannoy. Haydock. Sandown Park. The horses labouring into the dusk, the muted silks and hoof-beats fading into the drizzle. Men giving way to an unforeseen wistfulness, darkness gathering on the streets outside.

'What happened then?' Brown felt himself being drawn into the day.

'We finished off in the Legion . . .'

'Did you buy anything?'

'What do you mean?'

'Did you go into any shops during the day?'

'I don't remember.'

'The prosecution say you went into Woolworths and bought shoemaker's tools. An off-duty policewoman maintains that she witnessed you buying them.'

'I suppose I must of then.'

'What happened then?'

'Me and Will went to my house. I gave him a go on the bullworker.'

'Bullworker?'

'Expands the chest muscles so it does. You ever see Charles Atlas? Nobody messes with Charles Atlas. That's what they say, isn't it?'

'I don't know.'

'I put near an inch on my chest with it. I put about a half an inch on my upper arms and near a quarter on the neck. That'll give Harry Allen something to think about.'

'Harry Allen?'

'The hangman. He has to measure the neck and weigh you and then calculate the drop.'

'Who was telling you this?'

'The warder. The boy who brought you in here. Says the head can be tore clean off if they don't get it right. When he hits the trapdoor. I hear tell Allen has a whole book of calculations for all sorts of weights. It's harder to hang a woman they say. A woman's body would be a different mass. You'd snap a woman's neck like a twig.'

Beaten. Stabbed. Strangled. Robert always having to know how things worked. Keeping the whole thing at bay with the mathematics. Fascinated that the hanging had its own dark science, that there were men in thrall to its arts. He couldn't stop talking about it.

'Did anything happen in the room when you were using the bullworker?'

'I had my foot through one of the handles. It slipped and the handle flew up and hit me in the face, scraped me. I put some of the ma's foundation on the scrape to hide it.'

'What were you wearing that night, Robert?'

'Fawn shortie overcoat and this dark drape suit I got in London. And blue suede shoes.'

'That's not what the witnesses say.'

'What do the witnesses say?'

'The witnesses say you were wearing a light-coloured suit with a white shirt and a black-and-red tie.'

'That's the tie I lent to Will. That tie cost three pounds on the King's Road. Will was always going on about it. How the women would be throwing themselves at him. In the end I give in. Here, I says, borrow it if it means so much to you.'

'Witnesses don't mention what Mr Copeland was wearing.'

'He was wearing the light suit and the black-and-red tie.

He borrowed the suit.'

'What is your relationship with Mr Copeland?'

'Friends. Blood brothers. We done everything together. Tell us this, Mr Brown. Pearl was found half a mile from Damolly Cross.'

'She was.'

'Could she have run there?'

'Hardly.'

'I hear tell about people getting shot and the like who keep running. Not a drop of blood in them and them running like a four-minute-miler. The nerves keep the legs working. Do you think that could have happened with Pearl?'

'I don't think so. The police are saying she was dragged there.'

It would be a pattern with Robert. Going over the murder scene, constructing scenarios. Was Pearl beaten or stabbed first? Was the killer right-handed or left-handed? Did Brown think she had taken her clothes off first for 'matters of a consensual nature' as Robert put it, or had the killer torn at them in a frenzy? Brown had never come across this behaviour from a suspect before. Robert coming across as dogged and simple-minded.

Robert told Brown how he had danced with Pearl and with Joan Donergan.

'What happened at the end of the dance?'

'I waited for Joan Donergan. When she didn't come out I went home.'

'You didn't take a bicycle from outside the Orange hall?'

'I never seen a bicycle. I walked home and went to bed.'

Brown felt that Robert was holding something back. It seemed that he could follow Robert to the door of the dance hall but that afterwards he lost sight of him.

'Did you know Miss Gamble before the night of the killing?'

'I might have met her when we were small but I don't remember.'

'But you remember dancing with her that night?'

'I remember, but people wanted to dance with me.'

'Did you request "It's Now or Never" from the band?'

'No, I never. I asked for "Chattanooga Choo Choo" but they didn't know it so they said they'd play "It's Now or Never" instead.'

Robert a good dancer like his father before him. Showing the girls the new dance steps, the jive, the mashed potato. Getting Pearl up for the slow set, 'It's Now or Never', Robert's luck running out in three-two time.

~

McCrink went to the evidence locker and took out the bags of books they had taken from McGladdery's house. He tipped them out onto the desk. There were bodybuilding books and rudimentary self-help books. Improve Your IQ in Ninety Days. There were Reader's Digests and National Geographics. There were copies of Mayfair. There was a sheaf of Health and Education magazines featuring nude girls playing volleyball. The girls were blonde and smiling. They looked like naturists from before the war, Aryans given to mass gymnastic displays. McCrink preferred the Mayfair models. Girls in French maid's costumes and schoolgirl outfits, smutty and knowing.

The other bag contained novels. McCrink tipped them out onto the desk. Crime fiction and westerns. He flicked through. Riders of the Purple Sage. Ian Fleming. He picked out a Mickey Spillane novel, The Long Wait.

The cover shows a man and a woman in an undefined urban interior. There is what looks like an overturned packing case in the back. The man has been tied to a chair and is straining at his bonds. His white shirt is ripped at the shoulder. He has black hair and a square jaw. The woman is in the foreground, half-lying on the ground. She has blonde hair to her shoulders and is wearing a low-cut yellow dress. The illustration is composed in such a way that your eye is drawn to her face, to the exposed portion of her breasts. She is looking up at someone or something just out of frame. Her pencilled-in eyebrows are arched, and her gaze is calculating. She has a blowsy, gone-to-the-bad look about her, and the tied man is watching her with apprehension. She might untie him before she makes a break for it or strikes up an alliance with his captor, but they've both been on the receiving end of too many tawdry outcomes to make this a foregone conclusion.

The novel was subtitled 'The New Thriller by the author of The Big Kill'. McCrink turned it over to read the back. He ran his hand over the cover and felt the indentations in it. He opened the cover. It had been punched through. There were holes everywhere. He counted thirty. The holes seemed to be star-shaped. He rang Speers.

'The wounds on Pearl's body match the shape of a cobbler's file, the one that McGladdery was supposed to have bought in Woolworths?'

'I know that.'

'I've got something else. A paperback with stab wounds in it, the same shape.'

'He was practising his stabbing at home.'

'It proves he had a punch. It doesn't prove he was practising stabbing someone.'

'It'll be put to him in the box. I'd like the jury to hear him deny it.'

McCrink put on his coat and went outside. He walked down Mary Street to the canal. It was damp and foggy. He thought about the man and the woman on the cover of The Long Wait. He wondered if McGladdery had lost himself in their fictional jeopardies. If he had imagined himself abroad in their fogbound milieu.

Seventeen

In the silence of the billiard room Judge Curran studied the fall of the balls on the table. He potted an isolated red and left the cue ball flush to the cushion to line up the black for the bottom left. The Reform Club dining room had been busy that night. Ferguson had watched the judge walk between the tables. He saw the judge mark who was in attendance. The shipyard bondholders and shire bosses. The garbed clergy. He saw the judge's unyielding regard fall on their wives and the way they looked after him when he passed, some bleak appetite stirred. Ferguson had heard rumours about women on the judge's trips to London. Rumours that followed him through the gaming rooms of Piccadilly.

Three days previously a handwritten note had been delivered to Ferguson's office in Whiteabbey. It was from Constable Rutherford who said that he would be attending the High Court in Belfast as a witness the following day, and asked Ferguson to meet him.

Rutherford was waiting for Ferguson in the great hall. Ferguson had not seen him since he had appeared as a witness in the Patricia Curran case. He was wearing dress uniform. Many of the constabulary had been in the army or navy before they joined up. They had the bearing. Boots and belting spitpolished and shellacked. Ferguson shook hands.

'What can I do for you, Constable?'

'I brought a visitor to the Glen a few months ago. I been thinking about it. I told Mr West. He said that you and his Honour should know.'

'Who?'

'The Inspector of Constabulary, Mr McCrink.'

'What in the name of blazes was he doing there?'

Rutherford told him about the workmen's discovery of what appeared to be a large bloodstain on the floorboards in the master bedroom.

'What did you think?'

'I was on the Arctic convoys during the war. I seen men killed, Mr Ferguson.' Rutherford had served as a merchant seaman sailing on convoys from Southampton to Spitsbergen in the winter of 1943. One convoy was attacked by Stuka divebombers a hundred and twenty nautical miles north-west of Shetland. Travelling at fourteen knots in a heavy swell. The salt spray froze as it landed on stanchions and handrails and men were sent aloft to chip it from sonar relays and mast tines. Gannets and blackheaded gulls followed in her wake, waiting for the slit gash bags to be flung from her stern. They followed her by day and by night. Screeching in the night as though awful revels took place in the ship's wake. Rutherford had seen men killed, strafed by gunfire and shrapnel on the open deck during the attack.

'I seen butchery on board ship. I seen what blood looks like dried into a wooden deck. It resembles itself and nothing else.'

'Tell no one else about this, Rutherford. What's done is done.'

'The convicted murderer Gordon has been released.'

'Released and taken care of.'

'Then there is nothing to be gained.'

'No, Constable. There is nothing to be gained.'

Curran listened in silence as Ferguson told him about his meeting with Rutherford.

'What do we know of this McCrink?' Curran said.

'Native of the province. Career detective. Joined the London murder squad. He was regarded as a high flyer. Then he requests a transfer back to Ulster. No explanation given.'

'Find out. A detective who does not believe his own evidence is fatal to a case. Particularly a case which depends on circumstantial evidence. Who is appearing for the defence?'

'Brown. As you know he has the reputation of never having lost a man to the rope.'

The judge rolled the white along the cushion to strike the black ball. The black hung in the jaws of the pocket for a moment and then fell. Ferguson respotted the ball as the judge walked to the end of the table and bent to calculate the angle on the next red. He potted the red then went to a side table. He poured a whiskey and siphoned soda into the glass. As he bent over the bottle and glass Ferguson thought he looked like some stoop-backed necromancer bent to his decadent elixir.

'What about Bratty? The man charged with the homicide of the girl in Hillsborough. There was a sexual dimension to that crime as well, wasn't there?' Curran said.

'I spoke to the Minister for Home Affairs about Bratty. He is of a mind to commute the sentence.'

'Then it will have to be McGladdery. Brown will lose his man.'

Brown came to the gaol every Tuesday at two o'clock. He sat with Robert for hours going over the events of the night of 28th January. What time did he arrive at the Orange hall? Did he speak to anyone on the way in? When did he first set eyes on Pearl? Robert understood that they had to work their way towards the main event of the night. Brown had yet to bring up Robert's journey home from the hall. These conversations would be difficult, halting. First the night had to be remade, contexts established, clear roles given to each character. The evening was not as Robert remembered it. A dance at a parochial hall with mill girls and shopworkers began to appear as something shadowy, a dimly-lit masque. In his memory the dancers seemed like people from the old times moving in silence around him, dancing some ghostly and sinister pavane.

'I am obliged to say that if you plead guilty it is probable that the capital sentence will not be imposed,' Brown said. 'And if the sentence is imposed there is a greater chance of a clemency appeal succeeding.'

'I can't plead guilty if I never done it.'

'That is true. However, I have to inform you of the options.'

'I'm pleading innocent.'

'Fair enough. That brings us to the second matter.'

'What's that?'

'Whether you should take the stand or not.'

'What do you mean?'

'The Crown's case is built on circumstantial evidence. They have no witnesses to the actual murder and obviously no confession. In circumstances like these, the accused often exercises his option not to testify.'

'So I keep the mouth shut. Does that not look bad with the jury?'

Robert's approach to the case was dogged by his visions of dramatic robed jurists, by his misuse of legal vocabularies.

'The judge will instruct them to the effect that they must not base any opinion on the accused declining to testify.'

'Why would I not testify when I'm innocent? I can tell them everything I done that night. I can put them on the right road. I've a few things up my sleeve.'

'It's your decision, Robert. The problem is that an experienced prosecutor can guide you into saying things that you do not really mean. He can lay emphasis on parts of your testimony detrimental to your case, and deflect the jury's attention from aspects that may be beneficial. My advice would be to stay out of the witness box. But the decision is yours. Think it over for a day or two.'

'What's he up to?' Hughes said that night.

'Fuck knows,' Robert said.

'Boy thinks you can't defend yourself on the stand. It's your right to get up on the two hind legs and let them have it. An innocent man. It's wrote all over your face.'

'You don't understand legal strategy though.'

'He'll strategy you into the arms of Allen is what he'll do.'

'Me and Mr Brown discussed the matter at length.'

'Length. Six foot of hemp. That's the length we're talking about here.'

Robert hadn't seen the way Hughes had been looking at him recently. Hughes slipping into the stereotype of treacherous sidekick. Hughes had spent six months listening to Robert and had decided to 'bring him down a peg or two', as he told other prisoners in the kitchen.

'He thinks he's a gaolhouse lawyer. Discussed the matter at length my arse. He'd sicken your hole going on about writing books and Russian spies. Russian spies my fucking eye. He says he's going to be world bodybuilding champion. I've seen bigger muscles on a sparrow.'

Hughes also said he didn't like the way Robert talked about Bratty. 'It was Bratty this and Bratty that, but mainly he kept saying that if they commuted Bratty they'd have to commute him. Plus, he said, "Bratty admitted doing it and I never done it."'

Robert borrowed law books from the prison library. Textbooks on evidence and criminal intent. He started dropping legal phrases into his conversations with Hughes. He talked about the defence of provocation and the defence of diminished responsibility. He spent days reading about the great criminal trials. Regina *vs* Cole. Regina *vs* Dalton. He told Hughes he was developing expertise in the field of the criminal mind and the criminals who committed them, their storied lives. Enraged husbands, poisoners. He imagined himself as a cosmopolitan murderer. Subtle, clean-shaven, capable of nuanced atrocities that would be elegantly debated in court by men in wigs. He imagined lengthy appeals, courteous exchanges with members of the higher courts. His name spoken of with grudging respect in the law courts and the Bar library. Women watching spellbound from the public gallery, recognising in Robert the exercise of a higher calling.

At the end of June he told Brown that he intended to take the stand in his own defence.

'I'd say he has Brown tormented with talk about the law,' Hughes said. But Brown understood the necessities that overtook a man fighting for his life, and knew that you couldn't deny someone who had uncovered a sense of last-ditch heroics and was determined to pursue it for all it was worth.

'How do you stand for a man that you know is guilty?' Robert asked Brown one day.

'You cannot know he is guilty until the court finds he is guilty. That is the mechanism of the law,' Brown said.

Even though the day was warm outside, the interview room was cold. Brown had suffered from constant colds since he had started to come to Crumlin Road. He shivered in bed at night. He felt that he carried something back to the hotel from the prison. He went to the doctor and was given antibiotics. He felt that he was suffering from nineteenth-century prison agues. He felt racked by chills and gaol fevers.

'It's the basalt in the walls,' Robert said, 'it absorbs the moisture.'

Black basalt quarried behind the mountain and drawn in carts to the city after dark, the dressed blocks stacked two deep as though cut from the substance of the night itself. The stone became the material of retribution. The stuff of punishment gathered on the site and assembled. It was necessary that the manner of building be sufficient to the recorded crime. The design of the prison based on Pentonville Prison in London, built as a model gaol. The prisoner was to be isolated, the architecture worked to direct the mind inward. Regimes of silence were enforced, inmates were to move about the prison without speaking under pain of flogging and forfeiture of time. The light of heaven would pour in from skylights, the eye drawn upwards. The prisoners were provided with Bibles and moral texts. They were to lay themselves bare before heaven and be shriven of their crimes.

As the summer went on Robert's thoughts were not drawn upwards. He kept thinking about the basement at the bottom of C Wing. Hughes told him that the gallows was struck down after each execution and rebuilt anew each time it was required. His mind kept returning to the unlit chamber, the dismantled machine of execution. Its stacked beams. He kept asking the head warder, McCulla, if he could see it.

'You'll be seeing it soon enough and seeing it plenty,' McCulla said.

During his interviews with Robert in Crumlin Road gaol, Brown brought up the river-crossing incident from the week when Robert was under twenty-four-hour surveillance.

'Why did you walk through the river?'

'They were following me everywhere. I says to the peeler outside the house, if you want to follow me, then follow me across the river. I did it for the laugh.'

'What happened then?'

'This other policeman picked me up on the other side of the river. Johnston.'

'What do you mean picked you up?'

'He put a gun to the side of my head and told me he'd blow my fucking brains out if I didn't get in the car.'

'Was he on his own?'

'There was another policeman in the front of the car. He kept his face turned away the whole time so I couldn't see who he was. They took me to Corry Square.'

'Johnston says there was only him. That he took you back to Corry Square to fix you up with dry clothes.'

'I never seen any dry clothes. They took me there to make me say that I done it. They kept asking me about the suit, the light-coloured suit. Johnston and his crew of local boys. Coming at me in teams. They kept at me all night.'

'When you say all night? According to their account you arrived at the barracks at 2.20 p.m. and left at 4.25 p.m.'

'I got home at about twelve that night after they threw me out.'

'There is no record of this interview.'

'Record or not, Johnston told me he was going to make sure I swung for Pearl. When I said I never done it he only laughed. I got the feeling there was somebody else telling him what to do. He kept going out of the room and coming back with new questions.'

They were slamming fists on the table. Where are the clothes you were wearing that night? The clothes. The fancy duds. The London gear. Tell us where they are so we can fucking bury you in them. Coming at him in relays. You asked her for a kiss, didn't you, Robert? You wanted something more. You fancied a little tit and she wouldn't give it to you. You'll be took out of here in a box unless you give us something, McGladdery. There's no Her Majesty's Inspector of fucking Constabulary to help you here. Where'd you get the cuts on your face? Did Pearl scrab you? Is that why you hit her?

'They kept trying to get me to confess, Mr Brown, but I kept the mouth shut. Because I never done it.'

Eighteen

In the final weeks leading up to the trial it seems that Pearl has been left behind. There are photographs of Robert in the press. Agnes is quoted. Brian Faulkner and Harry West give non-committal statements on the administration of justice. There is speculation as to whether Robert will take the stand. Then another photograph of Pearl emerges. It appears to be a professional photograph, posed and studio-lit, although it is hard to tell from the yellowing, low-resolution photograph in the archive. She is seated with her back to the camera, her head angled so that she is looking back in the direction of the photographer. The photograph shows a different person from the laughing girl of the commonly used shot. Pearl looks exotic in this photograph. She is half-turned, looking at the camera over her shoulder. It has the stylised look of a Japanese portrait, the eyes upturned at the corners, the skin flawless. The face has the expressionless set of a geisha, the heavily made-up eyes and the tight pursed lips. She could be a character from one of Robert's crime novels. You imagined her abroad in some vice-ridden oriental milieu, a Hong Kong waterfront bar, glimpsed in the opium-haunted spaces.

~

A week before the trial McCrink visited Doris Curran again. The previous day he had consulted with the clerk of the High Court in Belfast as to how the judge to try the McGladdery case had been appointed.

'It depends on the list,' the clerk said. He was a tall thin man with moles on his face. McCrink couldn't look at him without thinking about growths, malignancies, things that ate away at you from the inside. 'In the case of a capital murder case then it would have to be a judge of the High Court. There is a policy of rotation.'

'But a judge can remove himself.'

'If there were some species of personal involvement in the case, it would be expected.'

'And the hangman?'

'I beg your pardon?'

'The hangman. Who appoints the hangman?'

'The executioner is appointed by HM Inspectorate of Prisons in consultation with the prison governor.'

McCrink arrived at Holywell just before dark. The car radio reported storm force ten on the north channel and the trees alongside the car park moved as though some large shambling thing was trying to force its way through. Through the shrubberies he could see the windows of the hospital, well-lit and provident public buildings.

The hospital corridors were quiet. A man in a white gown passed him, his lips moving in some office of the mad. Doris wasn't in her room and a nurse directed him to the day room. The day room was a conservatory built on to the back of the hospital. Doris was on her own, sitting on a wing-backed chair facing out of the conservatory windows into the turbulent night. She was wearing a dressing gown and her white hair had been combed out. She motioned to him to sit down beside her.

There was a regal tilt to her head and McCrink wondered what deformed queenship she had allotted to herself. The tiled room seemed filled with her madness. He remembered the phrase from the textbook. Delusions of exalted birth.

'Good evening. Please take a seat,' she said. Her diction was precise. There were formal boundaries to be observed. The table in front of her was covered with trinkets, seaside keepsakes, Minton figurines.

'Have you come far?' Doris said.

'From the south,' he said, 'from Newry.'

'Newry? My husband the judge is familiar with that part of the country.'

'You must be mistaken. Your husband is a city man.'

Doris Curran turned to him. Malice unnamed deep in her eyes.

'Lance Curran was reared in the mountains beyond that town. Beyond the Fews as it is called. Reared, or dragged up. I do not care to recall which. Seed, breed and generation.'

'His family?'

'His family are all deceased. They are interred in a grave-yard there. His father and his brother brought him down on horseback and paid for him in cash to board at the Royal School.'

McCrink thought of the Currans, father and sons, ridden down in cohort out of the haunted drumlin country to lay down cash.

'They came down out of that country and then rode back and never stirred themselves out of it again. On the night of my daughter's death my husband was on the telephone,' Doris said. The telephone again, McCrink thought, she always talks

216

about the telephone. It was the first time she had mentioned the night of Patricia's death directly.

'Patricia was wilful,' Doris said, 'even Lance thought she was wilful.'

'What happened?' McCrink said.

'I don't know how she got outside,' Doris said, 'she was inside and then she was outside in the rain. Lance was on the telephone.'

'Where were you?' McCrink picturing the Curran house on the night of the murder, running feet, cries from the dark outside, trees tossing in the night wind.

'Lance knew,' Doris said. McCrink kept his eyes fixed on her, trying to find the meaning in her disconnected tale, the underlying threads. Doris like some cackling seer bent with age tossing herbs on the fire, calling up visions.

'Knew what?' McCrink knew he was lending himself to the scene, feeling like a supplicant come to avail of the old magic.

'He put me in the pantry,' Doris said in a whisper, 'then he was gone for a long time. I heard him telephone Patricia's friend to ask if he had seen Patricia. But he knew she was dead when he telephoned. He was lying.'

'Because he asked where Patricia was when he already knew she was dead?'

'He was lying. Do you not believe me?' Doris's tone changing, she was hunched and shrewish now. 'If you don't believe me you can look,' Doris said, 'go to the top of the house. He hid the phone records in the house. That's where they are. There's a box of them up there in the maid's room. Where is that nurse?'

A nurse came to the door and called Doris. Doris stood and took McCrink's hand.

'So good of you to come,' she said, 'please come again. My children do not call. It is thoughtless in them.'

McCrink nodded. He did not point out that Desmond was in South Africa and that Patricia had been in her grave for nine years. He watched as the nurse led her away, a slight, shuffling figure. The nurse carried the tray with the trinkets and figurines. She told McCrink that Doris normally kept the tray in her room. The nurse seemed to think it a normal thing. She understood the value of keepsakes, of charms and amulets held against inner dark. McCrink did not speak. He thought about Doris locked in the pantry at the Glen while Lance Curran drew the threads of awful night together. Doris standing in the chemical dark full of cleaning products. The smells of Daz and of Omo. Feeling the weird mechanics, the chemistry of things.

Nineteen

The trial of Robert McGladdery for the murder of Pearl Gamble opened on 9th October at the autumn assize in Downpatrick. There was a sizeable media presence with reporters from all the main national papers as well as the local papers. When Robert was asked his name he spoke out in 'a loud, clear voice'. He was wearing a 'dark suit, light-coloured shirt and tie'.

McCrink sat in the public gallery. He could see Agnes McGladdery in the upper tier of the gallery and Margaret a few rows along and Ronnie below her.

The first morning's evidence was taken up with testimony regarding the discovery of Pearl's body. Sixteen-year-old Charles Ashe gave evidence of finding a green button, a brown shoe and a blood-saturated handkerchief at Damolly Cross while out walking greyhounds. He brought them to the Gamble house where Mrs Gamble identified them as belonging to Pearl. The police were called and a search for Pearl commenced.

The youth told how he had stood awaiting the squad car at the roadside. He said he had five greyhounds leashed and muzzled at his side. The prosecution council dwelt on the greyhounds, creatures bred for hunt, their muzzles hidden by leather bands, giving them a look of medieval gorehounds. The prosecution counsel drawing out the image, letting the taint hang in the air.

Johnston was called to give evidence of the discovery of Pearl's body. He was wearing full dress uniform. Hide belt and buckler, brass buttons, the boots brought to a high gleam with a red-hot poker, a heavy Smith & Wesson revolver holstered on the belt. Johnston filled the witness box and spoke with harsh command, seeming vested with authority that was exercisable in jurisdictions beyond the human.

He related how other items of Pearl's clothing were found at the entrance to the stubble field. A black silk scarf, another brown shoe, a pair of black shoes. Her handbag, brush and comb. Later in proceedings Ronnie would explain that Pearl had brought a pair of brown shoes with her for walking home. Her 'skirt, blouse and intimate garments' were strewn across the stubble field. Johnston described how he had discovered a patch of bloodstained earth and had fetched a bucket and shovel and filled the pail with bloodsoaked soil. Pearl's body was discovered at Weir's Rock at 10.20 a.m. The photographs of the scene and Pearl's body were handed to the jury. McCrink knew what they were looking at, the quality of light unique to such scenes. You could see how the jurors' minds worked back from the photographs to the assault, the ghastly night scenes. How the scattered clothing led to the body, the intimate garments, *the rustling underthings.* You could see then how their eyes turned to Robert in the dock, sitting there with an abstracted air as though he was only marginally involved in the proceedings.

Johnston gave evidence of interviewing Robert. He described 'abrasions' under his right eye, and cuts on the thumb and forefinger of his right hand.

Details of the cause of death were given by the pathologist. Death was caused not by the puncture wounds, one
of which had pierced her heart, but by the ligature applied
to her neck.

Beaten, strangled, stabbed.

Johnston gave evidence regarding the blanket surveillance of Robert during the two weeks following the murder.
Brown questioned him regarding the river incident where
the soaking wet Robert was brought back to the station.
Johnston insisted that the only purpose of bringing Robert
back was to dry his clothes. He denied putting a gun to his
head and telling Robert that he'd 'blow his fucking brains
out' if he didn't get into the car.

During the day's evidence Robert listened intently to the
legal argument and consulted textbooks. He leaned back
in his chair with a serious expression when witnesses were
called to the stand. McCrink watching from the body of the
court thought that he was seeking postures of innocence,
that he wanted the jury to see him as pained, caught in the
brow-furrowed perplexity of a man wrongly accused, but
that another part of him responded to the theatrics of the
court, the gavotte of gesture and rhetoric. The dancer, the
bodybuilder. Robert feeling the regard of the public on him
but not aware of the price of that regard, the blood tithe.

Robert had never seen his QC, Brown, in his court garb
before. He thought he looked like a medieval figure, a
bewigged and frock-coated attendant. Everyone in the court
appeared to him like figures of legend. It was a feeling that
would grow during the seven days of the trial. Those in the
public gallery were small and far away whereas those called

before the court loomed in his mind. He looked up at Judge Curran and remembered how he had discussed the killing of the judge's daughter with Mervyn and how Mervyn had said he would swing for a man that would do such murder. He noticed that Judge Curran did not look in his direction. That night when he was returned to Crumlin Road he told Hughes that he thought the Judge would try the case fairly.

'He's the same sort of man as myself,' he said. 'The rest of the QCs and all's a bit scruffy-looking. Judge Curran's robes and all is perfect. Knows how to wear his clothes. There's not a crease. Dead sharp he is and talks polite to the whole crew, no matter if they're Queen's Counsel or the cleaner. And fair as they come. A bit on the dry side, but fair.'

McCrink watching from the body of the court had observed that the judge was polite and scrupulously fair. Like Brown he came to the conclusion that Curran was concerned less with probity than with ensuring that all avenues of appeal be cut off.

The afternoon's proceedings concerned the events of the night of 28th January. It was agreed that Pearl arrived with Ronnie Whitcroft at 10.30 p.m. and that Robert McGladdery arrived with Will Copeland at 11.30 p.m. There was no dispute that Pearl danced two or three times with McGladdery or that she left in a car about 2.15 a.m. with two other men and three girls after a 'short talk' with Joseph Clydesdale.

The court adjourned at 4.30 p.m. with Judge Curran saying they would deal with the events of the night in more detail the following day. Margaret was waiting for McCrink outside the court. McCrink got into her Renault.

'You don't care who sees you?' he said.

'They all know.'

'I'm still married.'

'They all know that too. '

They drove back to Newry. It was the first cold day of the year, squalls of hail blowing through the gap in the mountains that marked the frontier to the south. They drove down into Newry and across the quays, dockers bent with coal sacks over their heads against the sleet and soaked tinker children gathering the spilled coals by hand, smoke from their rain-damped fires wreathing in the dark and making of it a scene of labour from some benighted olden city.

'You could be back in the dark ages,' Margaret said.

'You get that feeling in the courtroom. Something's not right about the whole thing.'

'Let the town deal with it in its own way,' she said.

'Even if McGladdery's innocent?'

'You're a brave boy to come talking about innocence in this town.'

'If McGladdery is innocent,' he said, 'and the judge is guilty?'

When they got back to her flat she asked him whether he had ever seen a man hanged. She pressed him for the details, the condemned man's demeanour. She pictured him pale and unearthly.

'They say that women get excited at executions. Is that true? That they experience arousal?' Her detailed clinical talk. 'Experience arousal' – as though it was a procedure to be undergone. She brought him into the bedroom and lay down on the bed. She thrashed and moaned and pushed at his body as if she was trying to divest herself of some old pain.

223

Tuesday 10th October. The Downpatrick Assize resumed at 10 a.m. Judge Curran took the bench. The prosecution admitted into evidence the soiled shortie fawn coat found in the septic tank, along with the other items of clothing. The jacket lay on a table in front of Judge Curran during the day's proceedings, stiff with ingrained ordure from the tank in which it had been suspended. The jurors' eyes were drawn to it. They had the sense that something beyond evil had slipped its bounds in the January night, had walked abroad attired in the putrid garment. The prosecution also produced the dark drape suit that Robert said he had been wearing. They were to put thirteen witnesses in the witness box to testify as to what Robert had been wearing that night.

Maud Wilson, the wife of the caretaker of the Henry Thompson Memorial Hall, said that Robert had been wearing a 'greeny' suit. A machinist, Edith Henry, said that Robert had been wearing a 'dark' suit. Shop assistant Maureen Matier said that the suit McGladdery had been wearing was 'darker' than the one in court.

Teddy Cowan said that Robert was wearing a 'fawn shortie overcoat', and that 'his suit was light blue'. Heather Sybil-Kenny, described as a linen designer, said that Robert was wearing a 'chocolate-brown shortie overcoat with leather buttons' and a 'watery-blue suit much lighter than the one in court'. Patrick Morrow also said that the suit McGladdery was wearing was 'much lighter' than the one in court.

The prosecution strategy was to prove that Robert was telling lies when he said that he had been wearing a black suit. The jury would be asked to conclude that he had been wearing a light-blue suit and had concealed that fact because the suit was probably bloodstained and had been concealed or destroyed.

Esther Henning said that Robert was wearing a light-coloured suit. Samuel Moffit said that he had seen a man skulking in the bushes outside the front door where bicycles were left. A bicycle had been stolen that night and it was suggested that the killer had used it to get to Damolly Cross where he lay in wait for Pearl. Moffit said that he thought the skulking man was wearing a 'gaberdine coat'.

Brown cross-examined each of the thirteen witnesses. He suggested that they might be mistaken. He was soft-spoken, apologetic. He tried to prise them away from hard-won certainties. He knew how difficult this thing was, this bearing of witness, learning to address the picked-over artefacts of Pearl's last hours, the allusive nature of this midwinter dance in what now seemed a far-off province of the night, the death-haunted hours in the Orange hall.

'That doesn't feel right either,' McCrink said outside. He stood on the pavement with Margaret. It was evening, rain blowing down the pavement, coal smoke in the air, cheap imported aggregate that tainted the rain.

'What's wrong?'

'They all remember too clearly. Eye-witnesses aren't usually that reliable.'

'You think they've been put up to it?'

'I don't think so. But sometimes people remember what they think they should remember.'

They stood in the rain, pedestrians passing swiftly, their heads down beneath umbrellas and hats, their faces strained.

After dark Hughes and Robert would lie awake talking. They spoke softly so that the guards would not hear them. They talked about things they remembered from their childhood, the retold stories that were like objects handled and worn smooth. Enduring lights-out intimacies. This Robert was different, Hughes said afterwards. He would listen to Hughes, be attentive to the material, the dense contoured narratives of childhood. Robert told him about Will Copeland. The way they were friends. Blood brothers. It was the way men did things, Robert said. They saw the lifelong in things, the lasting companionships.

'He'll see me right,' Robert said, 'all the stuff we done together. We were blood brothers.'

'I hear tell he's being called by the prosecution,' Hughes said. 'I wouldn't put the house on him backing you.'

'The truth will come out, you'll see,' Robert said. He was that sure of himself, you'd of believed him, Hughes said afterwards. He kept saying that all he had to do was get up on the stand.

In later years Hughes would come back to these nights. He said they were like men from the past telling stories by firelight, the murmured yarns, passing tales one to the other as keepsakes, the handed-down wisdom of their race.

~

On the third day of the trial the prosecution focused further on the events of the night. Gladys Jones, an officer in the Rangers, took the stand first. She described how she had seen Robert dancing with Pearl.

226

'I remember the second time, McGladdery was trying to hold Pearl tightly towards him and had his head bent down towards her face. She kept turning her head away from him.'

Brown asked her how many times Robert had danced with Pearl. She replied two or three times.

'Pretty, dark-haired' Joan Donergan was called to the stand. She was asked what Robert had been wearing. She said he had been wearing a 'shortie fawn overcoat'. Brown cross-examined her. He asked her when she had first seen Robert. She said that she had first seen him in the entrance hall where he had 'picked her up and swung her off her feet'. Brown asked her how many times she had danced with Robert. She replied that she had danced with him six times.

McCrink started to see another narrative emerging. Robert going to the dance. The way he picked Joan Donergan up and swung her around. It is a good-humoured, flamboyant gesture, the night's bounty in front of you, a pretty girl laughing. He could see Robert smiling and nodding.

But the jury's attention kept returning to the soiled coat on the table in front of the judge's dais. They were still convinced that this was part of the real story. It belonged with the skulked-through bushes outside the hall, the idea that the hall itself represented some kind of waypost on the dire path to the stubble field and Weir's Rock.

Ronnie took the stand. Her eyes were dark with fatigue. She placed her hand on the Bible and spoke the oath. For a moment she seemed lost in recollection. She had been taken to country tent missions when she was a child and it had had no effect on her. She wasn't the religious kind but something of that past was felt in the courtroom when she put her hand on the book, the taking of covenants and saying of psalms, the laying of hands on holy writ and the speaking in tongues. When she spoke her voice had the conviction of scripture. Robert told Hughes that she looked like a different person. The ride of the town, he said, speaking as if from the pulpit, the storyteller transformed by the story.

The jury listened to her. They had seen how Ronnie was dressed when she came into the courtroom. The lipstick that was a shade too bright and the peroxide beehive, the black mascara and the falsies. They disapproved of her to start with until she began to talk, taking them through the night, the last person to speak to Pearl before she met her killer, the dense textured moments. They went along with Ronnie, granted her permission to be garish and overdressed.

She told how she had walked to the hall with Pearl and how Pearl had seemed changed that night, elevated in some way, the swaying walk, eyes downcast, people stepping out of her way as though some court voluptuary came their way.

'They were afraid for to ask her to dance. They couldn't take their eyes off her but they were afeard,' Ronnie said, 'till McGladdery took her up, that is.'

'How many times?'

'Three, I think. The last time I seen him go up to the singer of the band for to request a song.'

'What song did the band play when he came down to ask Miss Gamble to dance for the last time?'

'They played "It's Now or Never".'

The jury looked at each other. The song title implying that Robert had put final terms of some kind to Pearl. The title of the song infused with sexual threat, the libidinous vibrato

228

of Elvis Presley setting down the carnal ultimatum. McCrink could see that Robert was shaking his head.

Ronnie went on to describe how they left the dance at 2.15 a.m. She remembered how cold it was, water frozen in the guttering. The lights were turned off in the Orange hall and they milled around in the lee of the ill-lit venue. This was the hardest part of the night to remember, the Orange hall behind them and the scriptural hall done in red-brick Gothic looming over them. People going off in couples. Not much is being said. All the work has been done in the hall, the lingering glances, the feints. The commerce is in the open now. There is an air of rut about the scene outside. They've got down to the point of the night, the sensuous marrow of it, standing in rows against the back wall of the hall. The tit. The bush. The box. Ronnie is pulled in by McKnight who stands with his back to the railings at the war memorial. She looks up at the bronze putteed infantryman on the plinth, bayonet fixed as though he might lead out an army of the night.

'Where was Pearl at this point?'

'Pearl went up Church Avenue with Joseph Clydesdale.'

'Was he a boyfriend?'

'Pearl didn't have a regular item but you'd miss something if you didn't have a charver of a Saturday night.' A charver. Ronnie dropping into the port town argot, the cant, the garrison slang.

Speers and Johnston had interviewed Clydesdale at length about this episode. Clydesdale did not know what had possessed him to ask Pearl up the Avenue and had assumed she would refuse. But she had gone with him, walking silently alongside. Clydesdale had noticed her make-up and dress, the way it made her look oriental, a figure from the olden times bonded to concubinage or other service.

'I never dared put a hand on her when we got up there,' he said. 'I gave her a kiss on the lips but you wouldn't have dared try nothing.'

There was a pulling back. A drawing together in the matter of self. Clydesdale said that she hardly seemed to be there any more. 'She went quiet on me,' he said, as though a silence had descended like awful night, a hush falling through the memorial oaks and unlit approaches of the Avenue.

After fifteen minutes Pearl and Clydesdale came down Church Avenue. Clydesdale went back to his friends. Ronnie had got a lift for Pearl with two local men, Billy Morton and Derek Chambers. They were joined in Morton's Ford by Pearl's cousin, Evelyn Gamble, and Rae Boyd. Chambers and Morton in the front seat and the four girls squeezed into the back. The car full of Saturday-night banter. Ronnie getting stick for the beard rash on her chin. Pearl crushed up against the pressed-steel bulkhead of the car, staring out of the window. Chambers drove carefully, watching out for black ice on the unsalted road, the laden-down Ford going through the gears as it climbed towards Damolly Cross, the other dancers dispersed.

'What happened then?'

'Pearl's house was nearest. We dropped her off at Damolly Cross. That was the last we seen of her.' Ronnie stopped. There was no point in adding any more. She had told the story of Pearl's last moments enough times to know that the ornamentation had fallen away. Her account had a bare, stripped-to-the-bone feel about it.

Ronnie was cross-examined by Brown. The QC had only one question.

'Did you meet another car on Damolly Lane?'

'We did. We met a car coming down the hill just at the bend.'

The prosecution put the other inhabitants of the car on the stand. None of them remembered meeting another car on Damolly Hill.

~

Robert and Will Copeland are missing from the scene outside the hall. In evidence Robert would say that he had waited for Joan Donergan, the pretty dark-haired one, the girl he had danced with six times, but that when she had not appeared he had gone home. The caretaker Wilson said that he had seen McGladdery leave the hall at 2 a.m. Robert maintained that he was there at 2.15 a.m. which would not have given him time to get to Damolly Cross to attack Pearl. Will Copeland's whereabouts were not established.

Twenty

During the trial Judge Curran maintained his routine at the Reform Club. Each night he had dinner alone at the same table in the oak-panelled dining room. The walls were lined with portraits of plumed marshals and viceroys sent out to other lands to rule and gather spoil, and the judge was at home among their melancholy, corrupted faces.

After dinner he played bridge in the members' room or billiards in the billiard room with Ferguson. He did not mention the case. Ferguson did not expect him to. On the evening of the 10th a porter came to the billiard room to say there was a policeman downstairs who wanted to see Ferguson.

Ferguson went down to see the Whiteabbey policeman Rutherford waiting in the foyer. Ferguson took him into an anteroom.

'Your man. McCrink. The Inspector of Constabulary.'

'What about him?'

'He's been visiting Mrs Curran. He's been going up to the mental to see her.'

'Has he now?'

'Talks to her for hours.'

'And does Mrs Curran talk to him?'

'So they tell me. She does have good days and bad days.'

Ferguson returned to the billiard room. Judge Curran stood at the window looking out into the October night, the night's traffic on Royal Avenue below. Ferguson told him what Rutherford had said.

'I will not have my wife troubled in this manner,' Curran said.

'What does he think he's at?' Ferguson said.

'What does a man like that value, Ferguson?'

'I'll find out.'

'Does he have a wife?'

'Used to have. Long gone.'

'Like your own,' Curran said.

'Yes. Like my own.'

'What sort of town is Newry?' Curran said.

'Used to be prosperous but run-down now. They're dealing people. There's many a man would fleece you at a market but they wouldn't turn a hand to do a day's work. Built on a marsh.'

'A marsh?'

'They have a dyke to keep the sea back.'

'Like the Dutch. Except the Dutch are a hard-working, God-fearing people.'

After Doris's incarceration in Holywell Mental Hospital Ferguson had travelled to Rotterdam by ferry with the judge. They had played roulette and pontoon in the saloon of the ship. As they approached the harbour the judge stood on deck. He seemed to approve of the country that he saw. There was a hard-won look to the polder landscapes, the drained flatlands and dykes, the North Sea slobs and bents.

'I have heard that smuggling is rife in the area.' Curran kept his back to the room, staring from the window, contemplating renegade nights on the borderlands, the marsh town reeking of illicit commerce.

'There's not much up there you could put on an affidavit

and bring into court,' Ferguson said. Unless that affidavit was constituted by frontier ordinance and writ.

'A mongrel breed then. Hawkers and pedlars.' Mongrel enough, Ferguson thought, but then you'd wonder if there was a bit of the mongrel in his lordship. Since the murder of Patricia and the sectioning of Doris Curran Ferguson had quietly made enquiries into Curran's background. He had not been able to find out anything about where the judge had been born, or his education. It was Ferguson's experience that when someone's history could not be uncovered it meant that they did not want it to be uncovered. Curran turned back to the room, his face pale and ascetic in the electric light. A member of some wintry cohort ridden down in order to pass judgement.

The judge had conducted the trial according to the book so far, Ferguson thought. A man of law. But Ferguson knew the judge. He was devious and conducted his affairs like a courtier of old. He's got something up his sleeve, Ferguson thought. There was not one shadow of doubt that McGladdery would pay for the happenings of that night nine years before when Curran drove through Whiteabbey in parade with the blood-sodden body of his daughter laid out across his knees. What had Curran said that night in Douglas? 'Justice is a by-product of our system of law, not an end.' If the word mercy had been mentioned that night Ferguson had not heard it.

~

Will Copeland took the stand on the third day of the trial. He had been called by the prosecution and he did not look at Robert as he took the oath. The prosecuting QC took him through the events of 28th January. He confirmed that he had been drinking with Robert during the day and that he had gone back to the house in Damolly with Robert. Copeland's answers had a flat, coached sound. He was asked if he had seen the chest expanders in the house, the bullworker.

'Yes. Robert showed them to me.'

'Did he try them out?'

'Yes.'

'What did he do?'

'He put his foot through one of the handles and pulled the other handle up towards his face.'

'Did the chest expanders slip at any stage and strike Robert in the face?'

'I didn't see the bullworker slip.'

'Did you notice any marks on the defendant's hands?'

'There was nothing wrong with his hands.' It was the first time Copeland looked at Robert. Nothing more than a glance. McCrink wondered if anyone else had seen it. It was the kind of look he was used to from the London assizes, the Monday morning processional of pickpockets and call girls, a slippery and faithless glance.

'What did the defendant do before you left the house?'

'He changed the dark suit he had been wearing. He removed the garments he had been wearing that day.'

'The dark suit?'

'Yes. He removed the dark suit and put on a light-coloured suit along with a red-and-black tie and a light-coloured shortie jacket.'

'Did he offer you anything?'

'No.'

'The defendant didn't offer you any item of clothing?'

'No. I proceeded to the dance at the Memorial Orange Hall wearing the clothing I put on that morning.'

The QC took Copeland through the events of the evening. He said he had seen Robert dancing with Pearl.

'How many times?'

'Approximately three times.' *Proceeded. Approximately. Garments.* Policeman's language, McCrink thought. Copeland on the stand using flat copper's lingo. He could see Johnston watching the witness from the public gallery, the sergeant wearing civilian clothes, a suit with a broad check so that he looked like a reprobate vaudevillian, a sheen of sweat on his face, his small eyes fixed on Copeland.

'When was the last time you saw McGladdery?'

'I seen McGladdery dancing with Miss Gamble at approximately 12.30 a.m. He then proceeded to the bandstand and asked the band leader to play a popular song that had been in the music charts.'

'What was that song?'

'The song was called "It's Now or Never".'

McCrink saw Robert write something on a piece of paper and push it across the table to Brown. His face was white. It was late in the day and the dark was closing in and Robert's face stood out in the penal gloom of the courtroom like that of a medieval sinner who awaited the penitential fire and the jury looked back at him and their faces seemed to suggest that if fire was required then they would deliver him to it.

'Where did Mr McGladdery go then?'

'I don't know where he went.'

'You didn't see him again that evening?'

'I don't know where he went.'

*

Brown cross-examined Copeland. He asked him again whether he had borrowed any clothes from Robert. He asked him if it was true that he often borrowed clothes from Robert. The King's Road shirts and crêpe-soled shoes, the fancy London duds. Robert strutting down Merchants Quay with that out-of-town look to him. Suggesting that Will was jealous of Robert, the big-city mannerisms and the fancy talk he came out with, the West End patois picked up on Dean Street and Berwick Street.

'Where were you in the two days following the murder?' Brown asked.

'What?' It was the first time McCrink had seen Copeland rattled.

'You weren't seen in your usual haunts.' Copeland hadn't been seen in the British Legion. He hadn't been to Mervyn Graham's gym. He hadn't played darts in Hollywood's or stood with the unemployed men outside the dole office on Bridge Street. Brown listing the places Copeland normally frequented, letting the jury know what they were dealing with here, lives adrift in the snooker halls and no-hope bars of run-down, provincial towns, prey to bad faith and lack of fidelity. Copeland not seen in these slouched-through land-marks for forty-eight hours after the murder.

There was a lull in proceedings while the Attorney General debated points of law with the judge. The courtroom was whitewashed and the October sun shone through the windows high in the wall above the public gallery, dust motes floating in the air. Robert leaned over to his QC and whispered, 'It's like High Noon or something in here.'

237

Robert read crime fiction during lulls in the trial, or when he was waiting to be returned to Crumlin Road prison. He swapped books with the QC, Brown, who liked Westerns and who seemed to understand the rarefied fictions that are sometimes required to get you through a difficult time, and nodded at Robert to show that he was happy to go along with the motif.

Robert was a fan of Western films and imagined that he could detect a pioneer seriousness in proceedings. He could see himself as a dusty loner, a slouch-hatted fatalist who knew a bad end when he saw one. Matters brought to a head in a plank-built courthouse on the outskirts of town. He wanted to adopt a posture of gruff fortitude in the face of the townspeople who made up the jury. There were accommodations which had to be made in the end, and he knew what was needed to impress a jury of shopkeepers and saloon-owners. They were clapboard stoics with limited time for his high plains drama.

The final prosecution witness was the pathologist who had made the link between the shape of the shoemaker's file and the wounds on Pearl's body. He had also examined the copy of The Long Wait which had similar puncture wounds in the back cover. The pathologist pointed out the shape of the file, related it to the unusual shape of the wounds on Pearl's body.

The scientist described the shape of the shoemaker's file and the star-shaped puncture it caused. He held the book in his right hand and the file in his left as though he were weighing them one against the other. Pointing out the hasp of the file, the way it found purchase on the welt of the boot. The jury swayed by the pathologist's mastery of the everyday qualities of the tool, the way he was able to use the journeyman vocabularies.

In later years the pathologist was to talk about the 'break-through' when it was pointed out that the wounds on Pearl's body were the same size and shape as the indentations in the paperback. You get the impression that the marks in the book started to take on more significance than the wounds on the body. The prosecution was able to imply that Robert had practised his stabbing technique on the book at home, which implied premeditation. But more than that it appears that Robert's story, in the mind of the jury and of the public, had merged with that of the hunted couple on the cover, the faithless girl and the struggling man in a fix of their own making.

'So much for blood brothers,' Hughes said when Robert was returned to his cell that night. 'Copeland has you done up like a turkey for his lordship.'

'He's been brainwashed,' Robert said, 'they've got into his head. He didn't look like himself.'

Robert had read about such things. There were implants they put in your skull so that they could make you do what they wanted with radio signals. The way they talked was a giveaway. They spoke in flat, robotic voices. He'd read about the Chinese in Korea. Prisoners transmitting through tinny loudspeakers at night.

'You only had to listen to him,' Robert said, 'but I don't pay no mind to them anyhow.'

'Why's that?'

'I'm up on Monday. I'll lay it all out for them. They'll have it on a plate.'

Have your head on a plate, Hughes thought to himself.

Twenty-One

Margaret didn't like dancing. The Friday evening of the trial McCrink took her to Henry T's on Hill Street. She sat at a table off to the side drinking gin and watching the girls dance in the dresses they'd bought in C&A. Margaret had taken to wearing flat shoes, slacks and cable-knit jumpers. The clothes emphasised her loping walk, made her look sexless and eager.

The dancing girls carried gloves and patent-leather handbags, their hair shaped into beehives, the smell of Silvikrin hanging in the air.

'I keep expecting to see you in a nudist magazine,' McCrink told her, 'you and a bunch of humourless Aryans, playing volleyball in your pelt.'

Outside they waited for a taxi in Margaret Square. They were the only people at the rank, the traffic sparse, tyres hissing in the rain. A ragged troupe of tinkers moved through the square and then were gone. Across the road a Teddy boy had backed a girl up against the wall. He had his hand between her legs. He was talking to her as he fondled her, easing her into the territory, the roughshod terrain, the taste of tobacco on his lips and the wall pressing into her back. The man stopped talking. The girl opened her eyes and looked at Margaret.

'You want to take notes or something?' she said.

When they got back to her flat she opened a bottle of Gordon's. She looked pale.

'I can't believe the way that girl talked to me,' she said.

'Forget about it,' McCrink said. She poured a glass of the Gordon's and drank it down without tonic.

'You'd like me to forget about it, wouldn't you? You'd let a slut talk to me like that in the street.' The Newry accent coming out, like something that seeped from the fen the town was built on, a marsh stink rising upwards.

'Don't drink any more of that.'

'I'll drink what I like. Why didn't you arrest the knacker bitch, Mr Policeman?' Her eyes were glittering and she was moving her hands in a wringing motion, working her way into it, finding the unstable rhythms, her sentences staccato, spat-out.

'You could have me put away. I'd be like a suffragette. You'd have me like Mrs Pankhurst in Wormwood Scrubs with a feeding tube down my throat.'

'That's enough.' He felt that he'd found himself adrift in a mad devising of the town. He imagined cracked laughter, scurrying feet outside the window.

'People won't talk to you in this town. They know what you are. They can smell a uniform coming a mile away.'

'Margaret, please.'

'Take me away from this town. Isn't that what they say? Or take me somewhere. Take me to the pictures. Take me for a drive.'

'It's the middle of the night.'

'Then talk to me.'

'I'm trying to talk to you.'

'You aren't really. We don't have much in common, you and me. The detective washed up in a dead-end job and the provincial librarian, unwed and unwanted.'

'We have plenty in common.'

'We have one thing in common.'

'Don't.'

'I see. You want me with my mouth shut and my legs open.'

'Don't be crude.'

'I'm not being crude. I'm just being truthful. You'd rather I just stayed on my back. It's my best side. Everybody says so.'

'Don't get hysterical on me.'

'I'm not hysterical. Is that the best you can do? Is that supposed to be the crushing retort, Eddie? If that doesn't work then get the truncheons out, the handcuffs?'

In the end she fell asleep on the sofa. She lay on her back, her feet together, looking like something from the early church, pale, martyred. She woke at four o'clock.

'I'm sorry,' she said, 'it happens like that sometimes.'

'What happens?'

'They said I had a breakdown. In my twenties. They gave me ECT. Wired to the mains for my own good.'

The rubber gag between the teeth, the duress to the body, the back arched, the heels drumming. He took her hand.

'Did you?'

'What?'

'Have a breakdown?'

'I don't think so. I went a bit off the rails is all. They had me committed. The doctors signed the forms. That was it. When I got out they gave me the job in the library. Told me to stay put.'

McCrink knowing he wasn't getting the full truth. Knowing that wasn't the way the town worked. The story had to be pieced together, dredged out of the alluvial mud and silt.

~

On Saturday morning he left her sleeping and drove to Castlereagh. McCrink went down to the archive, showing his warrant card at the door. The door was unlocked and he went in. He realised that these rooms were the heart of the place he had found himself in. Deep in the earth, temperature-controlled. Thousands of lives archived and stored in grey metal filing cabinets. People who saw themselves as ordinary were transformed by the process of having their lives examined, their mail opened, photographs taken without their knowledge. The dense, storied matter of their lives was acknowledged in this place. Their importance in the scheme of things was recognised. The act of watching made their lives shadowed things. Nuances were teased out. The unexplained was given its full weight.

He requisitioned her Special Branch file. Margaret had been seen at meetings of the Communist Party and other political events held in Christian Science halls and second-hand bookshops with posters of revolutionary leaders on the wall. He realised that she had always been drawn to the illicit. She had always held secret positions within their relationship. He could imagine her sitting on a folding chair among the trade unionists and Trotskyites. Intense men with enamelled lapel badges. He could see her among their dreams of upheaval. Her earnest face. Her furtive heart at home with the dogmas, the tendencies, the schisms.

Her father had been a trade-union official. She had been photographed marching through the town with her father and other trade unionists, seeing themselves as figures in history, marching alongside the work-booted radicals of long ago. The men who had accepted invitations to the Soviet Union and East Germany. You could see it in their faces. That they'd toured the tractor factories and fraternal institutes. That they had hearkened to the East's dour and smoky hymnal.

He saw they were lost in some deep human need for the clandestine, the secret muster, gathered in the dark. To imagine themselves among companions, keepers of the secret.

Margaret had kept a flat in the University area where she attended political meetings in the students' union. There were photographs of her leaving a Socialist Party meeting. There were several men around her. They were bearded, one of them wearing a beret. They were going for the dissident look, the breakaway radical. Trying to persuade the world that they had set up a liberation front. They saw themselves in historic terms as exiled radicals, plotters on the margin. Two of the group were named in the file as security service informers. Several of them had been seen in known homosexual haunts, gents' toilets and canal banks. McCrink wondered which one she had been sleeping with. He knew she liked danger, the threat of discovery.

Her admission to Downshire Hospital was noted, and the length of her treatment. It was noted that she had been released 'into the care of her parents' and that 'no further subversive contacts were observed'.

McCrink pulled Speers's file. There were details of assignations with other men's wives, a tawdry subtext running through a steady career ascent. The ascent had stopped in 1955. Speers had been found in a hotel in Bangor with an underage girl. 'No further action' was taken. No further action needed to be taken, McCrink thought. Speers would do what he was told.

Agnes spent the trial in a state of bewilderment. She saw her so-called friends from the newspapers in the press gallery but they would not meet her eye. They put her aside like any worn thing. She wished to ask the police and lawyers about what occurred in the courtroom and what was her role as a mother but they would not answer. They acted like they were the owners of the whole world but they weren't because she had her place too. There was more than one tale to tell of the fate of Pearl Gamble. There was a man sat across from her who was in the papers to do with the case. She asked the usher who he was and the usher said that is McCrink, Her Majesty's Inspector of Constabulary. Agnes saw him outside the court with the Mackin girl from the library. He'd do well to do some inspecting in that department and then he wouldn't look so full of himself.

They said they were going to put her on the stand to talk about suits but then they didn't. That sergeant, Johnston, had come to the house looking for a light suit but she said Robert did not own a light suit but only a dark one. We'll see about that was all he said with a smile on his face that was like the gleam from a plate on a coffin lid. Afterwards in Newry court-house she heard the Crown solicitor saying that they wished her to be declared a hostile witness. Yes, she wanted to say, I am a hostile witness when you come to my house and turn it upside down. He might have been a trial to me and a harsh gift from a father who turned his back but I would not have him prey to a man the like of Johnston.

Sometimes when she saw him in the dock it was like she was seeing him for the first time, not a man like he thought himself but a little boy like when he would swim in the pool at Warrenpoint and say look at me Ma look at me. She wished with all her might that when he went to London he had stayed there not come back to a town of decay.

Robert was sat up in the dock trying to put the smart head on him like he understood what was going on. She knew from the start he was in for a fall. Her heart forbode her when she heard he was to be put on the stand. Robert could not stop himself. He had to know how things worked and he had to act like he knew it all. As well as that he had that white face on him that you seen when he was about to have one of them headaches. Agnes could see that the prosecutor was a man like an icy knife and besides there was the judge sat on his bench like a man from the testament who puts his hand in the fire but burneth not.

~

The courtroom was full to capacity on Monday morning. It was known that Robert would take the stand. He was to be cross-examined for seven hours. The night before Hughes had seen Robert sitting on his bunk with his head in his hands. Hughes had asked him what was wrong and Robert had said it was nothing. Nevertheless the next morning Hughes said there wasn't much sign of the big courtroom lawyer. There wasn't much old chat out of him that morning, Hughes said, and a big white face on him fit to put the frights on you. You would of felt sorry for him.

Robert was escorted to the witness box by an usher and the oath was administered. It was a moment he'd read about a hundred times in crime novels. The innocent man faces down his accusers. The truth, the whole truth. Putting one hand on the Bible and raising the other. He wanted everyone to see the importance of it, the idea of a vow taken, a man sworn before his fellows. But the Bible was a grubby and stained paperback, and the usher muttered. His own voice sounded cracked and unconvincing. He felt as if he was outside his body watching himself take the oath.

From the start the story was going in a different direction. He didn't recognise himself as the figure that began to emerge from the prosecution case, the night stalker, the unsated abroad in the dark. How he had befriended Pearl, danced with her.

'You asked for "It's Now or Never". That was your request for a dance with Miss Gamble?'

'I never asked that. I asked for "Chattanooga Choo Choo", but they didn't have it.' Everything coming out of his mouth seemed unconvincing, their version of the night gaining in the telling. She turned you down. You were enraged. You swore to get your revenge on her.

'Why were there marks on your hands?' the judge asked suddenly. Robert was confused. He didn't know that the judge was allowed to ask questions like that. Curran demanded that he demonstrate the shoemaker's grip on the instrument. Robert seeing the way the jury was looking at him, approving of the judge's line of questioning, the miscreant made to account for himself.

'Everybody knows that a cobbler gets marks on his hands.' He could see Mervyn in the public gallery and wanted to get him up on the stand to tell them that. He wanted Mervyn to hold up his shoemaker's hands, scarred and notched with tool-marks. But it was too late.

'What happened to the files you bought that afternoon?'

'I want to explain that later on. It's important I don't tell you now.'

He could see Agnes watching from the gallery. He could see that look on her face that said you're trying to be too smart, son, as usual. Tell the man what he needs to know. Part of him wanted to admire the story that was emerging from the cross-examination, the jury being guided towards the old tales, the fireside tellings of the innocent and the guilty.

It was mid-afternoon before they came to the matter of what he had been wearing that night, the suit, and the shortie jacket laid out on the evidence table, the sleeves crooked and the shoulders hunched. Robert was still struggling to get back to the testimony he had imagined giving, the dense, scripted moments. He felt harried. He couldn't gather his thoughts. Sometimes a question had been put to him two or three times before he answered. The night of the murder itself starting to slip away as the prosecution closed in on the matter of what Robert had been wearing.

'Why did you ask the police for thirty-six hours to turn up the light-coloured suit?'

'I lent the suit to Will. I wanted to ask him about what had happened to it.'

'What about the jacket?'

'That's the whole thing. I left the jacket in the cloakroom at the hall. When I went to get it, it was gone. It was either stole or Will took it on me. He kept saying how much he liked it. I needed to get talking to him, but I couldn't when the peelers were following me around all the time.'

McCrink could see that the jury didn't believe him. That they thought he was trying to shift the blame onto Copeland.

'The files. That's what I wanted to say earlier, the shoe-making files were in the pocket of the coat. That's why you couldn't find them in the house.'

Robert looked from face to face. He realised what had happened. He could see the character he had become in their eyes. The rat. The weasel. The man who would do anything to get out of a fix. Gibbering in the shadow of the noose. The courtroom was silent. He looked up and saw 'pretty' Joan Donergan in the public gallery. He wanted to tell them again about how he had picked her up and swung her around. How they all wanted to dance with him that night, how he made them feel fleet and graceful. The questions kept coming. Did he hide the bundle of clothes in the septic tank behind the house? Did he lie in wait for Pearl? Robert blurted out answers, contradicted himself. The mouth that was doing the talking seemed to belong to someone else.

Brown asked him about the river incident. Robert told him how Johnston had put the gun to his head, the threat to 'blow his fucking brains out'. The wording sounding improbable, some desperado phrase from a film.

In the end there was unease about Robert's testimony. He did not show himself to be a model citizen. His explanations of what had happened to the clothing seemed far-fetched. But his denials of involvement in the death of Pearl Gamble were vehement and repeated. 'I had nothing to do with it.' 'I didn't kill her.' 'It wasn't me.' During a cross-examination lasting almost seven hours, Robert did not crack, and Attorney General Brian McGuinness was unable to make any serious inroads into his defence.

Twenty-Two

On Monday afternoon both counsels delivered their closing statements. The prosecution went back over the main points of their case. McGuinness admitted that the evidence against the defendant was all circumstantial, but was 'none the worse for that'. The shoemaker's file bought in Woolworths, the witnesses who testified as to what McGladdery had been wearing. The jury were reminded that Pearl 'had been known' to McGladdery before that night. He conjured up the picture of the accused practising his stabbing technique on the copy of the Mickey Spillane novel The Long Wait. He invited them to recognise the type. McGladdery was a drifter, a no-good, a corner boy who had tried to shift the blame for his crime to his friend. Pearl had rejected his advances that night and he had lain in wait for her at Damolly Cross, beaten, stabbed and strangled her. McGuinness dwelt on Pearl's nakedness, the stripped remains, eyes opened to the unholy night, her nude, violated stare.

Brown's defence was measured. The evidence against McGladdery was all circumstantial. Each strand of the prosecution case was open to interpretation. The witnesses were not consistent as to what the defendant had been wearing. A hand other than Robert's could have placed the bundle of clothes in the septic tank. Robert had only met Pearl in passing as a child – he did not know her. The marks in the paperback were not proof of a stabbing technique being 'practised'. There was no fingerprint or forensic evidence. No eye-witness testimony as to Robert's presence at the murder scene. Robert's explanation as to what had happened to his shortie jacket was plausible. Despite Robert's demeanour in the witness box it was possible that Will Copeland or someone else had taken the jacket from the cloakroom at the Orange hall that night.

Brown made much of the river incident. Was it believable that the police had taken the defendant into Corry Square so that his clothes could dry? He could have dried his clothes at home, or changed into fresh clothes. Brown said that the jury must believe Robert's story about being interrogated by teams of detectives until late at night. If they had lied about that, what else had they lied about? What stealthy hand had placed the bundle of clothing in the septic tank?

With regard to the evidence of what Robert had been wearing, Brown pointed out that the lights in the hall had been low during the dance, and that the air was full of cigarette smoke. That it was possible for certain materials to shimmer and appear lighter than they actually were. He said that eye-witnesses were often mistaken, even multiple eye-witnesses, not that they were lying but that they were drawn into the current of a story and their accounts were shaped by it unbeknownst to themselves.

Brown told the jury that the night yielded up more than one version of events. Could anyone have carried Pearl over half a mile from Damolly Cross to Weir's Rock? He reminded the jury about the car that Ronnie Whitcroft had seen driving towards Damolly Cross as she was driven back down the hill.

Brown closed on the matter of motive. Pearl was only one

of a number of girls that Robert had danced with that night. Despite what the prosecution had said, he barely knew her. One witness had suggested some discord between them when they danced, but no one else had noticed anything. Robert's attention seemed to have been focused on Joan Donergan. Much weight had been placed on the request for the Elvis Presley song 'It's Now or Never', allegedly requested by Robert for his final dance with Pearl. But Robert had in fact asked for a different song. The marks on Robert's hands were consistent with the use of a shoemaker's file. The marks on his face tallied with his assertion that there had been an accident with the bullworker.

During both closing statements Robert seemed dreamy and absent. He did not look at either counsel, or at the jury.

On 17th October 1961, the second last day of Robert's trial, a petty thief, James Hanratty, was arrested in Liverpool and charged with murder. On 22nd August Michael Gregston had been sitting in a car with Valerie Storie at a layby on the A6 when they were approached by a man wearing a black suit. After abducting the couple and forcing them to drive around Berkshire for several hours, the man shot Gregston, raped and then shot Storie, who was crippled but survived. Hanratty was picked out of an identity parade by Storie after each of the men on the identity parade repeated the phrase used by the murderer, 'Be quiet, will you, I'm thinking.'

Despite a lack of forensic evidence and strong alibi evidence, Hanratty was found guilty and sentenced to death in what became known as the A6 murder case. He would be scheduled to hang on 22nd February 1962.

There was widespread disquiet following the conviction. The case of Ruth Ellis was referred to. Ruth Ellis was a nightclub hostess who had been convicted of shooting and killing her lover, David Blakely, outside the Magdala public house in Hampstead on 10th April 1955. Ellis admitted to the murder during unsupervised police interrogation and in reply to a direct question from prosecution counsel during her trial. Shortly before her execution she was visited by the Bishop of Stepney, Joost de Blank. He repeated the phrase she used. 'It is quite clear to me that I was not the person who shot him. When I saw myself with the revolver I knew I was another person.'

Despite her admission of guilt, doubts persisted about the quality of the police evidence and the ability of Ellis, whose hands had been damaged by rheumatic fever as a child, to fire six accurate shots from the heavy Smith & Wesson revolver. Twenty-eight-year-old Ellis was hanged at Holloway prison on 13th July 1955 by Albert Pierrepoint.

Threads of petty thievery and vice run through both accounts. Ellis had given birth to children by two different fathers. She worked as a nightclub hostess. Hanratty was a petty criminal and car thief. Gregston and Storie had been conducting an affair when their car was approached in the dark approaches to Shepperton village. Storie was subject to a violent assault before she was shot and left for dead.

There were shadowy figures in each background. Ellis said in the days before her execution that she had been driven to the Magdala pub by a friend called Cussen who had then given her the weapon. Her solicitor, whom she later dismissed, was a friend of Cussen's. Observers were puzzled as to why, when she confessed her guilt under questioning by prosecution counsel, she used the exact form of words that would guarantee a conviction for murder rather than manslaughter and so put her on a path to the scaffold. Ellis was also friendly with the procurer Stephen Ward, who ten years later was a central figure in the Profumo scandal.

A world of fences, half-alibis, small-time roguery. Girls who worked as hostesses in seedy nightclubs. The Black Cat. The Magdala. There was a feeling that they still operated within the confines of wartime shortages. Much of their lives had an improvised feel to it. They had been brought up in the era of rationing and post-war shortages and they hungered for the threadbare glamour on offer. They appeared in the News of the World, brazen, no better than they should be. They bring to mind the photograph of Myra Hindley, the sluttish mouth and brassy unrepentant stare.

Observers at McGladdery's trial said that he did not seem to be fully aware of what was happening to him. There is a theme of absence running through these cases, people inattentive to their own cause. Ellis, Hanratty and McGladdery. In each case they seem complicit in their own downfall.

That night when Robert was taken back to Crumlin Road, Hughes was waiting for him with a torn-out front page from the Telegraph.

'They commuted Bratty,' he said, 'detention at Her Majesty's pleasure.'

'It doesn't matter,' Robert said, 'it's too late for me anyhow.'

~

The following day was set aside for Judge Curran's summing-up and the beginning of the jury's deliberations. McCrink took his place early in the public gallery. A verdict was not expected that day. There was a sense of the court ceremonials coming into their own as the verdict approached. The ill-fitting wigs and shabby gowns. The archaic commands. The words of condemnation given their due weight. Lance Curran had prepared extensive notes and he read from them in a monotone, moving through each aspect of the case and giving it due weight. At first Robert appeared to be following him, but after a while he drifted off. The details of the case were like something that had happened to someone else a long time ago. A dusty, archived murder. Something you read about in an old newspaper you found lining a drawer, Judge Curran being meticulous, dry as a bone, working his way through the forensics, the time of death, the body temperatures. McCrink saw him looking up at Robert at that point, staring at him over the top of his glasses. McCrink sat up. Malice hanging like ectoplasm in the silent courtroom. Patricia Curran and Pearl Gamble. McCrink shivered. He felt as if cold nineteen-year-old hands were drawing him downwards into some elaborate devising of the underworld. Judge Curran started to deal with the dry clothes incident which Brown had made much of in his closing arguments.

'Before you would agree there is any knavery on the part of the police force you will want strong evidence and not merely the say-so of a man charged by this court.'

Curran moved on to the issue of what Robert had been wearing on the night of the murder.

'Thirteen witnesses said that McGladdery wore a light-blue suit. You will be very slow to say they were all mistaken.'

McCrink saw the barrister Brown half-rise to his feet as Curran was speaking, then sink back into his seat.

Judge Curran finished his summing-up by reminding the jury that they must deliver a unanimous verdict and they withdrew to the jury room. Forty minutes later, they were back.

McCrink had met Speers and Johnston in the foyer outside the courtroom.

'He sabotaged McGladdery's case,' McCrink said, 'the judge deliberately pulled the rug out from under him.'

'It wasn't much of a case to begin with, the murdering little shit,' Johnston said, 'the fatherless little fuck.'

'Who put the clothes in the tank?' McCrink said.

'The jury will tell you that, and that's not going to take them long by the look of it,' Speers said. 'The clothes were in the tank. This town takes care of its own.'

'And who takes care of you?' McCrink said. 'I saw your branch file. The hotel in Bangor? That's enough for them to own you for the rest of your natural life. I know the way it works.'

'You and McGladdery's got something in common, you know that?' Johnston said. 'You come back here in your fancy London duds and act the big shot. We took McGladdery down and we'll take you down too.'

'That's enough, Sergeant,' Speers said, 'let me talk to the inspector.'

McCrink and Speers faced each other in the court foyer.

'Maybe you'd like to go outside and express your reservations about McGladdery to Mrs Gamble out there,' Speers said. 'Do you remember going to that house?'

'You decided McGladdery was guilty and went after him

on that basis. You never looked at anyone else.'

'It's up to the jury to decide if he's innocent or guilty.'

'No it's not. You and Judge Curran already decided.'

'Do you know what you should do? Go home out of this and get your own house in order. See to that woman of yours, the librarian. Maybe you'll look after her better than you did the last one.'

McCrink looked up to see the court ushers move among the people in the foyer informing them that the jury had come back. He started to walk towards the courtroom and found himself face to face with Agnes McGladdery. She was wearing a yellow dress and her make-up was garish; she resembled a forlorn Pierrot, a face turned to the crowd in lurid woe. The ushers were telling people to take their seats in the courthouse and McCrink saw the judge's tipstaff slip through his chamber door like a man who knew that bad tidings were at hand. Brown was talking to the solicitor Luke Curran and shaking his head. McCrink knew that a jury out for such a short time was not a good sign. At the courtroom door Mervyn caught McCrink by the arm.

'What's happening, Mr McCrink? It's all changed.' There was a sense of something long-incubated coming to pass, plans come to fruition. McCrink wondered how much of it led back to the judge's door. Speers and Johnston went into the court-room in front of him, followed by the robed and bewigged attendants of the prosecution, the court ushers and tipstaffs.

~

Years later one of the jurors, Jack Landelis, described what had happened in the jury room. 'I took an A4 sheet of paper and tore it into twelve pieces and passed it around. I says, on that piece of paper write either guilty or not guilty, and then we'll start discussing it.'

From Landelis's account there did not appear to be any deliberation at all over any aspect of the evidence. There would not have been time for any deliberation. The jury returned with a verdict forty minutes after retiring. Each piece of paper carried a guilty verdict. Later in the interview Landelis discusses McGladdery's demeanour in court. 'He didn't come across as a goody two-shoes,' he says, and laughs.

Contemporary accounts of the McGladdery case report the guilty finding and the sentence of death passed on Robert McGladdery by Judge Curran. Curran asks if there is any reason 'why judgement of death and execution should not now be awarded to you'.

Robert replies, 'There's a whole lot of things I could say, but it wouldn't make any difference. I understand that your Honour has a duty to perform, but there is no man in this court who can say I murdered Pearl Gamble for I didn't. I am innocent of the crime.'

The coverage is muted, carried on the inside pages of the newspapers, reported as second or third item on the radio news. Compared to the coverage of the investigation the guilty verdict was low-key, the newspaper accounts faltering when it came to the sentencing. McGladdery pale and guilty in the dock, the sentence handed down, Lance Curran placing the square of black silk on his head to pronounce the death penalty, scenes that appeared to come to them out of the past, the flickering melodramas of early cinema.

Both Curran and McGladdery seem aware that the moment should not be understated, that a level of the high-flown is required, that in the face of last things, a certain amount of formal rhetoric is acceptable.

You are reminded of the cover of the Mickey Spillane novel found in Robert's room, the man struggling with his bonds, his eyes fixed on the faithless woman.

However, once Robert had spoken he sat down again and seemed to take no more interest in proceedings. Observers in the public gallery remarked on his apparent lack of emotion.

That night people gathered on high streets to see the images of the case. It was the start of the era of mass production of televisions and the sets were made available through high-street outlets. There was a feeling that the new medium would know how to address the verdict and sentencing. People stood rapt, watching the silent footage of McGladdery being escorted from Downpatrick courthouse into a prison van. There was some kind of high-spec theatrics at work in the televisual images. Through the transmission static there was a burnish on the scene, a futurist hue.

When the coverage cut away to the murder scene at Weir's Rock, it had the eerie look of studio-lit fictions. People understood that new truths were being made available to them. The world of rumoured happenings, sightings, half-truths, the allusive and fleeting values of the medium.

McCrink stopped at the Ardmore Hotel on his way into Newry. Margaret was waiting for him. They watched the news in the television lounge. The hotel looked across to Damolly and they could see the street lights along the terrace of mill houses where Agnes McGladdery lived, the stubble field and Weir's Rock rising up in the darkness where the lights ended.

'The execution date has been fixed for the 7th November, but McGladdery has appealed,' McCrink said.

'I wonder what his mother's thinking now,' Margaret said.

'Brown has a few weeks to prepare for the Court of Appeal. If that fails then the only other option is an appeal for clemency to Brian Faulkner.'

'Will any of it work?'

'They commuted Bratty. They won't want to commute another one. And there's something else.'

'What?'

'Curran.' The judge pronouncing sentence. The judge taking the blood that was owed him.

'What are you going to do?'

'The judge sabotaged McGladdery. I'm going to sabotage the judge.'

'You can't do that. You know the place you're in.'

Nyuk. The town of thieves. McCrink drove home to Rostrevor past the old counting house. The tinkers were awake. You could see shapes against the firelight. They never sleep. They wander lost through their own narrative. They are night's children. No one knows them.

Twenty-Three

McCrink parked a hundred yards from the entrance to the Glen and walked to the gates. On the way the car radio had forecast gale-force westerlies. The waves were coming over the low sea wall opposite the gates to the Curran house. Seaweed and shingle had been carried over the wall onto the roadway, and the wind whipped the bare trees on the shore side, broken branches littering the pavement, the night in disarray.

Once McCrink had stepped through the gates of the Glen, the wind died a little. He walked up the driveway, glancing into the trees. The place where Patricia Curran's body had been found. You felt as if there was a storybook evil abroad in the tree shadows. A killing from the Carpathians or some other remote and mountainous province. He could see it when he shut his eyes. A community huddled on the edge of a forest. A place of blood feuds. Of wolf-prowled outlands. Old terrors from his childhood returned. He imagined eyes watching him from the trees. He thought of a fabled man-beast from an old book of hours.

The Glen was windowless now, builders' skips and shuttering on the lawns, and it had the look of a theatrical prop, a painted set of a gloomy mansion, put there to further the cause of overwrought fictions. But when McCrink stepped into the hallway he could feel the retained cold in the building, hear his feet on the parquet floor and could remember the way he

261

felt when he stood looking down at the body of Elizabeth Figg in Dukes Meadows and when he had stood at Weir's Rock in the townland of Damolly. This was the place. These were the death-realms. By torchlight he felt his way up the stairway, the brass-bound stair rods loose beneath his feet. On the second turn he looked for the servants' stairway going upwards to the attics and roof spaces, the garret rooms. The narrow stairs took him to the second floor. He opened a small door onto a cor-ridor where the flooring had been lifted so that you had to walk on the bare joists. The roof beams were visible and in places slates had been blown away so that the corridor was exposed to the night. The beams creaked and the slates of the old house shifted against each other. McCrink realised that he was above the room with the bloodstain on the floor, the master bedroom. *Beaten, strangled, stabbed.* Doris Curran had known where she would send him. There was an atmosphere of contrived dread, madwomen abroad on night-time heaths, the sound of the wind rising to a shriek. Doris raised in Broadmoor, the prison for the criminally insane, Doris counsel of the leering mad, guide and mentor to the blasted places of the soul. The box of phone records was where she had said it would be, sitting on the dressing table of the maid's room. McCrink approaching it as though it were a kind of wergild, bounty from a mad-woman's hoard. He lifted it and took it downstairs.

He drove away from Whiteabbey with the box sitting on the passenger seat beside him. He felt as if he had come into posses-sion of the deed and codicils to all the doings of the Currans, a bequest willed onto him out of the rancorous night.

~

McCrink drove to Newry and went to the phone box on Hill Street. He booked a call to Len Barrett at the Express in London. He waited for several minutes to be put through, the call routed through the cross-channel interchanges, listening to the cable hum, lost in the transnational networks. He got through to the Express building and waited on the line for Barrett.

He could hear newsroom noises in the background as he waited on the line. The presses would be turning for the morning editions. He remembered being in the place at night, feeling the whole building move to the vibration of the machinery, the production staff coming and going, chapel heads, masters of print unions, men of conviction and inner strength, burly, shirt-sleeved. Operators of vast and complex printing presses. He looked through the misted windows of the phone box, the street empty at 11.30, the blurred shapes of the mannequins in Foster Newell's window, regret archived on provincial streetscapes.

'Barrett?'

'This is Eddie McCrink.'

'What do you want at this time of night, McCrink?'

'Have you been covering the McGladdery case?'

'Small fry here, I'm afraid. The big news is Hanratty and the A6 murders.'

'I think McGladdery's been stitched up.'

'You'll have to do better than that. Thinking isn't proving. McGladdery's the kind of small-town hood that people like seeing strung up. If they think about McGladdery at all over here, which they don't, it's hang him and good riddance. Even the anti-death penalty crowd would be glad to see the back of him. Gives murderers a bad name.'

'What if I show you something to do with the judge who pronounced sentence on him? He's the father of Patricia Curran. He's up for privy councillor.'

'There was talk about him at the time of that murder.'

'The parents of the girl's boyfriend got a call from Judge Curran asking them if they had seen Patricia. The parents swore blind the call came after the girl's body had been found.'

'I remember. So you think that if you take down the judge, they'll have to retry the case.'

'They'll have to consider commuting at least.'

'But you can't prove any of this. The parents could be mistaken.'

'They're not.'

'How do you know?'

'I have the phone records from that night. The calls from the Curran house are timed.'

'How did you get those?'

'Patricia's mother gave them to me.'

'Jesus, McCrink, you're in deep water in that place. Send me the phone records and I'll have a look.'

~

Robert McGladdery's appeal against his death sentence was heard on 16th November. The appeal court president was Justice H. A. McVeigh, who had been defence counsel for Iain Hay Gordon in his trial for the murder of Patricia Curran. There were nine grounds for appeal out of which three main grounds were identified. The first was that Robert's demeanour on the days following the murder was not consistent with someone who had committed a sordid crime and who was under relentless surveillance, and that the trial judge should have brought the jury's attention to this. The other two grounds concerned Judge Curran's remarks in his summing-up when he said that the jury should be slow to infer any 'knavery' on the part of the police on the word of a man 'charged before this court'. Brown pointed to the implied undermining of the accused man in Curran's phraseology. Brown's approach to this issue suggests that he believed there was a concerted effort to make the facts of the case fit McGladdery as the killer, to the exclusion of all else. It suggests that the police were willing to go to almost any lengths to prove McGladdery guilty.

Brown brought up the word 'knavery' used by Judge Curran. It was a word not in common use, a medievalism, it conjures up a world of vassals and lieges, courts where dark pranksters wander gloomy banqueting halls in cap and bells.

The final main ground of appeal was the judge's suggestion that thirteen witnesses had identified McGladdery as wearing a light-coloured suit. Brown contended that this was a determination that could only have been made by the jury. By commenting on it, Curran had effectively removed one of the central planks of the defence.

After several hours' deliberation the Appeal Court rejected all nine grounds of appeal. The execution date was fixed for 20th December. McGladdery's last hope was a grant of clemency from the Minister for Home Affairs, Brian Faulkner.

Robert was moved to the death cell in the basement following the failure of his appeal. Brown visited him every week to update him on the progress of his clemency appeal. Brown had contacted organisations who advocated the end of capital punishment and several had embarked on lengthy correspondences with him.

Robert exercised on his own in the prison yard after the other prisoners had been returned to their cells. During the trial he had set aside the account of his life but now he took it up again. Mervyn continued to visit him and he would ask Mervyn for details of things that had happened in his past.

'You think you remember things but when you go to write them down they're different,' he told Mervyn. He asked for dates and times, the past becoming indistinct, dissolving into textures, the lough fogs hiding the town from his gaze.

'Sometimes I feel like I'm away in the head,' Robert said.

'I wish you were away in the head,' Mervyn said, 'at least then they'd put you in the mental.'

Robert didn't tell Mervyn that he was glad to be where he was instead of in the mental hospital. Will used to talk about it all the time. Will said he'd seen it many's the time, the Downshire Hospital, the bedlam with its high red-brick walls. Will talked about padded rooms and doors with no handles. He said that an inmate had escaped and strangled a woman in her own bed. When Robert went up Damolly Hill in the dark he waited for the sound of padding feet in the darkness at his back. Not looking behind him for fear of what he might see. The vacant face, slack-jawed, dribbling.

'I know what Pearl must of felt like,' he told Mervyn.

'Maybe you'd be as well not talking like that,' Mervyn said.

'What are they saying in the town?'

'They're saying you must of killed Pearl.'

Robert could hear them working on the gallows from his cell. The trapdoor hung from crude brass hinges. When the carpenters tested it it could be heard on B and C Wings. Robert kept getting pieces of information from the prisoners who delivered his meals and his mail. The knot on the rope was a sheepshank or some such, an artful arrangement with an improvised look to it.

On the Sunday night after the appeal he was woken by the head warder, McCulla, playing a torch on his face.

'You wanted to know about the scaffold? It's finished now so come on and get your fucking look.'

Robert followed him out of the cell and down the corridor, feeling the cold, the black basalt chill. McCulla opened the door of the execution chamber. There was something comical about the thing. Unserious. The knocked-together look of the whole structure. The fresh-sawn planks and shining bolt-heads. Wood shavings lying on the ground under the gallows.

'There's no rope,' Robert said.

'Allen'll be here with his kit any day now,' McCulla said. 'I'll let you know, don't worry.'

~

Robert McGladdery's appeal for clemency to the Minister for Home Affairs, Brian Faulkner, was turned down on 5th December 1961. Across the top of the letter informing Robert's legal team of the decision, Faulkner has written in pen, 'Let the law take its course.' It is hard to know why he felt that he had to add this touch to a document that already stated his determination not to grant clemency in clear legal terms. It is as if Faulkner saw the outworking of the legal system as represented by the formal, typed letter as one thing, and the law itself as another.

James Brown told Robert about the failure of his clemency bid on the evening of 5th December. He said afterwards that Robert didn't show any emotion. As with the delivery of the guilty verdict Brown wondered about Robert's reaction. It wasn't so much that he didn't show emotion, but that emotion was in fact absent, an observation made by others at his sentencing, the same absence noticed in Ruth Ellis and James Hanratty at their murder trials.

'I'm going to finish what I'm writing about my life,' Robert said, 'there's time for that.'

The warder McCulla was as good as his word. He woke Robert on the morning of the 23rd and handed him a piece of paper. The words on it were printed in a heavy hand.

> Execution Box No 2
> Contents
>> Ropes 2
>> Block and fall 1
>> Straps 2
>> Sandbag 1
>> Measuring Rod 1
>> Piece of Chalk 1
>> Pack Thread 1
>> Copper Wire 1
>> Piece Cap 1

'What do you think of that, McGladdery?' McVeigh said. 'What do you think of that?'

Robert understood what each part of the apparatus did, apart from the copper wire. There was a reassuring old-fashioned quality to the list. Plain artisanal objects. He liked the idea that the whole thing would be gone about in a workmanlike and everyday fashion. He remembered a phrase that Mervyn had used when he was showing him how to cut leather.

'Measure twice and cut once, isn't that what they say, Mr McCulla?'

'Measure twice and drop once in your case, McGladdery,' McCulla said.

'Tell us this,' Robert said, 'what's the copper wire for?'

'You'll find out brave and soon,' McCulla said.

'I just like to know how things work.'

'Is that why you stripped Pearl to the skin? You wanted to know how girls work? You wanted to get yourself an eyeful?'

~

McCrink rang Harry Ferguson and arranged to meet him in the Slieve Donard Hotel in Newcastle. McCrink drove down the coast in gathering dark on Monday evening. There was static in the air, thunderheads out at sea, outward-bound freighters just visible on the horizon. McCrink had made the call but felt that it was he who had been summoned, Judge Curran's election agent waiting for him.

The crowds were sparse on the front at Newcastle. McCrink could see figures moving in the amusements, the first drops of rain falling as he parked in front of the hotel.

He found Ferguson in a glassed-in annex. He was sitting in a wing-backed armchair facing the sea. He looked like a keeper of secrets, a spymaster. Something about him made McCrink feel uncouth. A provincial policeman, rustic and untutored.

They sat in leather chairs looking out over the golf links. Golfers moving on the tees and the greens, taking shelter under the salt-lashed palms on the shoreline.

'I wondered if you'd like a transfer back to England.'

'I'd prefer to stay here.'

'I read your file. Your commander in Scotland Yard reported morale problems. There were some family matters.'

'My marriage.'

'The women. It's always the women, isn't it, Eddie? I visit with Doris Curran in the mental hospital. No one else visits with her. Apart from you of course. She thought her daughter was a difficult girl. These things are always complicated.'

It was the way people like Ferguson worked. Hints and asides and things left hanging in the air. McCrink knew he was being warned off Judge Curran again.

'Why did Faulkner not commute McGladdery's sentence?'

'He's already commuted Bratty this year. Besides, how they're seen on the mainland is important to boys like Faulkner. They like to have the hard men on their side. And the hard men like to see murderers swing.'

'What do you think about Judge Curran's part in the trial?'

'What do you mean?'

'In his summing-up. He hung McGladdery out to dry. He undermined his defence.'

'The jury were going to convict him anyway. You could see that. They wanted to.'

'He had a chance up until Curran opened his mouth.'

'He never had a chance.'

'I think he had a chance.'

'It'll make a difference to your career, you know. A perverted murderer sent to his maker in your first year as Inspector of Constabulary. You've got a backwater posting now. A hanging could get you a big job.'

'Just as long as McGladdery is executed. Whether he did it or not.'

'If the court says he did it, then he did it, and there's not a thing you can do about it.'

'There is something I can do.'

'Your friend Barrett at the Express.'

'How did you know?'

Ferguson waved a hand in the air. McCrink thought about the Special Branch headquarters, the miles of files, the telephone intercepts.

'He's waiting for me to give him the go-ahead to publish the phone records on Judge Curran. It'll prove he was lying about the night of Patricia's murder.'

'What do you think happened that night?'

'I think that Patricia was killed in the house and her body was carried outside. Doris Curran was diagnosed with paranoid schizophrenia. There are documented instances of sufferers killing loved ones under the influence of delusions.'

'I would confirm that diagnosis before I went any further. Besides, if that is the way it happened, it is simply a case of a man desperately trying to protect his wife. It's understandable.'

'An innocent man was convicted of the crime. He might have gone to the gallows.'

'But he didn't.'

Ferguson bent down and undid the catch on the briefcase at his feet, holding it open for a minute before closing it. McCrink saw the brown cardboard folder inside. It was the file containing the phone records from the Glen.

'How did you get that?'

'The world moves on, Mr McCrink. The papers are full of Hanratty and the A6 murders. There's no conspiracy. Nobody cares about McGladdery. Or about Pearl for that matter. Barrett's editor didn't want the story. He traded the file back to me in the hope that I'll give him a break on some future story. That's the way it works.'

Ferguson got to his feet. 'You might think I'm here to mark your card and you might be right. But as I said, I read your file. A woman can be a ruination of many's a man. When you get the chance to rebuild you should take it. McGladdery is nobody's angel. Let the Newry boys deal with it. And don't go back to the Glen. Patricia Curran is dead.'

'What do you know about a woman ruining a man?'

'I know the same things you do. My wife's long gone. Out of my life and into a bottle. And by the way, if I were you I'd check out the Special Branch file on your new librarian friend. Read it more carefully this time. She's still a ward of court. She can be committed against her will at any time. You could go to see her at Holywell instead of Mrs Curran. Who, incidentally, won't be receiving any more visitors.'

McCrink watched Ferguson from the window as he walked across the car park. The wind blew his raincoat out behind him like a cloak, a ragged, flapping thing. He looked like a figure from history, a hunched janissary laden with corrupt knowledge. McCrink knew he should take Ferguson's advice. Judge Curran and McGladdery. He had a sense of preordained happenings. The scene outside darkened as the light went behind the mountain and night fell on the town so that McCrink could see the promenade lights through the rain. Ferguson had crossed the road to Main Street and was making his way along it, an air of bad tidings in his wake. McCrink thought about the killer. The lack of forensic evidence left on the clothing. A frenzied attack but the killer left no traces of himself at the scene. He took out his notebook and read what he had written down about the items left in the septic tank. Vest. Coat. Tie. Black leather shoes.

He drove back to Newry. When he went into Corry Square Speers and Johnston were at the front desk.

'Something we can do for you, sir?' Johnston said. McCrink looked at Speers. Johnston made no move to leave the room. He wore his tunic open and his uniform hat pushed back on his head.

'The clothes in the tank. Why was the suit not there? Why go to the risk of being seen putting the jacket and the shoes and tie in the tank and not put the suit in?'

'Maybe the suit wasn't bloodstained,' Speers said.

'Then why hide it?'

'Maybe he set light to the suit, burned it in the grate,' Johnston said.

'He wouldn't burn the suit and not burn the rest of the clothes.'

'I don't get your point, sir. You'd near think you wanted McGladdery to get off,' Johnston said.

'The jury did not deliberate over the evidence at all.'

'They deliberated as much as they needed to.'

'It's McGladdery,' Speers said.

'We nailed him,' Johnston said, 'us and Judge Curran.'

'That's the way it is, Inspector,' Speers said.

'That's the way it is around here,' Johnston said.

The next day the Newry papers reported that the hangman, Harry Allen, had arrived in Belfast. The Reporter carried a photograph of Allen. A tall man with a moustache and hair Brylcreemed back from his forehead. He is wearing a bow tie and there is a carnation in his buttonhole. The photograph seems to have caught him in motion, turning towards the camera with a glass in his hand, interrupted in the act of charming a lady. He has a sensuous mouth and mournful showman's eyes.

'What is it about hangmen?' McCrink said. Men plucked from obscure occupations and set upon the stage. You wanted them to be burdened with the loneliness of their calling. You wanted an awareness of last things. Instead you got second-rate theatre barkers.

'It's all about the theatre,' Margaret said, 'village entertainments on the edge of the forest. People know that bad things are lurking just outside the lamplight. You have morality plays. Actors dressed as Famine and Pestilence.'

There seemed to be a requirement that there be an unprofessional element to the execution process. The clergyman with his head bowed to his breviary. Everyone gathering around the prisoner, amateurish, bumbling.

'They're all like that. The guillotine. The electric chair. They're like something you put together in the garage.'

'It can't be seen as being professional.'

'There's always stories of things going wrong. People

274

twisting at the end of a rope.'

'Massive voltages. Body fluids heated to boiling point. A look of surprise on the executed man's face.'

'It goes right back to medieval times. They brought a relish to it. The prisoner disembowelled and his entrails held up in front of his face.'

'The way that each branch of the citizenry has to be represented. The clergyman, the doctor.'

There was more to it than that, he thought. The public did not want the process to become too professional. It was important that it be gruesome. They wanted the prisoner anatomised, rended. They wanted the viscera engaged with, the very matter and substance of the person. They wanted the death-tics, the spasms, the ghastly twitches.

'It all reminds me of being in hospital,' she said. 'They give you a piece of rubber to bite on before they put the thing on your head, the electrodes.'

'You're not going back to that.'

'You can't say that. I'm going to protest outside the prison tomorrow morning. They could send me back but somebody has to do something. You've gone very quiet on your big campaign to bring down Judge Curran.'

'You never told me you were still a ward of court.'

'What's that got to do with anything?'

'Nothing.'

'How did you know?'

'Ferguson.'

'I see.'

~

He stayed in her flat the night before the execution. He let himself in at seven o'clock and found her asleep on top of the bed. He left her and went out. The town was fogbound, the sound of traffic muffled. The design of the mill buildings at the end of Canal Street based on eighteenth-century Venetian palaces. You thought of cloaked figures hurrying through the evening gloom, stilettos wielded. The merchant buildings along the Mall resembled some Weimar street, the banking functions fallen into disuse. The overblown architectures of lost eras, gaunt remnants standing alongside the canal.

At the end of Hill Street he saw the Frontier cinema, the lit frontage seeming to harbour some old lonesomeness. The film was Ben-Hur. It was what he needed. Happenings on an epic scale. The thunderous chariots bearing down. Themes of betrayal. Covert sexual undertones.

He bought a ticket and went in as the newsreel was starting. He took his seat in the dark, watching footage of nuclear tests on Bikini Atoll. The dark fusion. The nano-events at work, the trance clouds, shaped and verified in the heavens, boiling upwards. And the roar of the explosion, the dream-percussive, awe rolling over the far-off ocean. McCrink understood. You weren't here to be educated. These newsreels were here to instruct you in the terror to come. You were supposed to think about the seeping radiation, the deep cell damage. How someone can be altered on the fundamental level.

In the foyer after the film he saw Will Copeland with a group of others. *Will wanted them to be blood brothers. He said they should take solemn oaths. That they should be bound for life and if something happened to one then the other should take a terrible revenge.* McCrink felt Copeland's recreant gaze on him. *Where*

276

were you in the two days following the murder? He wondered if Copeland had seen the book in Robert's room that night when they were getting ready to go out, The Long Wait, the woman poised for flight, the man straining against his bonds.

McCrink walked down Hill Street past Foster Newell's, then crossed onto the Mall. He passed Mervyn's shoe-repair shop. There was a light on in the back. He tried the door and found it open. He went in and lifted the flap of the shop counter and went into the back room past the lasts and glues and ranked files, the rank organic smell of the adhesives in the cold night air.

Mervyn's darkroom was in the back of the shop. Duplicate photographs of the murder scene and of the autopsy hung above a photographer's bath. The crossroads at Damolly, the roads leading off with a choice of endings but each destination fraught. McCrink wondered what meetings between travellers might take place at such a spot, what journeys related. Next was a series of shots of the girl's clothing, the hapless mislaid items scattered on the fellside. Beside them the photographs of the body at the crime scene and on the autopsy slab. Nude, pornographic shots that looked like photographs of different women taken over a period of time. Looking asleep in some of them. In others posed against the landscape. Women laid out on the hillside like carrion. A directory of the dead. There was a series of close-ups of the girl's face, the eyes open and glazed, the lips parted.

He turned to see Mervyn standing in the back door.

'I didn't kill her,' Mervyn said.

'I didn't ask you if you did,' McCrink said. 'But if I had the time back I would have had you in to Corry Square and sweated you. You and Copeland and half the men in this town, and Bratty too for that matter.'

'What are you going to do?' Mervyn said.

'Nothing. You can stay here with your girlfriend.' McCrink backed out of the room and through the cobbler's shop. He found himself on the Mall again. The fog smelt of the silt exposed at low tide as he tried to find his way back to Margaret's flat, adrift in the river stink and corpse murk of the place, bearings lost in the marsh town.

~

That night Harry Ferguson played billiards with Judge Curran at one guinea a ball. Curran did not refer to the execution due to take place the following morning. He spoke about his bid for a seat on the Privy Council.

'I trust I have Faulkner's support?'

'His hand is strengthened by taking a hard line on crime.'

'He only thinks his hand is strengthened. They do not care about Faulkner in Westminster. Nevertheless there is a seat for the Province on the Privy Council to be filled and it is partly in his gift.'

'You have his support. McCrink is unlikely to upset the apple cart. He won't be seeing Mrs Curran any more.'

Curran bent to the table. He crooked his fingers on the baize and placed the cue across the bridge.

'The mentally ill are less morally intact than ordinary people,' he said.

You're some boy to be talking about morally intact, Ferguson thought. He chalked his cue. He bent to the table. Ferguson and the judge played on into the night.

~

When McCrink got back to the flat Margaret was awake. She had taken a Bible from the shelf and it lay open on the bed beside her.

'The Bible?' he said.

'I couldn't think of anything else.'

'My father used to read to us from the Bible every night.'

'Did you ever think about the name Holywell? I wonder if there is a holy well there?'

A place steeped in belief. Rags hanging from tree branches, miraculous medals and rosary beads tied to the lower limbs. A place where the halt and the barren came to pray.

'I'm not sure a cure's that easily got.'

'No. You're probably right.'

'Where was Pearl buried?'

'The Meeting House graveyard.'

'And we know where Robert is going to be buried.' In a yard at the back of Crumlin road prison, quicklime poured on his corpse. A high-walled, sunless yard.

'They used to say that nothing would grow in the yard where murderers were buried,' Margaret said. The names of murderers recorded in some prison register. Ellis. Hanratty. McGladdery. Execution by hanging gave the names a weight that they did not have in life, a feel in the mouth. You felt the death-timbre on the tongue as you spoke them.

'They should give the body back to the mother.'

'Would she take it?'

He went to the window. The streets below still shrouded in fog. The moody small-town streetscapes. The mansions of long-dead merchants. The town built on marshland. The warehousing along the canal empty and shuttered. The river a fetid tidal sump. Upstream dyeworks discharging toxic leachates into feeder streams. A dank, malt odour from the feed mill on Merchants Quay. Further up the river there were derelict tanneries and malthouses. The sea fog drifts through Boat Street, Sugar Island, the Buttercrane, Chancellors Road, Exchequer Hill. The dead do parlay in the shadows.

She got up before dawn. He heard the front door closing and the car started outside. He picked up the Bible from the bed and turned it over in his hand. Every night his father would take down the Bible from the shelf above the wireless, the scuffed King James, and read to them, the reverenced script, his father leaning forward in the forty-watt light, reading almost painfully as though each word had to be earned, a man straining to bring truth out of the darkness, bent forward in heartfelt telling.

Twenty-Four

Agnes had stood on the steps of the courthouse looking at her son being led in handcuffs in front of a crowd that bayed. She could see women looking down their big long noses at her. A woman vexed by the world. A woman with a son on trial for his mortal life in a country courthouse. It was like Robert to place a mother's heart in jeopardy. She did not understand why they had such appetite for her son's death. She did not know which precedent might apply. When you have a heart that is scarred from too much use. Her life was like a story that had been told in the wrong way. Men were a weakness in her that she had to admit. Hers was a life crowned with fault.

Agnes liked to read romances. Mills and Boons and other romantic fiction. This was something she had passed to her son. The desire to read. She could read three romances a week. When she worked in the mill the other girls would laugh and say she'd always got her head stuck in a book.

Most women agreed that Robert was lucky in his mother. That many's another young girl would have set a child aside into a home if things had been let get that far at all. A visit to Nurse Scour would soon put paid was what the other women said when one of the mill girls got put in the family way.

But Agnes was not like that, for what father would not return for a son if he knew and leave mother and child forsaken to the world? She kept him as token and keepsake of her love and it was no fault of hers that he turned out the way he done. The badness in him was not her doing.

The day before he was hung the Reverend Norman Dugdale came to her door to see if she would visit Robert one last time. He said that we are all condemned persons in the eyes of God. She put on hat and coat there and then and drove to Crumlin Road prison with Reverend Dugdale and they were admitted by the gaol gate. When he saw her Robert started to go on slagging her the way he always did and she had to remind him that they were in the presence of clergy when Robert says clergy my eye this time tomorrow I'll be in the presence of the man himself or maybe the devil. Then he looked her in the eye and says I never done it Mother you can tell them that, trust him to make such a statement to taunt a mother for the length of her days. Then he took some paper from his pocket and handed it to her. Here Ma, he says, this is what I wrote about myself.

She went home that night and sat blind on the sofa. She did not know what she was doing. She took a box from the back kitchen and set it outside in the black night the way Robert done when he was small, to catch a meteorite he said, but when she went out in the dawn none had fallen. Then she remembered the paper he had given her so she opened it and started to read.

My name is Robert John McGladdery and this is my account. I was born in Tinkers Hill on that very night the neighbours said it was so cold even the stars looked froze fixed to their setting in the night sky so that I never minded cold even in this gaol in the chill midwinter.

I seen the hangman today he came to my cell to

measure my neck he was a sad-looking string of a character for all he stretched many's the man. I tried to get him talking for I am sure he has a tale or two to tell but he kept the mouth shut. He put the tape around my neck and weighed me and made me stand up to measure me and I says it's like I was joining the fire brigade or the army and he looks at me as if to say I know what army you're joining the one in the shadows.

I try to keep fit in the prison the governor came to my cell and asked me if there was anything that I needed and I made a suggestion that a gym would be a good idea. Good man he says it's a pity there's not more like you in here. Get me a draughtsman pencil and lined quarto and I will draw it for you I said as well as a programme of weights. You want it called after you as well? McCulla the chief warder says. That wouldn't be bad I thought the Robert McGladdery memorial gym will suit me. I have a daughter McCulla says and I've a little plot out the back of this gaol will suit you and some quicklime too.

I thought that if I told my life like a story like the ones you get in Reader's Digest where someone faces terrible odds and overcomes them etc. My mother Agnes McGladdery what can be said about her she done her best. I wish she'd stayed home nights when I was small the wind was loud in the slates it roared dear God it roared.

I wonder what it will be like the last night do they still hang at dawn I forgot to ask. Does the condemned man get to eat whatever he likes or is there a last cigarette? The condemned man. Sometimes I feel like a ghost to myself a being who wanders at night.

I often put the question to myself did I murder Pearl the mind is a strange place. Did I act unknown to myself? The answer I have to say is no I was in full possession of my faculties at all times. As it is I feel like a character in a tale the murderer McGladdery with a sound like a man blackhearted and dangerous.

The story of my life. I was neither brought up nor let alone. My mother moved from place to place until she settled in the village of Damolly. Her demeanour to me was always one of regret. For example she would say it would have been better if I'd never had you or left you in a bucket. What about my father I asked her she says you don't have a father did you not notice? She always had a tongue in her head. I seen her strip a grown man to the bone with words.

I knew I was different. From the start I had headaches and seen bright lights during the headaches. How often do these episodes occur the doctor asked me and I says once or twice a month since childhood. The doctor must have told the head warder McCulla for he came to my cell. I hear you get headaches says he well I'll make sure you get a fucking neckache to go along with it.

I hear them working at night on the scaffold the sound of sawing the sound of hammers. I asked them could I have a look at it but they said no that it would not be good for my morale. I says what sort of morale do you think I have waiting in a cell to be stretched you're some set of comedians. Mervyn comes to see me but he's the only one. I would like to see Will to say it's all right Will you said friends should do anything for each other and that's what I'm doing.

My mother Agnes McGladdery told me about this mill girl who was looking after me and who dropped me on my head and after that I cried and cried for days and would not take comfort but I'm starting to wonder now was there any mill girl or was she just something my ma had in her mind or maybe she dropped me herself. When I was small I used to dream of a father to take me away a sailor or something with a smell of tobacco on him who would pick me up and swing me around and say here you go son it's you and me.

The freighters would come up the ship canal to Newry and when you looked you could not see the canal so it looked as if the ships were sailing through the fields. I would say look Ma at the magic ships but she would say there's no such thing as magic in this world whatever about the next.

I remember dancing with Pearl. I seen her in Foster and Newell's she was like a china doll and when you danced with her you'd be afraid she'd break. I remember we talked but I can't remember what we talked about. Mr Brown says that if I want to say I done it and say sorry then it would count towards my clemency but I can't say I done something when I didn't especially when that thing is to leave a girl lying bare to the world. Mr Brown looked at me funny when I said that and says he would do his best by me. Strain every sinew was the words he used. Don't strain every sinew I says a torn sinew is a bad man I know from the bodybuilding but Mr Brown is not a man to get a joke. I says the same thing to Hughes just before they moved me out of his cell into the death cell.

I says I can't say I done it and he looks at me and says either you never done it after all or you're stone fucking mad either road they shouldn't hang you. Hear hear to that says I.

The governor asked me if there is anything I'd like special in the cell and I says is there any chance of some barbells and a skipping rope to keep up the cardiovascular system. He looks at me funny as if to say what are you doing keeping fit we'll be stringing you up in the heel of the hunt you'll have no need of a cardiovascular system. But a healthy body leads to a healthy mind and a good attitude.

McCulla come to me and said that the prison reform trust had told him to ask if there was anything I needed. As far as he was concerned he says they had built the only thing I needed down the corridor from the death cell but he was obliged by law to ask. McCulla was getting on my nerves so I says to him I would like a bullworker to exercise with. I thought that I'd gone too far and McCulla would do the hangman's job for him but all he said was he would report my request back to the reform trust and to the governor. When I told Mervyn he said you've shot yourself in the foot there why didn't you keep your big beak shut?

If somebody asked me the happiest things of my life I'd say one would be dancing you'd float around the room. Another would be to be sitting with Mervyn fixing shoes. And the last would be standing on the high board at the baths you could see for miles around you, the ships on the lough, the water and people far below you. Your heart was in your mouth with the fear but your head was clear.

~

Robert McGladdery was hanged at Crumlin Road prison at 8 a.m. on 20th December 1961. The Met Office reported the city fogbound for several days preceding the execution. The night before Robert's death the Reverend Norman Dugdale accompanied Agnes McGladdery to the prison to see her son. After his execution the newspapers reported that 'his last wish was that his confession be made public.' This was 'revealed by officials shortly after the execution at 8 o'clock that morning'.

The officials were not named but a letter to the governor of Crumlin Road from the prison chaplain, the Reverend W. Vance, was subsequently released to the press.

Sir
I wish to inform you that prior to the sentence of death being carried out on Robert A. McGladdery he accepted full responsibility for the death of Miss Pearl Gamble. He further informed me that he disposed of the light suit in question by burning it. He also stated that he wished his confession to be made public.
> *signed*
> *William John Vance*

The letter appears to have been conceived for the purpose of removing any doubt that might exist in the public mind regarding the hanging of Robert McGladdery. The language seems to be that of a lawyer rather than a chaplain. The phrase 'accepted full responsibility' is strange and appears to be carefully chosen. It is less than a full confes-

287

sion. The reference to the burning of the light suit seems designed to clear up any lingering doubt about a main plank of the prosecution case.

It would be expected that a man in Robert's position who wished to make his peace on the eve of his execution would express remorse, and perhaps give some insight into what drove him to commit the crime. This is absent. Instead the letter finishes with a justification for making public the preceding assertions.

The six witnesses to the execution included the Reverend Vance and the prison governor. At 7.55 when Robert was led into the execution chamber the observers saw him eyeing the scaffold, turning his head from side to side to look at it. They said afterwards that he appeared agitated. It seemed to confirm his criminality, a gaunt, harried figure in the shadow of the gallows, cowed by its everyday rigours, the nailheads and unplaned planking.

'Agitated my eye,' the warder McCulla said, 'he was looking for the copper wire that he seen on the hangman's list.'

It was important for Robert to understand things and give them their place in the world. When Allen put the cap on him he wondered why it was called a cap when it was in fact a hood. The only thing he could hear was the voice of the pastor. He remembered Mervyn talking about the parable of the talents and when he asked him what a parable was Mervyn said it was just a story.

Twenty-Five

The Police Training College at Enniskillen has a small collection of artefacts and documents relating to notorious cases. It is based on the well-known collection at Scotland Yard and is also referred to as the Black Museum. One glass case contains the contents of the bundle found in the septic tank at Damolly. The black shoes, the red-and-black tie and the shortie fawn jacket. The jacket appears to have shrunk to the proportions of an article of clothing belonging to a child. It is hard to imagine the squalid allure it once possessed.

Another case contains pieces of evidence preserved from the Patricia Curran case. There are photographs of the crime scene and of the Glen. The art folder she had been carrying the night she was murdered. The yellow juliet cap she had been wearing. Her raincoat. It is difficult to imagine the significance attached to these items at the time of the murder. The dyes are faded, exposure to sunlight has aged the fabrics. But there is an intimacy to the objects, and a sense of trespass about looking at them. Despite the sunlight and dust motes floating in the museum air, it is an unquiet place.

Lance Curran was appointed to the Privy Council in 1962 and moved to London. Doris Curran never left Holywell. She died in 1970 and Curran remarried in 1972. You go back to the photograph of Lance Curran inspecting the guard of honour at Downpatrick Assize in 1961. Curran is aware of the camera. The Curran family are always aware of the camera. The faces of the soldiers are hidden but they stand like members of a grim yeomanry bidden to his side.

A left-hand turn from the Belfast Road leads to Damolly village. The heart of the village is a dog-leg of about twenty workers' houses on a bend in the road. The McGladdery house is in the middle of the terrace. They are built in granite with stone lintels and red-brick window surrounds. The houses are well maintained, mostly in original detail, although towards the bottom of the hill some of the houses have been rendered in white, and diamond-paned PVC windows and other details have been added. All of the houses have satellite dishes pointed towards the sky, towards the lonely orbits, the hubbub of the world gathered and directed out to the edge of space, into the meteor dust and photon streams.

The way the road ends brings you up short. The road takes a turn left and there is a box-girder bridge across the weed-choked river. The road is closed with four large concrete blocks and the other end of the bridge is barred by an overgrown grass bank. Beyond the bank the land falls away and the eye is level with the shining roofs of an industrial estate. Then the land rises and you can see the retail park, the roundabout and bypass. The way to Weir's Rock blocked by post-industrial clutter, but underlain by the ghost paths, Pearl Gamble walking home. A steep, stubble-covered hillside rears above the houses.

By the end of the 1960s Newry and its surroundings would have the highest unemployment in western Europe. There was a grim civic pride about the unemployment rate. There was an epic quality to it, a dustbowl scope to the economic collapse. The lines of men, shuffling, downcast, outside red-brick labour exchanges.

From the beginning the police had decided that Robert had killed Pearl. He had danced with her that night. He had asked the band to play 'It's Now or Never'. No one had seen him leave the dance. No other possibilities were considered. Robert did nothing to help his cause. In reaction to intense police surveillance he allowed an air of malign tomfoolery to descend over him. He led them through the town, mocking them.

Robert McCartney, QC was a solicitor's apprentice and sat in the public gallery during the trial. He pointed out that the law had been changed in England, effectively outlawing capital punishment in most cases. If Robert McGladdery had been tried there and found guilty he would not have received the death penalty. He added that although the evidence against the accused was circumstantial, there was no evidence at all pointing to his innocence.

Interviewed in later years, the juror Jack Landelis said that he would 'bring capital punishment back tomorrow'.

No one swims on the beach at Warrenpoint. There have been attempts to import sand to make a beach, but the tide has washed it away. The swimming baths closed in the late 1970s. They reopened twenty years later as a watersports adventure centre. For several years windsurfers set off from the lee of the baths, scudding across the tops of the waves, wetsuited, ephemeral figures, leaning into the wind. When the adventure centre closed the windsurfers left. The paint is peeling and the iron handrails are corroded. The pagoda-style entrance kiosk is empty. The Heysham ferry passes down the channel every night a hundred yards from the shore, its screws churning silt from the seabed, the wash booming against the pool walls, oceanic rumblings in the foundations of the baths, deep-water sounds.

The centre of the town is dominated by the cranes and industrial shedding of the docks. The dockside is lined with crumbling seaside buildings. The Victoria Hotel. The Liverpool. The Marine Tavern. Warrenpoint had once been a transit point. Passengers would travel from there to Liverpool where they would transfer to liners for the ocean crossing to New York and Boston. Ghost emigrants waiting to take ship, outward bound. There are odd turreted buildings along the esplanade, seafront Gothics, crumbling Victorian chinoiserie.

There are Eastern europeans from the ships on the street, small dark-skinned men with a down-at-heel look to them. There are ships from Riga and Gdansk, the great northern ports. There is a Baltic tang in the air.

The town keeps trying to go upmarket, but there's always an undercurrent around the takeaways, the Friar Tucks and Country Fried Chicken. Young men from Kilkeel and Rostrevor, from Barcroft and the Meadow, hood-eyed cliques marauding in the night.

People still come to the amusements during the summer. They eat ice cream at the Genoa. They walk along the front and lovers sit on the low sea wall. But these small resort towns are never about the present. They were built to look back to long hot summers that may or may not have happened, for the sun-dazzled memories of childhood on the beach.

There are nursing homes along the front housing the shuf-fling and the halting, the perplexed aged who know how the past can undo you. In the Stella Maris Home Margaret sits in a wing-backed chair looking out to sea. Eddie McCrink died in his sleep in 1987. Margaret had spent much of the next twenty years in hospitals and sheltered accommodation. She is very old. She thinks she sees people she knows walk-ing along the seafront and sometimes Pearl takes her place in this promenade of ghosts, that hint of the oriental about her with her slanted eyes and porcelain skin, the idealised look, refined and sensual with a hint of the grave about it as she passes the deserted swimming baths. Shading her eyes as she looks upwards towards a man's body in silhouette against the noon sun, a phantom olympian on the verge of flight.

Twenty-Six

Saturday 28th January 1961

Pearl was getting ready to go out. She wore a black pencil skirt and red blouse with a broad black leather belt that she had borrowed from Ronnie around her waist. She sat in front of her dressing-table mirror using a white foundation and dark eyeliner to bring out the natural paleness of her face and using a deep-red Rimmel lipstick which she could only afford with her employee discount. She knew that other girls sometimes slipped things into their pockets but Pearl liked to pay. She wanted to feel that she had earned things, and liked the expensive feel of the lipstick. She had her hair tied back from her face. Seen in the mirror her face is impassive, the geisha look back again. You can see her in elaborate dress, moving with tiny steps, with that hobbled gait. The face expressionless, knowing, suggesting carnal knowledge refined through the ages.

There is something of death in the oriental ideal. A waxen, lifeless look. There is a whiff of gravebreath about it, the sexual stakes raised as high as they can go. It's tempting to see Pearl as she prepared to go out that night, gliding from room to room, as though she were in some ricepaper-partitioned oriental residence. There is a feeling that shadowy assignations are awaiting her, the erotics of last things.

She was to meet Ronnie at the bottom of the Belfast Road.

The night was cold. It had snowed several days beforehand and there were still icy residues in shadowed areas and on the high ground. Pearl's mother called out to her to take a coat and hat but she put a wrap around her shoulders instead.

The following morning when Pearl had not arrived home her mother said, 'I was not unduly worried as I thought that Pearl might have decided to stay the night with one of her friends.'

There are other dances going on that night. The papers show that there are dances in Maxim's. In Thompson's Alfresco Rooms. The Clippertones are playing in the Flamingo Ballroom.

The dance was a fundraiser in the Henry Thompson Memorial Orange Hall. There was a military tone to the evening, the town's militias and corps represented. There were members of the Territorial Army and the Special Constabulary present.

Ronnie was waiting for Pearl at the bottom of the road. Ronnie was quieter than usual. She had always struggled with her complexion and Pearl had advised her not to wear so much heavy pan make-up which Pearl said 'blocked the pores'.

'Where would I be without my slap?' Ronnie said. The skin on Ronnie's face was blotchy and there were spots on her chin. People noticed the contrast between them. Pearl's still mask and Ronnie's pasty, badly made-up face. Ronnie had not mentioned McKnight for several weeks and Pearl had not asked. Ronnie had a temper sometimes. She could lash out and say cruel things and Pearl did not want to provoke her. Earlier that week they had gone to Falloni's for ice cream. Pearl went into the toilets with Ronnie. Ronnie had gone into one of the stalls and been sick.

'Are you pregnant or something?' Pearl said.

'None of your business if I am,' Ronnie said, 'least I don't have a block of ice between my legs, little Miss Frigid.'

Afterwards Ronnie followed Pearl out into the street apologising. She looked as if she was about to cry.

'I don't know what came over me,' she said, 'my big mouth.'

'I hate that word,' Pearl said. When it had been used about her in school she had gone to the library and looked it up. *Frozen or stiffened with cold; chillingly stiff; (of a woman) sexually unresponsive.*

'Course you're not,' Ronnie said, 'you're just not a slapper like me. The slut of the town. You got self-respect, Pearl. Give me ten years I'll be hanging out at the lock gates waiting for some big Russian freighter to come in. Hello Ivan, give us a few of them roubles and I'll keep you warm.'

Ronnie knew how to make Pearl laugh. Pearl knew there was no harm in her and allowed Ronnie to link her arm down the street, but the word hung in the air between them.

Ronnie had whistled when she saw Pearl dressed for the dance.

'You look like something from the pictures, Pearl,' Ronnie said, 'they'll not be looking next nor near me tonight. You look like you're headed for that Orchid Blue. Mind you, there'll be trouble if you try dancing in that skirt. If the seam goes on you then watch out Mother, they'll be looking all the way up.'

Ronnie hadn't seen this Pearl before. There was a level of sophistication. There was a cool, artful look. People made way for her as she walked towards the entrance of the Orange hall, the young men of the town gathered there. When they arrived at the Orange hall the music had already started,

Ronnie dancing to herself in the queue.

William Eglington. Joseph Clydesdale. Special Constable William Quinn. Their listed names already taking on the formal configuration of a witness list. It was 10.30 p.m.

Robert and Will Copeland arrived at the hall at 11.30 p.m. According to his own account Robert was wearing a shortie fawn coat. It is impossible to tell what he was wearing underneath, the air in the hall thick with cigarette smoke. On the way in Robert picked up Joan Donergan and swung her around. The night's chronologies coming into play.

Robert's first dance was a ladies' choice. One of the tennis girls got up with Robert, a Hannah Taylor whose father was a shipping agent. She looked back at her friends before she walked up to Robert. They acknowledged her with small, heartless waves. She had big hands and feet and Robert knew she would look good dancing. People watching would see a certain amount of ungainliness overcome, strivings for grace undertaken. The band were mixing waltz and jive music. They understood the times they were living in, the easing through things that was required, and they bent to their instruments.

Robert danced six times with Joan Donergan but he must have noticed Pearl. She stood out that night, people looking at her, surprised when she jived with the young men when she looked as if she should be performing something Eastern, a temple-dance, eyes lowered, shadows on screens.

Pearl danced a jive with him first.

'So you're the big-shot dancer,' she said. There was a wan bravado in her eyes.

'You need to put your fingers higher on my shoulder,' Robert said, 'bend your elbow.'

She could feel his hand on her back, above the waistband of her skirt. Robert moving her on the sprung dance floor, three beats to the bar, bringing her into the old films, the Fred Astaires and Busby Berkeley numbers, Robert moving with a kind of shuffle, loose-hipped and expert, everyone else on the dance floor looking stiff and formal.

Later Robert went up to the band and made his request and when he came down to Pearl they were already playing. This is the dance where Ranger Gladys Jones says that 'McGladdery was trying to hold Pearl tightly towards him', where he had 'his head bent down towards her face', where she 'kept turning her head away from him'. They are talking but it is impossible to know what they are saying. They move across the floor until they are lost in the dancing couples. It's Now or Never. Lost in Presley's backwoods tremolo. *It's Now or Never*, their faces fading away with the bass notes, the drawn-out vowel sounds.